THEIR DIVINE FIRES

THEIR DIVINE FIRES

a novel

WENDY CHEN

ALGONQUIN BOOKS
OF CHAPEL HILL
2024

Published by
ALGONQUIN BOOKS OF CHAPEL HILL
Post Office Box 2225
Chapel Hill, North Carolina 27515-2225

an imprint of Workman Publishing
a division of Hachette Book Group, Inc.
1290 Avenue of the Americas,
New York, NY 10104

Printed in the United States of America.
Design by Steve Godwin.

The publisher is not responsible for websites (or their content)
that are not owned by the publisher.

This is a work of fiction. While, as in all fiction, the literary perceptions and insights
are based on experience, all names, characters, places, and incidents either are
products of the author's imagination or are used fictitiously.

Library of Congress Cataloging-in-Publication Data

Names: Chen, Wendy, [date]– author.
Title: Their divine fires : a novel / Wendy Chen.
Description: First edition. | Chapel Hill, North Carolina :
Algonquin Books of Chapel Hill, 2024. |
Identifiers: LCCN 2024003555 (print) | LCCN 2024003556 (ebook) |
ISBN 9798889697152 (hardcover) | ISBN 9781643755175 (ebook)
Subjects: LCGFT: Novels.
Classification: LCC PS3603.H45547 T47 2024 (print) |
LCC PS3603.H45547 (ebook) | DDC 813/.6—dc23/eng/20240202
LC record available at https://lccn.loc.gov/2024003555
LC ebook record available at https://lccn.loc.gov/2024003556

10 9 8 7 6 5 4 3 2 1
First Edition

for Jun,
whose light shines the brightest

The Zhang Family Tree

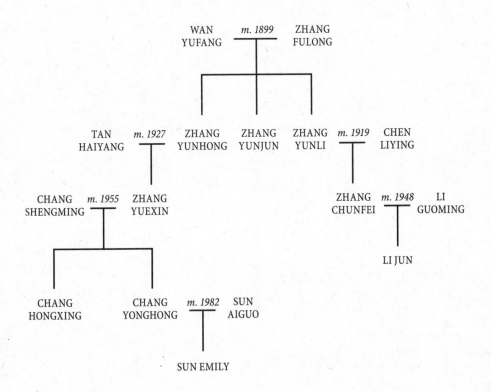

THEIR DIVINE FIRES

PART ONE

LIUYANG

1917–1939

A Pair of Silver Scissors

"DON'T BE AFRAID, Mei Mei. Hold the scissors like this."

But Mei Mei still hesitated. As she stood in the field, she watched the water ripple in the pond. The carp swam up to bite the surface with their hungry little mouths.

Da Ge bent down to grasp her hand within his. He showed her how to adjust her grip. Mei Mei stared at his long fingers enclosing hers, the ink stains on his fingertips. Her elder brother had the hands of a scholar.

"Mei Mei. Are you listening?" Da Ge touched her cheeks and she could see his dark eyes, framed by thick, sharply angled brows. "Do it quickly. In one cut." Da Ge's hand left her.

Mei Mei glanced at the house behind her. Inside, Ma Ma was wrapping the dumplings. Ba Ba was in his office, making medicines. Ge Ge was studying for his middle school exams. They did not know what she was about to do. But Da Ge did not give her time to doubt. He turned and knelt in front of her, baring the pale nape of his neck and his long, black braid. She touched it with the back of her hand.

Mei Mei wondered if he would feel pain when she cut his hair. Would it hurt him? Would it hurt her? Could she bear to do it?

The mountains at the edge of the horizon were gradually darkening in the evening light. Ma Ma had once told her the mountains were the ridges of a dragon's back—a dragon that guarded them. Mei Mei had often been comforted by the thought, but today, there was something threatening about its shape.

Da Ge's face was in shadow as he spoke. "You'd like the city, Mei Mei. Just outside the south gate, there is a mountain called Miaogao. If you climb to the very top, you can see all of Changsha."

Mei Mei had tried many times to imagine the city that had transformed her brother. Lately, he carried himself differently—taller and sharper, like a reflection in the blade of a knife.

"When I first arrived, I saw the strangest thing in the Xiang River. There was an orange cloud floating right in the middle of the water. If you ever come to visit, I'll take you to see it. They call it Juzi Isle—the island planted with a thousand orange trees. When you stand on the bank under the turning wind, you can almost smell the oranges flowering on the branch. The sight is like something out of a dream."

Da Ge fell silent. Then, he looked at her. "Mei Mei, will you do it? For me?"

Mei Mei softened. This was Da Ge, who had told her stories deep into the night. Da Ge, who had carried her on his steady shoulders. Da Ge, who had prayed beside her to their ancestors.

She looked down at the scissors in her hand, at how they burned under the setting sun, a silver fire setting her alight. Swiftly, she grabbed his braid with one hand, and with the other, she brought the scissors up to the nape of his neck.

She cut.

She half-expected Da Ge to cry out in pain, but he was silent. Was it done? Just like that? The braid was a heavy weight in her hand, and now Mei Mei wanted more. To cut the sun from the sky. Cut the light from the water. Cut the earth between the two of them.

"Thank you, Mei Mei." Da Ge felt the shorn ends of his hair, then rose to his feet. He took the braid and flung it into the pond. At first, the fish swarmed around it, biting eagerly. But soon, the braid sunk, disappearing into the depths. Da Ge began to laugh, his eyes glittering with tears. He picked Mei Mei up and swung her around, and the scissors fell.

Da Ge's hair tossed loosely around his face, and Mei Mei's heart eased. She couldn't help but return his smile. She had never felt closer to her brother.

But suddenly, there was another pair of hands on her, wresting her away.

"What have you done? What have you done?" Ma Ma, who always spoke softly, was almost shouting now. Her eyes were wide, and her breath came fast. All of her voice, her entire body, was an accusation.

"How could you cut your hair? How could you dishonor yourself, dishonor us, this way?" Ma Ma trembled as she looked at Da Ge. "When you cut your hair, you are cutting into the body we have given you. The one our ancestors have given you. You are cutting yourself away from us."

Mei Mei got up from the ground. She wanted to stand between the two of them, and she wanted to shrink away.

"I am not dishonoring any of us." Da Ge looked resolutely into Ma Ma's eyes. "The braid is our shame, a symbol of the Manchus. When we cut our hair, we are cutting it away. Honoring our country, our mothers, and our fathers."

Ma Ma let out a bitter laugh. "You want to be like them? Is that it? Those foreign devils?"

Mei Mei had never seen her so angry. She was like a creature from a story, one who came out of the wild, earthy places.

"No, Ma Ma. It is time to let go of the old values." Da Ge looked at her earnestly. "You said so yourself when Ba Ba wanted to bind Mei Mei's feet. You said all should walk freely upon the earth."

Ma Ma said nothing.

Mei Mei tugged on her mother's shirt. She moved between them. "It was me. I did it."

But neither was listening. Ma Ma pushed her away. Above her, they continued to fight, filling the sky with their voices. She pressed her hands against her ears and went to the dark place. The place that was safe, deep inside her. There, it was peaceful, like the pond filled with strands of slowly falling hair.

When Mei Mei opened her eyes again, she was alone next to the pond. Only the scissors remained, glinting through the blades of grass in the moonlight. She picked them up and held them before beginning to cut again.

THE NEXT MORNING, Da Ge was gone, having left before sunrise to return to Changsha. Ba Ba smeared Mei Mei's palm with a pungent yellow ointment, then wrapped a fresh bandage around her hand.

"You must not be like Da Ge. You must not learn from him. Next time, you will not touch the scissors. Do you understand?" Her father's voice was firm, his gaze forbidding. Though Da Ge had inherited the thick brows and wide, square jawline of their father, Ba Ba's features held a severity within them that had only sharpened over time.

Mei Mei nodded, ashamed. She had thought Ma Ma and Ba Ba would be angry with her, too, for cutting her hair—just as angry as they were at Da Ge. But instead, they were only sad, and now she had no desire to touch the scissors again.

Mei Mei fidgeted in the chair. "Ba Ba, how long will you be gone this time?"

Her father's eyes gentled. "For several days—perhaps even a week. I must tend to a little boy who is terribly ill." Ba Ba kissed her on the forehead. "You will be good for your mother, won't you?"

Her father sometimes spent up to a week on the road making his rounds to the houses of the sick in neighboring villages in Liuyang. He brought them pills and pastes in dark little jars. Mei Mei often watched him work, grinding the dried snakeskins, the dark grains of musk, or the red seedpods in the mortar until they turned into powder. A few times, Ba Ba had taken her along on shorter day trips. He would place her in front of him on the back of his mule and point out sights such as the giant stone turtle, frozen forever in time as punishment by the Heavens. "This is your chance to see the world," Ba Ba would tell her, "before you settle down and get married."

But Mei Mei didn't ever want to get married if it meant she could never see the world again.

The houses they went to were sometimes large, fine manors; other times, they were little more than shoddy hovels leaning against the trees. Ba Ba treated his patients all the same, and he charged only what the family could afford.

Mei Mei was scared of the patients who were dressed in rags, so skinny they seemed carved out of wood rather than flesh. Once, she even saw a young child half her size breathe one long breath, and then no more. But her father told her there was nothing to be frightened of. In this life, they are the unfortunate ones, he told her. But in the next life, they may be reincarnated into a lord or lady. It all depended on the karma one accumulated through good deeds.

She didn't want to be reincarnated as a beggar or maybe—if she was particularly bad—a cicada. She wanted to be a dragon in her next life. But to do so, she had to be good.

DURING BREAKFAST, MEI Mei observed her mother quietly from across the table. Usually, Mei Mei loved breakfast with just the two of them, in the golden spill of the morning when Ge Ge had already gone to school. But today, Ma Ma had been like a stone buried under snow.

"Are you still angry, Ma Ma?"

"No," Ma Ma said, though a frown lingered around the corners of her mouth.

Mei Mei had always been told that she looked just like her mother. Their noses were both rounded at the tip. Their double eyelids folded exactly the same. Their pointed chins were mirror images. They had the same red birthmark on their chest—the size and shape of a thumbprint. But Mei Mei had a gangly build to her that Ma Ma did not. A certain sharpness to her elbows and knees. A knobbiness in her knuckles and toes. If Mei Mei was the branch of a tree, her mother was the root. Mei Mei hoped that one day she would grow into her mother's grace. That her wrinkles, too—when she gained them—would make her seem as if she were always on the edge of a smile. But inside, Ma Ma was steely at her core.

After breakfast, Ma Ma braided Mei Mei's hair in two neat plaits and bound them tightly at their ends with string. Usually, Mei Mei wore her hair in two buns on the top of her head, but with the new, jagged cuts she had made, she could no longer. The braids, however, disguised the places where her hair was choppy and short. When she was finished, Ma Ma knelt and placed her hands on Mei Mei's knees. Then, she looked intently at Mei Mei and smoothed down her hair with both hands.

Ma Ma brushed a finger against the tip of her nose. "I've been think-ing of what your brother said yesterday." Ma Ma took Mei Mei's bandaged hand in hers. "Mei Mei, would you like to attend school?"

"School?" Mei Mei's heart began to race. She had always wanted to follow her brothers to school—the place that occupied Da Ge and Ge Ge's days and filled them with such stories. But the one time she had asked to go with her brothers, Ba Ba had laughed—not unkindly—and Ma Ma had shaken her head. "That is a place for boys," Ba Ba said. Afterward, Da Ge had caught her crying. When she told him of their parents' refusal, he had sat her at his desk and began to teach her characters.

Lighting an oil lamp, Da Ge had cleared a space on the table and laid out a sheet of paper. From a drawer, he pulled out a flat, rectangular stone with a shallow well. He carefully filled the well halfway with water, then ground the inkstone against it. The water slowly blackened.

Da Ge dipped the tip of his brush into the ink and made a series of quick strokes on the paper.

"Do you recognize this character?" Da Ge asked.

Mei Mei studied the marks. The ink was lighter in places where it had already dried but dark and glossy in others. She looked up at her elder brother and shook her head.

"Zhang. Our family name." Da Ge seemed disappointed but did not blame her. "I taught you once, a long time ago. It's natural you might have forgotten." Her brother wrote down another two characters. "Yun, for the clouds across the sky. Hong, for red, for happiness."

Da Ge taught her more words. His name—Yunli. Ge Ge's—Yunjun. The ink splashed down on the paper, one after another, like drops of rain. Before long, the paper was covered with Da Ge's slender, precise marks and Mei Mei's clumsy ones, some that bled into the other.

When they finished practicing, Da Ge stared down at her. "These are our names, Mei Mei. The ones that no one can ever take away from you. In them, there is the history of our family. For example, the Yun that marks us as siblings. The character you will never lose, even when you marry."

"Like my birthmark," Mei Mei said. This, she understood. It was the mark on her chest, Ma Ma had explained, that was passed down from mothers to daughters in their family. It came from an old legend in her bloodline—from a story that told of a daughter who had been lost in the mountains. Years later, when her mother found her again, a matching mark bloomed on both their chests—so they would never lose each other again.

"It is our history that sets us apart from other families," Da Ge said. "History that sets others apart from us." Da Ge was frowning now. "And when you marry, any name you take will have its own history. A history you can never part from, not even in death. That is why, Mei Mei, you must choose carefully. If only for your own sake."

But ever since Da Ge left for Changsha for his studies, there had been no one to teach her. So now, with every passing day, she could feel herself forgetting the words she had so painstakingly memorized.

Mei Mei looked up at her mother. "I want to go."

OUTSIDE THE HOUSE, Ma Ma opened the umbrella over them both. The road they took was wide and pooled with sunlight, the air still cool from yesterday's rain. The trees that lined the road buzzed with cicadas. In the fields, men and women waded through the damp earth.

Ma Ma took her hand. Mei Mei tried to hide the trembling excitement of her body. She didn't want her mother to think she was scared. She didn't want her mother to change her mind. She took careful, steady steps and kept her gaze fixed straight ahead. In the distance, half-obscured with fog, the dragon continued to sleep, curled around the outskirts of Liuyang.

By the time they reached the schoolhouse, rain was pouring upon their umbrella. It streamed down the black tiled roof of the schoolhouse like hair. They walked up the stone steps of the entryway and continued down a long, musty hallway that echoed with the shouts of the students in their classrooms.

Ma Ma and Mei Mei stepped into one of the classrooms. The room was crowded with boys Mei Mei's age—crowded with their chatter. Mei Mei looked at their faces, but her Ge Ge was not among them. He was in another classroom with other fourteen-year-old boys, laughing perhaps, as these boys were.

Ma Ma led her to the front, where an old man with a long white beard was standing. His coarse, dark robes added an air of solemnity, and to Mei Mei, he seemed like an immortal from a story, one who would be found walking barefoot through a bamboo forest, disguised as a humble teacher.

"Master Song," Ma Ma said, greeting him respectfully, "this is my daughter. The one I spoke to you about." Ma Ma smiled at the old man. "She's ten years old and very smart for her age. Her elder brother has already been teaching her how to read basic characters."

Master Song peered down at Mei Mei. "So, this is the little mei mei of Doctor Zhang's family."

"I was hoping," Ma Ma said, "she could join your class."

Master Song's brows drew together, and after a pause, he said, "I have heard that other villages are opening schools for girls." He nodded thoughtfully. "Perhaps you could find a place for her there."

The students watched. Mei Mei turned and pressed her face insistently into her mother's jacket. The pocket's knotted button dug into her cheek. Mei Mei didn't care. She wanted to go home, away from all the strange, prying eyes.

But Ma Ma persisted. "This school is the best. The other places would not be able to compare to the caliber and quality of its teachers. And the other schools are too far away. Surely, there is space for her." She looked down at Mei Mei, and Mei Mei looked back up at her—at the deep, encompassing black of her eyes.

"She is just one little girl, after all."

Master Song shook his head. "All our classes are full for the year. But I'm sure the good doctor would be able to find a tutor for her if he wanted to."

As Ma Ma and Master Song continued to push their gentle refusals toward one another, Mei Mei could feel her cheeks burning. She wanted to go back to the dark, quiet place, the place where she was free.

At last, Ma Ma took her hand again, and together, they left the classroom.

On the way back, the rain stopped, though clouds still gathered low on the horizon. Mei Mei ran ahead, trying to free herself of the hot, sickly burning inside her. She pointed at the bushes dotted white with hibiscus blooms, but her mother did not look.

Ma Ma spoke only once. "I'm sorry."

When they arrived home, Ma Ma went to her room. Mei Mei followed her, watching as her mother lay down on her bed with her hair still pinned up. She climbed onto the bed. Had the burning touched Ma Ma, too? She pulled out each pin until Ma Ma's hair unrolled from the bun. Mei Mei combed out the curls with her hands, arranging them like the rays of the sun.

Ma Ma rolled over. Her hair covered her face. "Not now, Mei Mei. Go play outside."

Outside, the sky was dark, then bright, then dark again. Soon, it began to rain. In the doorway, the jasmine's waxy green leaves beaded with water, while its pot thickened with mud. The rain washed down Mei Mei's two braids, but couldn't cool the fire gathering inside her.

The Arrival of a Stranger

WINTER MORNINGS, GE Ge went on his usual way to the school, while Mei Mei helped her mother feed the chickens inside their coop behind the house. The hens gathered around when she scattered the grain in generous handfuls. Her family owned a dozen hens, who kept them well-supplied with eggs. They also had one proud rooster, whose feathers gleamed darkly blue and green. But Mei Mei's favorite was the red hen with one white feather on its breast. That hen, too, had a birthmark like hers, and she named her White Flower for the mark. From time to time, Mei Mei would slip White Flower extra scraps of bok choy or celery and had even trained the hen to sit in her lap. Her brothers, however, were less affectionate. Ge Ge was always threatening to roast the rooster, who liked to chase him around their yard. And Da Ge, whenever he was home, was often tasked with slaughtering the hens who had stopped laying eggs.

In the afternoons, between chores, Mei Mei worked on her embroidery at Da Ge's old desk. She chose her threads carefully, and was fond of embroidering red swirling clouds as a kind of signature of her name. But in truth, she spent more time poring over her elder brother's old workbooks and retracing the words he had taught her. Ma Ma knew no characters—not even her own name—so Mei Mei had to learn on her own.

One morning, a monk was outside their door, begging for food. His head was shaven, and his feet were clad only in worn leather sandals. Ma Ma went inside the house and brought out a bowl of rice with pickled vegetables.

The monk thanked Ma Ma and sat down cross-legged right on the road. Mei Mei crouched down to watch him eat.

"Don't bother him, Mei Mei," Ma Ma scolded.

Mei Mei stayed where she was. "Master, aren't you cold?" she asked.

The monk smiled and shook his head.

Mei Mei shivered and wrapped her arms around herself. She looked at his feet, which were cracked and purple. Monks like him, she knew, chose a life of poverty and hardship, though she didn't understand why. She thought of the children she'd seen when she'd traveled with Ba Ba. They often cried out of hunger. They would tug at her sleeve and ask for food. That was when their parents scolded them, sometimes raising a hand, and they would apologize to Ba Ba for their children's behavior. But the worst was when the children were silent—hardly seeming like children at all.

A WEEK BEFORE the New Year, Mei Mei was startled by a terrible sound coming from the road by their house. She accidentally dropped the bowl in her hands, and the chickens swarmed around the grain that spilled out. The sound was so terrible—so full of pain.

It wasn't hard to miss the source of the sound: a boy lying on the ground. His right foot was trapped beneath his fallen horse, and his eyes were tightly closed. Mei Mei rushed over and crouched down. He was pushing weakly at his horse, who was still kicking wildly.

"Are you alright?" Mei Mei asked, touching his shoulder.

The boy's eyes flew open. He shook his head.

Mei Mei saw she couldn't lift the horse off his foot by herself. She began to get up, and he grabbed her wrist.

"Don't leave me," he said.

"I'm just going to get help," Mei Mei said, tugging at her wrist. Her heart was pounding.

"Don't leave," the boy repeated.

"I won't," she reassured. "I'll be back. I'm just going to find help." Then she added, "My father's a doctor."

At the mention of a doctor, the boy loosened his grip.

"I'll be back soon," she said. She hesitated, then reached out to give his hand a quick squeeze, the way her elder brother sometimes did to comfort her. She would never have done so to a stranger under normal circumstances.

Mei Mei ran instead to the Yus' house. Ba Ba was out attending one of his patients, and Mei Mei knew she had to help the boy as best as she could before he returned home for dinner. The three sons of the Yu family, Mei Mei thought, might be able to lift the horse just enough to free the boy's foot.

Mei Mei was relieved to find them all at home. They followed her as she sprinted back, their sister Ming trailing close behind. When Mei Mei got back, the boy lay limply beneath the horse, no longer trying to fight his way free. The horse, too, seemed to have given up and was only breathing in gasps.

The eldest Yu son clucked his tongue. "Looks like the horse can't be saved," he said, shaking his head. He pointed to one of the horse's hind legs, which had broken in the fall. Mei Mei hoped the boy's foot had fared better.

"The three of us will lift the horse, while you and Ming drag him out," the elder son instructed as the three brothers got into position.

But Ming shook her head and backed away. "I can't," she said. "It wouldn't be proper."

Her elder brother looked exasperated. He opened his mouth to berate her, but Mei Mei interrupted him.

"I can do it by myself," she said. She crouched behind the boy and wrapped her arms around his torso. His eyes remained closed. He had, it appeared, passed out.

The elder brother began counting from *one*. On *three*, the sons heaved, and Mei Mei dragged the boy out from under his horse. She knew it wasn't good to jostle a broken bone, so she tried to be as careful as she could, dragging him only just as far as she needed to free his foot.

"Where's Doctor Zhang?" one of the sons asked.

Mei Mei explained that her father was away. "But we should get him out of the cold and into the house," Mei Mei said. She looked at the boy's ankle, which was bent at an unnatural angle. "He'll need a splint."

She ran back into their house, through the inner courtyard, straight to her father's office, where she grabbed two pieces of bamboo and a roll of bandages and gauze. She had seen her father make a splint before, as she'd held the child's arm steady. Now the knowledge came back to her.

Ma Ma came out of the kitchen just as Mei Mei was rushing out the door. "What are you doing?"

"Someone's injured."

Wiping her hands on her apron, Ma Ma followed Mei Mei back to the boy outside. The Yu siblings crowded around curiously as Mei Mei carefully cut off his pant leg, which was stained with blood. There was a deep cut down the side of his leg, where Mei Mei had suspected there might be, and she cleaned up the blood as best as she could. She put pressure on the wound until it stopped bleeding. Then, she placed the splints on either side of his ankle, and fastened it firmly with the bandages.

"What now?" Ming asked.

"We bring him inside," Ma Ma said.

THE BOY WAS carefully settled into Da Ge's empty bed. Mei Mei peered into her brothers' room and watched the boy from the doorway. Now that the crisis had passed, Mei Mei felt embarrassed at how boldly she had touched him. She could still smell his sweat that lingered on her clothing. Everyone would see at once what she had done, just by looking at her. How she had clasped him in her arms.

"HE MUST BE some rich young master," Ge Ge scoffed when he returned home from school to find the boy in the bed next to his. Dismissively, he grabbed his erhu and went out in the courtyard to practice.

Judging from the boy's clothing, Mei Mei thought Ge Ge's guess was likely true. The boy was dressed in a thickly padded coat of fine blue wool, and his shoes and cap were embroidered with shining silk threads. His scattered sacks, which Mei Mei and Ge Ge had gathered up and brought inside, were also made of the highest quality cotton and filled with choice cuts of dried pork and fish and several purses of coins.

"What was he doing riding by himself on such an icy road?" Ma Ma asked, shaking her head. "And so young, too."

"Looks around my age," Ge Ge said.

Mei Mei dreaded the return of her father, who would be sure to scold her for her impropriety with the boy. But when Ba Ba came home, he didn't scold her—to her surprise. Instead, he nodded approvingly.

"You did a good job," he said, inspecting the splint.

Mei Mei ducked her head, pleased.

Ba Ba contemplated her for a few moments. "If only you were a son," he said with a sigh.

THE NEXT DAY, Mei Mei opened her eyes to the sound of the boy speaking. His voice came to her in muffled waves through the adjacent wall, but the sound still set her nerves alight. She wondered if he would remember how she had held him, and could feel her cheeks burning again. Mei Mei slowly braided her hair until the flush in her cheeks receded. Then, she took a deep breath and left the safety of her room.

At breakfast, Mei Mei kept glancing toward the closed door of her brothers' room. She was reluctant to ask her mother all the questions that filled her mind. She didn't want to appear too eager or curious.

When Ba Ba came out of the room and saw Mei Mei's expectant eyes, he laughed. Sitting down at the table, Ba Ba instructed Ma Ma on the kinds of porridges to make for the boy, who would need nourishing meals that would help knit the bones in his ankle together. When Ba Ba was finished, Mei Mei saw her chance.

"What's his name?" she asked.

"Tan Haiyang," Ba Ba said. "The son of Lord Tan."

Three generations back, there had been a member of the Tan family who had passed the imperial examinations and served the emperor himself. Now, of course, there were no more opportunities to do so—not for the Tans or anyone else. It had been over a decade since the last examinations and the nation was no longer interested in scholars—only in surviving the struggles that emerged after the fall of the emperors. But the Tans' standing remained.

Years earlier, Ba Ba had treated Lord Tan's wife for a persistent cough. In addition to a respectable sum of money, he had been gifted a set of heavy silver teacups. Ma Ma had quickly stored the teacups away, but Mei Mei still remembered the way they shone from the brief glance she got of them.

"The family is all in Changsha right now," Ba Ba said, "in their winter apartment."

"What is he doing out here?" Ma Ma asked.

"Apparently, Lord Tan sent him to fetch a document from their summer manor."

"All by himself?" Ma Ma asked.

"A chance to prove himself, perhaps," Ba Ba said absently. "I'll notify Lord Tan what has happened to his son. For now, the young master should remain here until his family makes arrangements. It's best not to move his foot any more than necessary. Thankfully, it's a clean break."

"Then, Ge Ge will have to sleep in the kitchen for a few more days?" Mei Mei asked.

"He won't be too happy about that," Ma Ma said.

FOR THE NEXT two days, Ba Ba stayed home to treat their guest. Despite Mei Mei's best efforts, the wound on his leg had gotten infected and oozed a yellow pus. The boy began to run a high fever, and Mei Mei was told to prepare clean, cool washcloths to help bring down his temperature. Once, Mei Mei slipped inside her brothers' room, but the sight of the boy lying so still and silent in the bed frightened her. That night, she dreamed of the moment she pulled him out from under his horse. But in her dream, she was careless, and his foot was torn clean off. And then, it was her being crushed under the horse, until she woke with a gasp.

LORD TAN HAD responded to Ba Ba's letter with one of his own, expressing his deepest gratitude. He and his eldest son, he wrote, were in Beijing on business, but he had made arrangements for his servants to ready their countryside manor for Haiyang's arrival once his infection was better. Lord Tan would be traveling back after the New Year and would stop by the Zhang house to pick up his son. If Doctor Zhang would be so kind as to continue caring for his son, he would be well compensated.

Mei Mei could tell that her father was irked by the imperious tone in the letter. "Lord Tan will deign to visit us in his own time," he told Ma Ma, shaking his head. "That is the way of these lords."

ON THE MORNING of the tenth day, the boy's fever broke, and he was finally able to eat on his own. Mei Mei was tasked with bringing him afternoon refreshments. Ma Ma handed her a bamboo tray laden with steaming porridge cooked in chicken soup, with a warning on her lips.

"Be careful."

Mei Mei gingerly balanced the tray in her hands and headed over to the boy's room. At the doorway, she hesitated. She was afraid of seeing again his motionless body. She thought for a moment of returning to the kitchen, but Da Ge had always told her to be brave—braver than she felt. Mei Mei entered the room.

The boy called Haiyang was lying in bed with his eyes closed. He seemed like a pearl nestled in the midst of the blankets that covered him, an entirely different kind of creature from her father or brothers. Mei Mei could hardly imagine them next to one another.

Haiyang did not stir, not even when Mei Mei set the tray down on his bedside table. But just as Mei Mei turned to leave, he groaned in pain and opened his eyes.

"Should I call my father?" Mei Mei asked.

"No need," Haiyang said. "He already gave me something for the pain." He tried to give her a smile. "Forgive me for not greeting you properly," he said.

"There's nothing to forgive," Mei Mei said. "I should be the one to apologize." She wanted to confess her improper behavior from the day she pulled him out from under his horse, but she couldn't bring herself to voice the words. It was humiliating enough—even more so if spoken aloud in the measured light of day.

"I should be thanking you for saving me," Haiyang said.

"It was nothing," Mei Mei said, blushing. This morning, Haiyang looked even more handsome than when she had first seen him, despite the pallor of his skin. And there was something so kind about his demeanor.

"I'll be forever in your debt," he said, before grimacing suddenly.

"Are you sure you don't want me to fetch my father?"

He shook his head. "But if you could fetch me some books or other distractions, I would be ever so grateful."

"Of course," Mei Mei said. "My elder brother is a scholar, and he has many books in his room. As many as you can imagine. He's studying at First Normal School right now, and he's very fond of reading." Mei Mei knew she was rambling, but she didn't know how to stop. The more nervous she felt, the more the words poured out of her.

"Do you like to read?" she asked.

"I do," Haiyang said.

Mei Mei selected a few of her favorite volumes of poetry from Da Ge's bookshelves. Da Ge had often asked her to fetch them to him whenever he was practicing his recitations, and she knew the location of each one.

"Here you go," she said, handing him the books.

"Thank you," Haiyang said. "It looks like I'm in your debt again."

A laugh escaped Mei Mei's lips, and she quickly composed herself again. She pointed to the cover of the book Haiyang was flipping through.

"I like that one the most," Mei Mei said.

"You know how to read?" Haiyang asked in surprise.

Mei Mei stiffened.

"I apologize if my question made you uncomfortable," Haiyang said. "My mother is an educated woman. My sisters, too. They often sit in on my lessons at home." He paused. "But of course, most women don't—"

"I know how to read," Mei Mei said. "My elder brother taught me," she added proudly. That day in the classroom was now so long ago, but still Mei Mei remembered. How her mother had walked home with her, her body a sadness.

Haiyang smiled. "Maybe you can read some of these poems to me, then."

"I can recite them even," Mei Mei said. She stared at the wall in front of her, the tips of her ears turning pink. "If you'd like."

"Please," Haiyang said.

Mei Mei always loved to listen to Da Ge's recitations and the way she'd feel enveloped by his warm voice. Da Ge would stride around the room, bringing the words to life with vivid detail. She knew all the words of Da Ge's favorite poems by heart. The one about the autumn moon shining in a pool of green water. Or the one about the soldier dying valiantly on the battlefield. But no one had ever asked her to recite them.

Though her voice was not as commanding as Da Ge's, Mei Mei tried to recite Li Bai's poems with Da Ge's same passion. For the first time, she felt as though she could truly understand the old classical poems, feeling as she had never felt before the grief and the longing. When Mei Mei finished and looked toward Haiyang, she found his gaze fixed on hers. There was a lofty grace in the tilt of his head and the sharp lines of his brow. Mei Mei couldn't look away.

"Might I be so bold as to ask your name?" Haiyang asked.

"They call me Zhang Yunhong."

He smiled. "What a beautiful name."

HAIYANG'S NAME IN its entirety, Mei Mei learned, was another name for the ocean—which was boundless and deep and everlasting. The name suited him, for his eyes seemed to her like oceans themselves. She had never seen the ocean but had read about it plenty before in books. In their writings, poets often spoke of the ocean, praising its rich blues and greens. But the ocean could also be terrifying. If you fell into the water, you might get swallowed up and lose yourself forever.

As the afternoon sun threw shadows across the room, Ma Ma came into the room with another tray of food.

"Let the young master rest." She set the tray down beside Haiyang's bedside and lowered the curtain before lighting a lantern. "Go downstairs to eat, Mei Mei."

Was it already time for dinner? How it had all passed so quickly.

WITH EACH DAY, Mei Mei and Haiyang's words came more and more freely. Soon, it felt as if they had known each other forever. Perhaps how vulnerable he looked lying in bed inspired a deep well of tenderness inside her. Haiyang was making steady progress in the recovery of his broken ankle, though the infection in his leg still lingered. Still, his cheeks had finally regained some color. When Mei Mei sat with him in the evenings, they seemed to flush even more. Mei Mei, too, felt herself flushing from the inside out, as if pinkening with the coming spring.

Mei Mei showed him her embroidery. She felt awash with pride as Haiyang admired the feathers on her birds, the curling leaves of her flowers. She watched as he tried to push the needle through the cloth precisely, stifling her giggles at his clumsy fingers.

In return, he told her stories of the world beyond her world—beyond even Ba Ba's world. The vast fields his father owned. The farmers in their wide-brimmed hats. The summers, on horseback, surveying the lands and traveling to Changsha on business with his elder brother and father.

Sometimes, they even spoke of the Great War outside China. Of Europe and Allies and Germany. The Empress Dowager, Mei Mei learned, had shipped many peasants over to Europe to labor for the war effort. They were doing the repairing work, passing secret messages. They were dying there, unwillingly, longing for home. How long would their ghosts wander until they found their way home again? Across oceans, cold mountains?

"It isn't right that we should fight their wars," Haiyang said. "Not when there's still so much work to be done to shape our own country." He glanced at Mei Mei. "What do you think?"

No one had ever asked her opinion on matters of politics in the way that Haiyang did. So seriously, and with such eagerness to hear her thoughts. Sometimes, she didn't have much of an opinion on countries outside of China—which seemed as distant to her as the stars in the sky. Sometimes, she could barely understand what he was asking. But she always did her best to answer him honestly.

"I agree," Mei Mei said. "But maybe this will bring us good karma, and others will help us in turn."

Haiyang also told her how he wanted to travel the country and write down what he saw, like the great writer Xu Xiake.

"You know Xu Xiake, don't you?" Haiyang asked. At the shake of her head, he told her about him, how he traveled all across China with one companion—a servant named Gu Xing. "Together, they went from town to town, recording all that they saw. Xu Xiake loved the mountains and rivers and followed every road to its end. It was not just the land that fascinated him, but the people, too. Often, he stopped at monasteries, recording the histories he found there. And he would talk with other local scholars deep into the night, raising his glass to the moon. He was like the wind if the wind had a heart and mind—traveling far and wide wherever he wished. He was one who truly lived as so few have ever lived—before or since."

Mei Mei felt her own excitement stir at his words. She imagined traveling the country with Haiyang. Imagined racing on the back of a horse, the wind in her hair and eyes.

Only the infection in his leg would hold him back.

"But I have faith your father will heal me." He turned to her with a brilliant smile. "Doctor Zhang is respected throughout Liuyang. And if I know my mother, she'll be going to Kaifu Temple to pray for his success."

Mei Mei nodded. "I, too, will pray for your health."

"With your prayers, how could the gods deny me?" Haiyang's voice was teasing, but his eyes were lovely and dark.

Yet last year, much of the temple had burned to the ground. Mei Mei remembered her mother speaking of it with the neighbors. It was an omen, the neighbors had said, of the troubled future. Of the flames yet to come.

The Girl Who Was the Hungry Ghost

BEFORE MEI MEI knew it, New Year's Eve was upon them. The east wind arrived with its warm and fragrant breezes. Everywhere, there was a sense of hope renewed. After all, it would be the year of the ram—a year of promise and kindness.

Mei Mei and Haiyang cut out red paper decorations in the shape of children and qilins, and Ge Ge begrudgingly helped Mei Mei hang them in the windows facing the inner courtyard. He didn't seem to have any fondness for their guest. Rather, he seemed resentful of having to give up his room, and had been staying later than he normally did at school to study. Mei Mei didn't mind. She enjoyed having Haiyang all to herself.

Mei Mei felt a mix of dread and expectation. Haiyang would be leaving the next day, but Da Ge would be coming home that evening. It had been over half a year since she had last heard her elder brother's voice, and she didn't know when she would be able to hear it again. She knew it wasn't easy to travel during the winter, and that he was busy, too, with his studies. But a part of her wondered if those were just excuses to avoid coming back home. After the cutting of his hair, Da Ge's relationship with Ma Ma and Ba Ba had not been the same. Their conversations were filled with weighted silences or muttered remarks that often left Da Ge looking stormy. Mei Mei wished she could ride Ba Ba's mule and go see him by herself.

In the morning, while outside feeding the chickens, Mei Mei watched for her brother. Was that shadow turning the corner his? Were those the sounds of his footsteps? Each time, she was disappointed. Not his shadow, not his footstep, but merely the branch turning in the wind.

But then, after Mei Mei and Haiyang had eaten lunch, it was Da Ge.

Mei Mei raced out of the house. She jumped over the threshold of the main door and leaped into his arms. Her elder brother dropped his bags to catch her, as she knew he would.

His hair was still short. Just as it was the day she cut it. He would never wear it long again, Mei Mei knew.

Ma Ma met them at the door. She regarded Da Ge from a few steps away. It was the first time they had seen each other since their argument, and Mei Mei held her breath. Then, she took Da Ge by the hand and led him toward their mother. Mei Mei took Ma Ma's hand, and she brought all their hands together.

At this, Ma Ma softened. Mei Mei stepped back to let them embrace. Ba Ba watched from a distance, and he nodded at Da Ge but did not smile. As was usual, no one spoke of Da Ge's hair.

It was the New Year, and so Da Ge had brought Mei Mei and Ge Ge each a gift. To Ge Ge, he presented a rattle-drum, painted on both sides with the image of a snake. "For the musician of our family," Da Ge teased. Though he complained he was too old for such a toy, Ge Ge rolled it between his palms. The wooden beads beat wildly against the skin of the drums. Mei Mei could tell he was pleased. He had always looked up, as she had, to their eldest brother. In that, at least, the two younger siblings were the same.

To Mei Mei, Da Ge gave a picture book called *Leigong and Dianmu*. He had seen a shadow puppet play about their story with a friend, Da Ge told her, and hoped she would enjoy it. The story, he explained, was a romance. "Leigong, the god of thunder," Da Ge said, "kills a human woman named Dianmu. The Jade Emperor resurrects her and makes her the goddess of lightning. Dianmu and Leigong are married and, together, they create storms overhead." He explained that death could offer up a new beginning. "There can be no thunder without lightning, no lightning without thunder. They are forever intertwined—inseparable."

Though Mei Mei loved the gift, she thought the story strange in his mouth—her elder brother was never one for romances. He always refused to see the matchmaker. Ma Ma had tried to persuade him, but he never listened. Mei Mei wondered whom he accompanied to the play, but she was more concerned with examining the pages of her new book, which were bound in white string. Some of the pages had text, while others had images, drawn in black ink. She marveled over the illustrations of women with long, flowing sleeves and shining mirrors that could light up the sky.

That afternoon, she showed the picture book to Haiyang. They bent their heads toward one another as they traced the characters with their fingers.

When Mei Mei looked up, she saw Da Ge watching them from the doorway. For a moment, he seemed like Ba Ba, on the verge of scolding her, a frown lingering on his face. She felt a flash of guilt—as if she were doing something wrong. But she wanted to spend as much time as possible with Haiyang. After all, it would be his last night before returning home. Soon, Mei Mei would only be able to imagine him, as she imagined the characters on the page.

LATER THAT AFTERNOON, Da Ge was standing by the pond, scattering crumbs into the water. Fish rose to the surface. Even after all these years, the sight of the carp reminded her of her elder brother's hair. How they had tried to devour it all.

Mei Mei crouched down and dipped her finger to the water. Immediately, her hand was swarmed with fish, biting at the tips of her fingers. For a moment, it seemed as if she were touching a brilliance of silver and orange scales—a ball of underwater fire.

"Do you think they are beautiful?" Da Ge asked. He watched her move her hand back and forth in the water, the fish following her fingers.

"Don't you?" Mei Mei asked, turning to look back at him.

He knelt down beside her and watched the water splash before them. Then, suddenly, he snatched a fish with his hands, raising it out of the pond. The carp squirmed fiercely in the air, but Da Ge's hold was tight and firm. At last, the carp stilled and only its mouth moved, gasping for water.

"They are beautiful, aren't they? Covered as they are in gold and silver," Da Ge said. "But although we feed and raise them until they are fat and plump, they do not care for us." Gently, he placed the fish back into the water. Its brightness quickly disappeared into the depths.

"They will never care for us," Da Ge said, his eyes cold. "Never forget that."

Her elder brother's anger had always seemed to her passionate and warm, like a stove fire on a winter's night. Now, it felt dangerous—something aimed at her.

AT DINNER THAT night in the courtyard, the table overflowed with dishes. Haiyang, with his leg elevated, sat beside Mei Mei, talking of all he would do once he arrived back home. He'd test his younger sister on her studies, as he was sure she hadn't been as diligent in his absence. Normally, he explained, he would tutor her for an hour every night. He was also sure that his mother—being the third wife of Lord Tan—would have several grievances with his father's other wives she'd want him to address. As Mei Mei bit into her nian gao, she caught Da Ge eyeing Haiyang across the table. Her elder brother proposed a toast.

"Now that the Great War is over, may our allies honor their promises to us. To our people who have given their lives. May China enter a new age." He raised his wine cup with both hands and tipped back his head.

Haiyang nodded and raised his cup. Ma Ma, too, followed. But Ba Ba looked down and swirled his cup without drinking, as if he could divine the future in the ripples.

In the evening, Da Ge led everyone outside the house to set off firecrackers. Mei Mei clapped her hands over her ears when the first firecracker was set off. Glowing sparks lit up their faces in the darkness. Mei Mei used to be frightened of the firecrackers when she was younger, but eventually she learned she had nothing to be scared of. It was the evil spirits and demons they were driving away. The ones who would snatch you away from those you loved. They might appear before you as a ghost even—a hungry one who had died unhappily.

Indeed, they might be like the hungry ghost that Ge Ge told her about. The one who had brushed against his ankle when he had waded into the pond. At first, he thought it was a fish, or maybe even a turtle, who was nibbling at his skin. But when he looked down, he saw hair swirling in the water beside him. And there was a girl's face, too, entirely white, floating just below the surface. Her eyes were closed, but at any moment she might open them. Perhaps it was their great-great (or maybe great-great-great) grandmother, who, it was said, drowned in the pond. She had been a child bride, after all, and didn't know how to swim. She must have died unhappily, with her life cut so short.

"So be careful when you step into the water," Ge Ge had warned, smiling a little meanly.

THE NEXT MORNING, on festival day, Ba Ba lit incense while Ma Ma put out offerings for their ancestors. Everyone took time to pray, conversing with the dead. Even Haiyang, having been carried outside by Mei Mei's brothers into a chair out of his consideration for his ankle, took the time to light some incense. Mei Mei felt the weight of her family's ghosts in the air.

Da Ge lit more firecrackers. But these were not for scaring ghosts away. They were for welcoming the new year. This time, Mei Mei grabbed one of the firecrackers and held it in the air. Sparks flew from her hands, and Haiyang laughed in delight. One day, Mei Mei wished, they might meet again. Mei Mei did not close her eyes but kept them open through the clamoring light.

LORD TAN ARRIVED shortly after lunch, in an elaborately carved carriage with fragrant sandalwood screen windows. The carriage, accompanied by several servants, parked in front of their house. Waiting respectfully outside with her brothers, Mei Mei watched as a large, pale hand pulled the curtain aside. A silk slipper emerged, followed by a black robe embroidered with clouds. Then, the wide, ruddy face of Lord Tan appeared. Lord Tan was a tall man with a short black beard. Haiyang, Mei Mei thought, didn't seem to resemble his father one bit.

Mei Mei was curious about this lord to whom they all now bowed respectfully. Haiyang always spoke of his father with admiration. He told Mei Mei of the time Lord Tan had fought off highwaymen in his youth. Of how he had survived a shipwreck and swam a whole day and night to find land. Of the time he had narrowly escaped death after being gored in the thigh by a wild boar during a hunt. But there was also a hint of bitterness in Haiyang's voice, especially when he wondered what pressing business matters had delayed Lord Tan and his eldest brother from fetching him. "I suppose the youngest son of the third wife ought to be considered the spare of the spare," he had said with a self-deprecating laugh.

Now, Mei Mei could see just what kind of man it was that Haiyang so looked up to. Lord Tan brusquely nodded at Ba Ba and demanded to be brought to see his son. Ba Ba led the way into the house, where Haiyang was sitting in the inner courtyard.

When Haiyang saw his father, he greeted him eagerly. But his expression, Mei Mei noticed, dimmed when Lord Tan only nodded curtly back. Ba Ba explained Haiyang's injuries and the treatment he had provided to stabilize the bones in his ankle and treat the infection in his leg. He informed Lord Tan of the specialized diet that Haiyang would have to be on for the next few months in order to stimulate his body's natural healing processes. Then, Ba Ba took Haiyang's pulse carefully, at three different positions on his wrist, to assess his health. Mei Mei hovered over Haiyang's shoulders.

At last, Ba Ba smiled. "Your vitality is strong," he proclaimed. "The infection is ebbing and your bones are healing. I foresee a complete recovery of your leg and ankle by the end of the year."

"Excellent," Lord Tan said. "You have exceeded your reputation, Doctor Zhang."

Ba Ba invited Lord Tan to sit on one of the lacquered chairs that had been brought into the courtyard for the occasion of his visit. Lord Tan sat down with a flourish of his robes. Ma Ma came in with a tray of tea and served Lord Tan, Ba Ba, then Haiyang, before calling for Mei Mei to follow her back into the kitchen. Mei Mei did so with reluctance but sat beside the window that faced the inner courtyard in the hopes of seeing what was happening.

The two men sipped some tea, and then Lord Tan took out a small glass bottle from his sleeve and extracted a little bit of snuff with the stopper spoon. After inhaling, he offered the bottle to Ba Ba.

Ba Ba accepted with a nod of thanks and turned the bottle over, admiring the painting on the outside.

"The detail of the portrait is beautiful," Ba Ba said. He, too, took some snuff before passing the bottle back.

"That it is," said Lord Tan, slipping it into his sleeve. "I commissioned

Master Su to paint my wife about a year ago. But he's so popular now that he's only just gotten around to finishing it."

"It's truly stunning," Ba Ba said.

"Have you ever seen the artists at work?" Lord Tan asked. "Their little brushes move so delicately inside the glass. It's amazing to observe."

"I haven't yet had the opportunity," Ba Ba said.

"Perhaps I can introduce you to Master Su."

Ba Ba smiled and nodded. "That would be most kind of you."

They spoke of the weather and the fields. All signs pointed to a promising spring, they agreed.

Stroking his beard with his left hand, Lord Tan complained that his youngest son had a weak constitution—he took after his mother. "None of my other sons have ever fallen off their horses," he said.

"The roads are icy in the winter, my lord," Ba Ba said.

"Have your sons ever fallen off a horse?" Lord Tan asked.

"No, my lord. But they do not ride as often your sons do."

"My eldest son," Lord Tan said proudly, "is a great rider."

"I'm sure he is."

"And your sons are your apprentices?" Lord Tan asked.

Ba Ba smiled with a hint of embarrassment. "I had hoped one would carry on my profession, but alas they have neither the mind nor heart for it. My last apprentice left three years ago to start his own business and family. Since then, I haven't trained a new one."

Lord Tan drained the remaining tea in his cup, then beckoned at one of the servants. The servant brought out a heavy purse and presented it to Ba Ba.

"For your troubles," Lord Tan said.

Ba Ba accepted the payment with thanks.

The servants then carried Haiyang to the carriage, taking care not to jostle his bound ankle. Mei Mei slipped out of the kitchen and followed anxiously behind. When Haiyang was settled onto the carriage seat, he bowed his head to Ba Ba and the rest of the Zhang family who were now gathered to see him and his father off. He thanked Ba Ba for rescuing him from his fall, for their hospitality—for everything. "I am forever in your debt, Doctor Zhang."

Ba Ba shook his head. "Nonsense." He handed Lord Tan's servants several jars of ointment that would have to be carefully applied to Haiyang's still-healing wound every night.

Mei Mei stepped forward and handed him a book of poems. "I'll miss you." She wondered if he would miss her, too. Since his arrival, her days had been filled with visions of poets galloping on horseback across wild plains, the sand-blown outposts of the Silk Road, the deep ocean everlasting, and the world beyond China. She couldn't bear to think of the silence his departure would bring.

Mei Mei wanted to hold his hand but held back. She felt the weight of Ma Ma and Ba Ba's eyes on her. Between the pages of the book, she had slipped in a letter in which she expressed everything she could not say out loud.

Haiyang smiled. "I won't forget you." He met her eyes. "We'll see each other again. I promise."

THAT EVENING, Mei Mei worked on embroidering a pair of horses racing across a wide open field while her elder brother talked to Ma Ma and Ba Ba. Their voices were hushed in the dark until Ma Ma lit a candle. The girl's name was Liying. Da Ge was in love. They wanted—no—were going to get married. He had already asked her parents and he wished—wished for blessings from his own.

"You and this girl plan to marry?" Ba Ba was incredulous. "Before you have even brought her home to see us?" His hand clenched into a fist on the table. "We know nothing of her circumstances, her character." He looked at Ma Ma. "And what of her family? What of her background?"

Da Ge furrowed his brows. "How could a matchmaker know her character better than I? Her character is far better than my own. And there is no shame in her family. Her father is a well-known, well-spoken tailor. She makes me happy. Happier than any other. When you meet her, you will understand."

Ba Ba shook his head in disgust. "I will never meet her!" On the wall, the shadow of Ba Ba's arm reached across the room. His voice bent back the flame of the candle.

Mei Mei crept between them as the two men stood. The tips of her fingers tingled. She touched her elder brother's arm and did not know if it was he who was trembling or her. "Don't fight," she pleaded, feeling like a child again.

But Da Ge and Ba Ba were not listening.

"How could you be such an unfilial son? How could you bring so much pain to your parents? First, your hair. Then, the student protests. And now this." Ba Ba's voice grew bitter. "Do you know how many tears your mother has shed? Do you even care?"

"Of course I care," Da Ge said angrily. "It is because I care—because I love—that I dare do this."

"You don't know the meaning of love," Ba Ba scoffed.

Sitting in her chair, Ma Ma was quiet, watching the candle as it folded down.

THE NEXT DAY was filled with tense silences. After breakfast, Ba Ba sequestered himself in his office. Ma Ma sighed and asked Da Ge to kill one of the chickens for lunch.

Da Ge borrowed one of Ba Ba's old, stained shirts. In the kitchen, he selected a long knife and tested the edge against his finger. "Mei Mei, come with me."

They went outside behind the house to the coop where the chickens were kept. Mei Mei called for White Flower to come sit in her lap and

stroked the hen's one white feather. She felt dull and listless. She wondered if Haiyang had read her letter by now, and what he thought of it. In
it, she had spoken of wanting to travel the world with him on horseback,
even if only in her dreams.

Mei Mei looked up at her elder brother. How did he know which one
was the one fated for death? Today, it might be a black one. Next year, it
might be a red one.

"Do you think you have chosen well?" she asked.

"Chosen well?"

"The one you call Liying."

Da Ge grinned and nodded. "Ba Ba will come around. There is no
stopping us, after all."

He bent down and picked up White Flower in his arms. At first, Mei
Mei thought he was simply admiring how lovely the hen had grown, but
then she realized what he was about to do. She sprung to her feet and
tried to reach for her hen, but Da Ge held White Flower out of reach.

"She's the oldest out of the bunch," he said. "And Ma Ma told me she's
stopped laying eggs."

"Choose another one," Mei Mei begged. Tears filled her eyes.

But Da Ge didn't listen. He strung the squawking hen up by her feet,
away from the others, and placed a bucket on the ground in front of him.
He held White Flower's head tightly with his left hand. With the other, he
swiftly drew the knife across the hen's neck. Blood poured out from the
cut, redder than a bride's falling veil.

A Trip Down the River

As HE HAD foreseen to Mei Mei, Da Ge and Liying were married. But Mei Mei could only imagine the three marriage bows she would never see. The bows to the heaven and earth, to the parents, and to each other. For though her brother had sent a wedding invitation, Ba Ba forbade the family from going, and no one dared protest Ba Ba's decision. They could see from the firm set of his mouth that he would not change his mind. Ge Ge played songs that entire week—festive wedding songs. Notes leapt into the air like sparks, each one tinged with a kind of longing. He curled his body around his erhu. None spoke of what they missed.

As the year passed, Da Ge's letters, always unanswered, came less and less. At times, Mei Mei asked Ge Ge to read them to her, as his voice had gained a timbre over the years that reminded her of Da Ge. Occasionally, Ge Ge would oblige, and the two of them bent their heads over the words their eldest brother had written. When they were finished, Ge Ge would fold the letters carefully along their original creases before putting them away in his desk.

In autumn, many harvests failed after a rainless year. The papers spoke of drought and hundreds of thousands dead. The people spoke of divine punishment and a crumbling, divided nation. There were no more emperors left—only warlords. Where would China be in a decade, a century? No one seemed to know.

Mei Mei went with her mother to give alms while Ba Ba was away. The two went to the temple to pray at Guanyin's feet. Ma Ma and Ba Ba believed that those who suffered or did good deeds would live a better life in the next. They were not like her brothers, who believed that everyone was only given one life. Mei Mei found it hard to imagine what her past life might have been. Perhaps her brothers were right, after all. She worried about Da Ge, so far away and so separate. She thought of going herself to visit him. Of slipping away in the night. But she did not know how to reach him or where he lived. She did not know how to read unfamiliar roads or navigate strange cities. She could not ride a horse like Haiyang or follow the wind like Xu Xiake. She could only visit Da Ge in her dreams.

By the time Mei Mei turned fourteen, her hair had grown so long it reached her waist. Whenever she braided her hair, she caught sight of the scar on her palm. It was a pale, thin line—barely noticeable. Something only she saw. Often, she thought of Haiyang. She wondered if he thought of her, or if he still had her letter. At night, Mei Mei practiced her characters on her own, trying her hand at calligraphy. But the two characters she practiced the most, over and over, were *hai* and *yang*.

The following spring, the rains were kept at bay for two months, and the water in the pond almost dried out completely. Most of the carp died off from disease. Where was the hungry ghost now? Mei Mei wondered. She took off her shoes and waded out in her bare feet. Her brother's hair was in there somewhere at the very bottom, mixed in with the bones of the fish. And in each strand, there remained a part of him. She put her hands in the mud, but never found what she was looking for.

Now, Mei Mei never sought out Ge Ge after he returned from school. She knew better than to disrupt him from his studies. More and more, his temper flared at the slightest provocation. "Don't bother me, Mei Mei," he would say. "I'm very busy." He would shut himself up in his room with his piles of books and burning candlelight. He no longer played his erhu in the evenings. He was solely focused on the county's primary examinations the next year, hoping to be admitted to First Normal School and follow in their elder brother's footsteps. After graduating, Da Ge had worked as an elementary school teacher while also tutoring on the side. Ge Ge wanted to do the same, though Mei Mei wondered if he would have the same patience for teaching as Da Ge had.

"He's simply worried about his exams," Ma Ma said as Mei Mei headed out after another such outburst from Ge Ge. Then, she added, "If you're going down to the river, take these clothes with you to wash."

So Mei Mei cultivated her friendships with the neighboring girls: Ming, whose three brothers had since moved to Changsha in search of work, and Fan Hua, who came from a family of fishermen. Ming always brought pillows to Mei Mei to be embroidered with flowers, while Hua insisted on birds on her dresses. Mei Mei didn't mind sewing for them or embroidering their requests. She liked to imagine her stitches being worn by other people, kept close to their skin. In return, Ming gave Mei Mei pots she painted herself, and Hua brought her fresh-caught fish, their eyes still glossy and clear.

"Perhaps you take after your grandmother," Ma Ma said, looking over the line of gulls Mei Mei had stitched for Hua. "They said the birds she'd sewn would take flight."

When Mei Mei was first learning to embroider, just eight years old, Ma Ma had searched through her room and pulled out a trunk made of dark purple wood. Inside, nestled against the red silk lining, there was a blanket, heavy with blue and silver threads. On the blanket were embroidered rows of swallows, head to tail, against a band of blue.

"I've never shown this to you, have I?" Ma Ma had draped it playfully over Mei Mei's shoulders. It was a wedding gift, her mother explained, from her grandmother. "Your grandmother passed a year before you were born," she told Mei Mei. "She used to tell me that her mother came from Xinjiang, the part that is furthest away, near Russia. It would explain her strikingly geometric style of embroidery. Your great-grandmother must have traveled a long way, don't you think?"

Mei Mei wondered how her great-grandmother had made her way, down into the heart of China, on the back of a horse, its hair windblown, tangled in her own. Her story, too, was windblown.

"One day, it will be yours as a dowry," Ma Ma said. "And the trunk, too."

The trunk was made of zitan wood—wood so heavy that it would sink in water.

"See?" Ma Ma said, knocking her knuckles against the side of the chest. "It's so strong, it'll protect you from anything."

Ma Ma gave Mei Mei the blanket for one night. Mei Mei wrapped the blanket around her shoulders and slept with it on her bed. In the night, she woke—breath short, a pressure on her chest. She threw off the blanket, relieved of the feeling pressing down, and stayed awake until she could breathe again.

ONE DAY, Ba Ba came home with a letter in his hand. Mei Mei, sitting with Ma Ma by the window, turned as her father entered the dining room. Mei Mei could tell the letter was from her elder brother by the handwriting on the envelope. As she threaded her needle, she watched Ba Ba out of the corner of her eye.

Ba Ba tore open the envelope and scanned the letter. His face turned red then white. He put down the letter on the table then picked it up again.

Mei Mei put down her needle. "What is it, Ba Ba? Has something happened?"

Her father said nothing. He crumpled the letter in his hands and stared at the table.

At his silence, Ma Ma rose from her seat and went over to him. "Is something wrong?" she asked, touching his shoulder.

"Your eldest son has just had a child."

"A child?" Ma Ma's eyes widened, and she pried the letter from Ba Ba's hands. She carefully flattened it out on the table.

"A girl," Ba Ba added.

"A girl," Mei Mei breathed out. A baby girl with Da Ge's eyes and his smile. She felt a sense of wonder at the thought, a joy so sharp it pained her. Mei Mei turned to her mother. "Can we visit Da Ge? Can we go see the baby?"

"No." Ba Ba shook his head.

"But Ba Ba—"

"No, Mei Mei." Ba Ba looked sternly at her. "They have made their choice. I have made mine."

LATER, HELPING HER mother in the kitchen, Mei Mei tried again.

"I miss Da Ge."

Ma Ma rinsed the rice with water, stirring it with her hand. Soon the water turned cloudy. "I miss him, too."

"Can we go by ourselves?" Mei Mei bent down to light the flame.

"Peace, Mei Mei," Ma Ma said. "Time will show us a way."

THE OPPORTUNITY CAME sooner than Mei Mei expected. At the end of spring, Ge Ge passed the primary exams and was ranked second in the whole county. The county recommended him, along with twelve others, to First Normal School.

Ba Ba proposed a toast at dinner in Ge Ge's honor—the first time he had ever done so. "To my youngest son," he said, raising his glass, "May he continue to bring honor to our family." He tipped back his head and drank down the rice wine.

They all followed suit—Ma Ma, Ge Ge, and even Mei Mei, who usually wasn't fond of the way the wine made her head feel clouded and dull. But that evening, Mei Mei only felt a warm glow from the wine sliding down her throat. Nothing could dull the bright pride that she, too, felt from having not one, but two brothers who were such respected scholars.

Perhaps, Ma Ma suggested to Ba Ba, she could take Ge Ge to Changsha to see the city where he might go to school. A trip to motivate him for his entrance exams. The entrance exams would be even more rigorous and would test him on his written, oral, and physical skills. Each spot was highly coveted, and Ge Ge would have to study like he had never done before in order to have a hope of admittance.

"Mei Mei could come along, too," Ma Ma added.

Mei Mei glanced at her big brother. The longing, the hope she felt inside, was reflected in his eyes. Mei Mei's hand curled into a fist beneath the table. How they both had missed their elder brother so.

The three of them waited for Ba Ba's reply. Mei Mei knew that Ba Ba could see through their flimsy pretense, but she hoped he would relent and let them go.

Ba Ba was silent for a long time. He drank down another glass of wine. Finally, he sighed.

"Go if you wish."

THAT EVENING, Mei Mei began work on a new piece of embroidery. One she had always meant to start. Slowly, patiently, Mei Mei wove together

her colored threads, night after night. Eventually, on the cloth, two cranes appeared. One drank from the water, while the other kept guard. A complete pair. And when she was finished two weeks later, it was time to leave for Changsha.

ON THE WOODEN sampan that Ma Ma hired to take them to Changsha, Mei Mei felt the waves too strongly to sleep. Not in the sick, lying-down way that Ma Ma felt them, but in a way that woke her. She felt the push and pull, tossing them along. Mei Mei turned onto her stomach on the bamboo mat that the old man had laid out for them, but she was stifled and hot.

Ba Ba had rented this very same sampan before, to cart him to and from his patients. The old man who owned and steered the riverboat was dependable, Ba Ba had told them—one of the few comments he had made at all about their trip.

The sampan was of a modest size, with barely enough space for Ma Ma, Ge Ge, and Mei Mei to stretch out under the reed canopy. Mei Mei had been frightened when she first saw it docked along the river. She had wondered, with how old and frail their skipper seemed, how the boat might fare against rocky waves—waves that towered above their heads like the ones in the old stories. She imagined the boat being torn apart and felt a tingle of fear.

But in the evening, the waves were calm. Mei Mei glanced at Ma Ma and Ge Ge, sleeping beside her. Rising quietly, she stepped out from under the canopy. On the other end of the boat, the old man sat on his bench, rowing, guiding them down the Liuyang River, west to Changsha. Mei Mei went over and sat down beside him.

Sitting beneath the stars, Mei Mei felt as if she were borrowing their light, every part inside her aglow. She had never traveled so far from home before.

"You know, my son, when he was little, used to sit there." The old man looked at Mei Mei. "He would accompany me on my trips ferrying people between cities."

He had imagined that his son would have had a child by now. "A grandchild—maybe a granddaughter like you," the old man said. But only his wife and he were left now, he explained. Perhaps in the next life then.

"And now, the years are getting harder. With rice so expensive these days, perhaps we will pass on more quickly than we had thought." The boatman sighed. "Maybe that's not such a bad thing—to be lost to the Heavens and the stars."

Ma Ma emerged to call her to bed.

ALL NIGHT LONG, the moon zigzagged with each turn in the river. In the shallow, muddy parts, cranes tucked their heads under wings. On land, houses were dark where people had drifted off to sleep, unaware of the violent brightness of the stars.

"Look there." The old man pointed to the images unfolding above. Ox-Star. Weaver-Girl.

Unfolding as she was.

IN THE MORNING, the sampan docked in the waterfront at the edge of the city. Ma Ma, Ge Ge, and Mei Mei stumbled out of the riverboat, wincing against the brightness of the sun. Carrying their bags, they followed the old man down the pier and to land. Along the waterfront, Mei Mei marveled at the stalls, full of fragrant candies and bright toys. She wrinkled her nose at the sour smell of sewage and rotting food that wafted over everything in the heat. They passed crowded rice shops, restaurants with paper streamers hanging from the doorways advertising their dishes, and the gleaming, painted doors of foreign consulates. Children in rags crouched in the street, begging for coins. Men roamed the streets, some even with short hair like Da Ge. And to her amazement, she saw two women with eyes the color of the sky and hair the color of yellow carp. They wore strange dark dresses that clung to their arms and breasts and waists before blooming like the cup of a flower. They were foreigners, the old man told them, from an island far away. Mei Mei watched the women until they disappeared into a building with a cross on its door.

Finally, down a narrow side street, they reached the small set of rented rooms where Da Ge and Liying lived. Red paper characters pasted on the door announced to the world their recent good fortune.

Mei Mei ran ahead to knock.

"Mei Mei?"

Mei Mei and her elder brother embraced. Da Ge didn't seem as tall as she remembered, but his hair was still the same—short and sweeping rakishly over his brows.

"I've missed you," Da Ge said, kissing her on her cheek. He turned to greet Ge Ge and Ma Ma.

"What are you all doing here?" Da Ge asked as he carried their bags into the apartment.

"Didn't you get our letter?" Ma Ma asked.

"Letter?" Da Ge shook his head.

Ma Ma explained Ge Ge's recent accomplishment and the opportunity it provided for them to visit.

"Ba Ba . . ." Da Ge hesitated but did not ask his question. Instead, he walked over to the crib in the corner of the room and picked up a small wrapped bundle.

"Her name is Chunfei." Da Ge's voice was filled with pride.

Mei Mei looked down at the O of the baby's mouth. It was such a soft, humid O. Mei Mei looked at the whisper curls of hair on her head. Like the froth of an ocean painted on silk. Mei Mei cradled her and felt her downy breaths on her cheek. She felt the baby's cheek, smooth as the side of an apricot.

All of them marveled at the baby. But Da Ge was the one shining the brightest when he looked at his daughter.

"How have you been?" Ma Ma asked.

"We've been well. Liying and I." Da Ge looked toward the other room, closed off with a curtain. "She's sleeping now. She mostly sleeps since the birth. But she'll be so happy to finally meet you."

Ma Ma piled gifts from home onto a desk beneath the window: candied kumquats for Da Ge, herbal supplements for his wife to replenish her blood, and boiled tea eggs.

Da Ge laughed and shook his head. "Ma Ma, don't bring me anything next time. We have enough." But he accepted the gifts gratefully, as well as the money Ma Ma pressed into his hand.

CHUNFEI WOKE AND began to cry, and Liying emerged from the inner room. She was both not like what Mei Mei had imagined, and somehow, exactly what she had. Liying had striking full eyebrows and an easy smile to match Da Ge's. She was only a little taller than Mei Mei and had high cheekbones. There was a mole beneath her left eye. But what was most striking was her short hair. Mei Mei had never seen a married woman with short hair before.

Liying glanced questioningly at Da Ge.

"This is my little sister," said Da Ge, "my little brother, and my mother." He turned to Liying. "They've traveled all the way from Liuyang to visit us."

A wide grin stretched across Liying's face. She knelt before Ma Ma and took her hand. "I hope you will accept me as your own daughter."

"Please, get up, get up." Ma Ma bent down and helped her to her feet. "You are my daughter now."

Liying then greeted Ge Ge before turning to Mei Mei. "Yunhong," she said, taking her hands. "It's so wonderful to finally meet you." She paused. "May I call you 'Mei Mei'? I feel we are already sisters."

Mei Mei nodded, handing her the embroidered painting she had worked on for so long. "A wedding gift for you and Da Ge."

"Thank you, Mei Mei." Liying examined her gift with a pleased smile. Liying admired aloud how intelligent the necks of the two cranes seemed, how softly rounded their bellies. "Yunli has always praised your workmanship, but your work surpasses even his words."

Mei Mei felt a glowing pride at Liying's praise.

"Who is who?" Liying wondered. "I must be the crane standing upright, looking out. Your brother is the one submerged in whatever he looks at. His head is always underwater." Liying met Da Ge's gaze with a smile.

IN THE EVENING, when the sun began to cool in the sky, Da Ge took Mei Mei and Ge Ge up Yuelu Mountain, leaving Ma Ma with Liying and the baby. They headed up the trail, up a steep, narrow path, passing by other visitors who were coming back down. Ginkgo and maple trees towered over them, providing shade from the afternoon sun. After some time, they reached a small outcropping of rocks. Looking down from there, they could see all of Changsha spread out before them.

"The Taiping Rebels came up here, too," Da Ge explained, "maybe to this very spot. Perhaps they stood here, as we do now, and looked down on the city, thinking of breaking its walls. But the Hunan Braves kept them back, defeated them, when the rest of the country had failed."

Da Ge surveyed the city before them, his eyes shining like pearls. "There are certain times in history—like now—when one is called upon to rise and fight," he said. Then, he cupped his mouth with his hands and shouted into the air. It was a sound filled with joy. Mei Mei followed suit, whooping down the mountain. Ge Ge did not, though he was grinning all the same. The three siblings stood on the mountain without saying a word, and the echo of their voices returned to them, again and again, until it was all Mei Mei could hear.

THE NEXT DAY was filled with conversation and laughter. There were many days, weeks, months to catch up on. After breakfast, as her brothers and Liying left to run errands and buy groceries, Mei Mei played with her niece, making shadow puppets on the wall. Fei Fei babbled and grasped at her hands, and Mei Mei tried to memorize her every feature, so she would not forget when she returned home. Fei Fei had Da Ge's eyes, as she had imagined, but the mole beneath her left eye was all Liying. And was there something of herself in Fei Fei, too? Mei Mei could only hope.

HER BROTHERS AND LIYING returned late in the afternoon, their arms full of groceries and flaky pastries that made Mei Mei's mouth water. The three brought with them the strange smells of the city—grease and sweat and the sun. Ge Ge recounted his morning with a flurry of words. He had been to every corner of the city, he boasted, and encountered so many new faces. He had even, he said with wonder in his voice, spoken to a Westerner. A missionary from England who had lived in the city for the last fifteen years and had witnessed firsthand the rice riots of 1910.

"And Da Ge was even speaking French," Ge Ge added.

"French?" asked Ma Ma.

"Some of our friends," Da Ge explained, "have left to work and study in France." He looked at Liying. "And so, we learned a little French ourselves."

"I want to learn, too," said Ge Ge.

"When you come here to study, I'll teach you," said Da Ge. In his grin, there was a promise.

THE THIRD DAY was their last. Da Ge took them all to the banks of the Xiang River. Walking beside Liying, Mei Mei looked curiously at her new sister's black shoes. They gleamed as if they had been coated in oil.

"Do you like them?" asked Liying, noticing her gaze.

"I do."

"They're from Shanghai." Liying lifted one heel to show it off. "A wedding gift from your brother."

Mei Mei admired the way they reflected the light.

"I felt so lucky when I married your brother," Liying said. "That I could marry for love when so many others could not." She stared at Da Ge, walking ahead of them. "Months after our wedding, there was a young woman in Changsha who killed herself in her bridal sedan chair. They say she cut her throat, preferring death over an arranged marriage with an elderly widower."

Mei Mei could imagine the young woman's fears of being married off to a much older man. All girls could. A widower was even more feared. Of what cause had his last wife died? Would you last longer than the previous one? For a wedding like that, the red of the sedan chair would not be one of celebration but despair. It would be an open wound, enclosing you. That was why one should marry someone kind. Someone with a gentle smile and endless stories to tell. Everyone knew the only way out of an unhappy marriage was at the bottom of the well, though she had also heard stories of mistreated wives swallowing gold rings. That was a slower death, she was told. But in both cases, you would become a hungry ghost. And in that way, you would finally have the power and freedom you had been denied in life.

"What was her name?" Mei Mei asked.

"Miss Zhao Wuzhen."

For a moment, only the clicking of Liying's shoes disturbed the silence between them.

Mei Mei lowered her eyes. "I've heard of others who have done the same."

"You're right. It was nothing new. Except this time, people were writing about it. They were coming to her defense." Liying's hand brushed against hers. "China is changing, Mei Mei. In ways that will be better for you and Fei Fei." She paused. "Don't you think so?"

WHEN THEY REACHED the banks, Da Ge paid a boatman to ferry them to the island in the middle of the river. It was a wide island, shaped like a leaf. Da Ge had pointed it out to her from the mountain. Juzi Isle was covered with orange trees, just beginning to fruit. It looked like a dream, as Da Ge had once described it to her. Through the rain, they paddled closer, the smell of citrus filling the air. Mei Mei dragged her hand through the lake, then let the water drip off. For a moment, she had no more thoughts about young brides with slit throats or rebels dying on a mountain. Instead, she saw how each drop of water gathered the sun within it. Everything a brightness.

A Longed-For Reunion

ON HIS LAST night home before leaving for First Normal School in
Changsha, Ge Ge brought out his erhu, playing songs he had composed
himself. Ba Ba and Ma Ma made an evening of it, inviting neighbors to
gather in celebration outside the house. Mei Mei strung up lanterns on
the doorway beams, while Ma Ma set down bowls of kumquats, sesame
crackers, and red bean pastries.

Mei Mei watched Ge Ge as he drew his bow. His eyes were closed as
he swayed back and forth. They had never understood one another in the
same way they each understood Da Ge, the common link between them.
But this evening, Mei Mei could feel Ge Ge reaching for her through the
music.

After Ge Ge's departure the next morning, the house was quieter than
ever. Turning the pages of the picture book Da Ge had given her, Mei

Mei traced the faces of the lovers separated by fate. Sometimes, she still imagined that Haiyang was the one on the page. Sixteen now, she felt a change sweeping through her. At night, she often dreamed of a flood, approaching from a distance, shaking the earth. Always, she woke just before she drowned, the back of her neck damp with sweat.

WEEKLY, MEI MEI went down to the river with Ming and Hua. In the last year, the river had grown wider and deeper from the recent floods that had devastated the countryside. Along the way, they picked the leaves of the wild hibiscus that lined the path. The hibiscus flowers were wide and white with a drop of red at the very center. Knee-deep in the water, they crushed the leaves between their hands and rubbed them into their hair until each strand shone like river stones. It was the older girls who had taught them the secret of how to soften and shine their hair with the oils from the leaves.

Lately, Mei Mei had been wondering about the kiss. One mouth against the other. Kissing. On the cheek between women was a kiss between sisters. When your mother and father kissed you, you were a child then. When your elder brother touched your hair before leaving, that was a kiss in its own way. A kiss against the surface of the water was a kiss against your other self. A kiss beneath the red veil was a marriage. A kiss hoped for, but not fulfilled, was not a kiss.

In the river, Mei Mei dove under the water. The water was icy with the promise of fall. Da Ge had taught her to keep her eyes open past the sting. To hold her breath against the desire to breathe.

She remained at the bottom, her hair floating around her. Her body in the current, taking flight underwater. Light flashed off the scales of small silver fish. In the book, light flashed off the hands of Dianmu as she brandished her mirrors. Her light always led the way, before the thunder.

Mei Mei combed through the sandy bottom with her hands. Above her, the legs of Ming and Hua moved back and forth in the water, glowing in their paleness. Mei Mei swam back up, breaking the surface.

"Here. Look at this." Mei Mei lifted her treasure out of the water.

"What is it?" Hua bent her head, peering at her hand.

A dulled knife, with a broken handle. Who had held it before her? Mei Mei scraped it against a rock, leaving behind marks of rust. Where the blade was scraped, it shone.

LATER THAT YEAR, Da Ge invited the family to visit again. In his letter, he spoke of a public lecture he would be giving for one of the newly formed peasant unions. His fight for the soul of China. But Ba Ba refused to answer.

"If only he had applied himself to medicine," Ba Ba said angrily, tearing the letter in two. "I tried so many times to teach him." Ba Ba looked down at Mei Mei. "Yunli could have been a great doctor, with his precise attention to detail. He could have healed the wounded and the sick. Saved countless lives." Pieces of paper drifted to the ground. "But now, he amuses himself with the so-called revolution."

Mei Mei had heard how the Hunan peasants working the fields were rallying against the rising cost of grain and taxation, how most of the harvest went to pay off their rents to the landowners. Then there were the annual taxes, keeping them forever in debt. And when the floods came for three years in a row, ruining the crops and raising the price of rice, they were left to starve.

All across the countryside, their anger sparked like firecrackers. They demanded lower prices and taxes. Some burned down the mansions of the landlords. Others joined up with outlaws and bandits to break into the granaries in search of food. No longer were people content to wait for their next life, for the lives of the peasants had never gotten better, not after the death of the last emperor, not after the death of the first president. And now, warlords, each crueler than the last, had divided up the country into their own little empires of influence. Their armies looted wherever they went. They hired Russian mercenaries to enforce their taxes on the peasants. And when the peasants in Hunan rose in protest, the local warlord Zhao Hengti stamped them out.

Mei Mei knew the fervor in Da Ge's eyes was born out of the suffering of the people. And perhaps revolution was inevitable, however hard it might be to imagine. How much more could the country transform—more than it had after ridding itself of the divine emperors? Sometimes, she, too, dreamed of a world turned upside down. One where she could roam as far as she liked—just like Xu Xiake.

THE NEXT YEAR, Ming told her that the Guomindang and the Communist Party held a joint congress in Guangzhou for the first time. She said that the Guomindang, led by Doctor Sun Yat-Sen, believed in the Three Principles of the People: nationalism, democracy, and socialism, while the Communists were guided by Lenin's Communist International. They had come together as the First United Front in order to fight against the warlords and reunite China. But it was an uneasy alliance, and everyone knew it, including the patients who came to call on Ba Ba and gossip on matters of state. The Guomindang hoped to absorb the Communist Party, while the Communists wanted to take advantage of the broader reach and influence of the Guomindang. And the Soviets, too, Ba Ba muttered at dinner, had motives of their own to increase their influence in the fractured country.

On the first day of July, Ming crouched in the river beside Mei Mei and said that her brothers had also joined the fight.

"They, too, want to seek justice for the common people," Ming said, scrubbing her father's shirts. "They said the peasants will rise again and again, even if they're stamped out."

Mei Mei wrung out her mother's dress, reflecting on Ming's words. There was that same haunting certainty in her voice as in Da Ge's. From her conversations with Haiyang years ago, Mei Mei had learned there had always been uprisings in China's history, but success, if it happened at all, was fleeting. And it was always the weakest and the poorest who paid the price. Still, she didn't blame them for trying. She knew what it was to want something beyond one's reach.

She only hoped there would be no more bloodshed. Not only for their sake, but for Da Ge's, too.

ON HER WAY back from the river, Mei Mei could make out the shape of a carriage in front of her house. Several servants stood in attendance, ignoring her as she approached. Adjusting the laundry basket in her arms, she walked slowly around the carriage, looking at the carved window screens. The decorative scenes looked familiar in a way that Mei Mei didn't dare hope.

In the kitchen, Ma Ma set a pot of tea and two teacups on a tray, alongside dishes of snacks.

"Who is the guest?" Mei Mei asked.

"That young master who stayed here for a time."

Could it really be him again? Her heart pounding, Mei Mei set down the laundry and took the tray from her mother's hands. "I can bring this to our guest," she said eagerly.

Inside his office, Ba Ba was taking the pulse of a young man sitting at the table, with his back to her.

"The circulation of your blood is full of vigor," Ba Ba said. "And I'm glad to see your leg and ankle have made a complete recovery."

The afternoon light filtered through the window, gilding the young man's profile. Mei Mei's hands trembled as she stepped across the doorway and the man turned and stood. His eyes widened before he gave a little bow.

"Miss Zhang," Haiyang said with a smile.

Mei Mei greeted him, unable to lower her gaze as was proper. Indeed, he had changed. Though he still resembled a pale scholar from a painting, his features had lost the softness of youth. Now, the refinement of their lines could be clearly seen. The delicate point of his nose. The graceful swoop of his jawline. The prominent angle of his cheekbones.

With an effort, she turned away, set the tray on the table, and served the tea. Her palms were warm and sweaty. The back of her neck prickled with heat. Haiyang sat back down. The conversation between him and Ba Ba resumed as if she had never interrupted them.

Ba Ba asked after the health of Lord Tan and Haiyang's elder brother. They were all doing well, Haiyang reported. His little sister, however, had passed away a year ago from ill health. Haiyang had wanted to invite doctor Zhang to treat his sister, but his father had insisted on waiting until he returned from a business trip. By the time his father arrived back home, however, there wasn't much to be done.

"But such is life," Haiyang said. The bitterness in his words betrayed his cavalier tone.

Mei Mei kept her eyes trained on the table. She laid out the little plates of fried twists of dough, dried pork strips, and sunflower seeds. She was slower than she needed to be, though not as slow as she desired. Haiyang's hand reached for a sunflower seed, and their hands touched for the briefest of moments before Mei Mei drew her fingers away. His nails, she noticed, had been shaped into little crescent moons.

Haiyang stood abruptly. "Would Miss Zhang be willing to give me a tour of the house? I didn't get to admire it in its entirety the last time I was here, being confined to the bed. But I do remember the views of the mountains were spectacular from every window."

"Of course," said Ba Ba. "She would be happy to." He turned to Mei Mei. "Show our guest the view from the pond, too."

"Would you lead the way, Miss Zhang?"

MEI MEI AND Haiyang stood silently in the long grasses dipped in the colors of the setting sun. Haiyang's face was also burnished with orange and red light. Mei Mei looked toward the pond before he could catch her staring again at him.

There were fewer carp than there had been years ago. Occasionally, they caught a glimpse of a mouth or a flash of a golden tail, but the water of the pond was, for the most part, silent and still.

"How have you been since I saw you last?" Haiyang asked, eyes fixed on the mountains.

"I've been well," she said. "And you?"

"Well, to start, my leg," Haiyang said, holding it out, "has completely healed—as you can see." He smiled at her, as brightly as he had when they were younger.

Mei Mei laughed. "Yes, as I'm glad to see."

"Now, I can run as fast as any horse."

Mei Mei laughed again. She could feel, suddenly, the weight of his eyes on her, and she flushed. It was strange seeing him again after so many years, but it was also everything she had imagined. There was so much she wanted to say to him, but the silence that resumed between them paralyzed her.

Haiyang broke the silence again. "One of my brothers was married last month," he said.

Mei Mei congratulated him.

"My father's now turned his sights on me," he said. "His last remaining unmarried son."

Mei Mei wasn't sure if she should ask if Haiyang had anyone in mind. A part of her was afraid to ask.

"I don't think either my father or I imagined I would live long enough to get married," he said.

"How come?" asked Mei Mei.

"The priest, when I was born, deemed my birth an inauspicious one. He said that I would die young and, upon my death, bring about the end of my family." Haiyang laughed. "My father chased the priest out of his house, but he is still a superstitious man."

Mei Mei felt a sense of outrage on his behalf. "Clearly the priest was wrong," she said.

Haiyang smiled sadly. "It was my sister who took my place."

Mei Mei felt like touching him then, and so she did, placing her hand on his arm.

"I'm sorry," Mei Mei said. "I know how much she meant to you."

"Thank you." Haiyang looked away. "Your kindness always made an impression on me. And the letter you wrote—" He paused. "I've always kept it. I can even recite it to you, if you want."

Before she knew it, he had clasped her hand in his.

"Have you thought about me at all?" Haiyang asked.

Mei Mei looked into his eyes. His gaze laid bare to her the depth of his feelings. "I have," she answered honestly.

He smiled, and Mei Mei let him turn over her hands in his. His thumb brushed over her scar.

"Then, perhaps, you feel the same about me," he said, "as I do you."

Mei Mei longed to tell him of the hooded crane she had once seen in the water of the rice fields. It had a long, curving neck, and its body was a wash of ink. It looked just like the ones she had embroidered once. It bent down to run its beak through its feathers. As she watched, it had glanced proudly in her direction before taking flight again. How she wanted to watch that solitary flight forever. For many nights afterward, in her dreams, the beating of its wings moved in her blood. Those wings were moving again through her now.

Instead, Mei Mei said, "I do."

His hands tightened on hers. "My father has plans to arrange a matchmaker for me in the next few months," he said. "But I have heard this matchmaker is willing to recommend certain matches in return for gifts, so to speak. Tell me your date and time of birth, and I will point the matchmaker in the right direction."

Haiyang took a jade bracelet out of his pocket. "When the matchmaker approaches your family, promise me you'll say yes." He held the bracelet out to her.

The bracelet was a green so pale it was almost white. Ornate carvings swirled around the bracelet: wisps of clouds, leaping fish, cherry blossoms in full bloom, even two cranes, flying side by side.

It was foolish to promise herself away. A promise was as good as an engagement, but one without the blessing of her parents. If anyone should find out, she would bring shame upon her family and herself. But Mei Mei thought of what Liying had said to her. The look of love in her eyes. Her black shoes shining in the sun.

"I promise," she said, giving him her hand.

And so Mei Mei hid his bracelet inside her pillow. Fall turned into a chilly winter. Winter into a spring without rain. The drought brought another poor harvest. The rice fields were empty of shadows. People crouched in the grass, digging in the dirt for roots. Once, on the road through the village, Mei Mei saw a mother lead her daughter by the hand, offering to sell her for food.

Mei Mei had no money of her own to give them. She could not take the little girl home. Her own helplessness yawned before her as she watched the two walk farther and farther away, the sun shining on their matted hair and hunched, bony backs.

At home, the congee became more and more watery. Deep lines settled around Ba Ba's mouth.

"It is hunger they suffer from," he said to Ma Ma. "Hunger which I cannot cure without food." He sighed. "Every day, women ask me to cure them of their pregnancies. For how can they feed their children when they cannot feed themselves?" He looked at the jar in his hand, filled with dark grains of deer musk that, when swallowed, could relieve the women of such burdens.

In the summer, her brothers unexpectedly returned, emerging out of a thunderstorm. Liying followed close behind, carrying Fei Fei in her arms.

Mei Mei stared at Da Ge as he stepped across the doorway. His wet hair curled around his face.

"Mei Mei?" Her elder brother opened his arms, smiling when they embraced. Mei Mei felt the rain drip onto her shoulders. She felt the warmth of him against her cheek.

"Hello, Mei Mei," Ge Ge said, unstrapping the erhu case he was carrying on his back.

Liying smiled and shifted her daughter in her arms. "Fei Fei, say hello to your aunt," Liying coaxed, but Fei Fei only buried her face in her mother's neck.

Ma Ma emerged from the kitchen, wiping her hands on a towel. When she saw her two sons, her eyes widened, and she rushed forward to bring her arms around the both of them.

"How is it that you're all here?" her mother kept murmuring as she touched their faces.

"What is this?" her father's voice swept over all of them. He stood at a distance, watching. Was it tenderness that passed through his gaze? Was it affection? It passed too quickly for Mei Mei to decipher.

"Ba Ba," Da Ge said, bowing his head. He gestured at Liying. "This is my wife, Liying, and our daughter, Chunfei."

Liying quickly stepped forward and bowed deeply before Ba Ba. Fei Fei squirmed in her arms.

In the face of Ba Ba's stony silence, Da Ge continued to speak. "We won't stay long. Only a night."

Ma Ma was pleased, at least, to see her sons and her second daughter. Mei Mei stared at the dishes laid out on the table; it had been so long since she had seen such a generous spread. Delicate bean sprouts in soy sauce and sesame oil. Fragrant tofu fried with black, gelatinous mushrooms. Rice steamed with sliced sausage and spring onions. Mei Mei's mouth watered.

"Thank you, Ma Ma," said Liying, "for such a feast." She placed a square of tofu onto Ma Ma's plate.

"Ma Ma," said Da Ge, "don't you think that Fei Fei has grown well in the last three years?"

They all looked at Fei Fei, sitting in Liying's lap, even Ba Ba. Fei Fei's eyes were half-closed, her head nodding against Liying's chest.

"She's beautiful," Mei Mei said. She glanced at her elder brother, whose face was lit by tenderness.

IN THE EVENING, Ge Ge played his erhu for their parents, and Mei Mei took the opportunity to slip outside. There, lying on his back in the grass by the pond, was Da Ge. His eyes were closed, but she knew he wasn't sleeping.

"Have you come to scold me," Da Ge asked when she neared, "for provoking Ba Ba with my presence?" He did not open his eyes.

Mei Mei pulled her knees up to her chest. "He'll come around in time."

"Perhaps." Da Ge opened his eyes. "Though I'm afraid we don't have much time."

"What do you mean?" Mei Mei said.

"Nothing," Da Ge said.

She wanted to reach out and pull at his sleeves to make him answer, but she did not. She was no longer a child. "Tell me the truth."

Da Ge smiled. "Nothing has happened yet," he said. "But we may not see each other again for a while. We'll all be going to join Mao Zedong in Shaoshan, where they say he's organizing the peasants still."

It was growing darker, the night settling into the earth. The trees rustled quietly with the wind. Somewhere, in the reeds that bordered the pond, a frog croaked.

"Liying and Fei Fei, too?" asked Mei Mei.

"Yes. They will come with me."

"What about Ge Ge? What about his studies? What about your teaching job?"

"Now is not the time for studies," Da Ge said. "Now is the time to have courage. The Guomindang have driven Mao Zedong out of power and sent him back to Hunan. They want to keep the common people down. Keep their own brothers and sisters down." Then, he added, "But we will aid Mao's work for the people. And those who step on the backs of others will one day meet their reckoning."

"But why . . ."

"All things worth having come at a cost," Da Ge said. "The world is going to change. Not the earth, the rivers, or the mountains, but Man himself, who has always ruled or been ruled. The rich will walk with the poor as brothers, the land shared freely by all."

"It has never happened," Mei Mei said, "not in the thousands of years of China's history."

Da Ge smiled. "It's impossible to imagine now," he conceded. "What are dreams, if not to dream the impossible?"

"But—"

"Mei Mei," he said. "I've made my choice."

The next morning, as Mei Mei stood in the doorway watching them walk away in the direction of the river, she wondered if her parents knew why Da Ge had returned and where he was going. Liying carried Fei Fei in her arms. Ge Ge wore his erhu case on his back. Da Ge carried enough food to last them on their trip across Hunan. Their march was steady and somber.

IN WINTER, Ma Ma called to her through the darkness of the room, through the last hours of the year.

"Come sit beside me, Mei Mei."

Mei Mei sat on the ground and leaned against her mother's legs. How thin they felt that winter, like bamboo in snow. Ma Ma had gotten thinner after Da Ge's last letter, which informed them that they had fled with Mao Zedong to Guandong to avoid Zhang Hengti's wrath and alluded vaguely to the work they were doing—the work for the country.

Ma Ma gently undid Mei Mei's braids and combed through her loose hair with an ox-horn comb.

"Next year, you will be nineteen. A year older than when I was married to your father."

Mei Mei turned her head, but she couldn't make out her mother's face in the darkness. She could only see the pale shapes of her arms reaching toward her.

"My match to your father was arranged," her mother said. "I had never met him, but his virtues were known to me even then. He was a promising young student from a good family. Everyone spoke highly of his intelligence and piety."

Ma Ma stroked her hair. "My mother wanted a scholar. Someone who, like her, did not care for bound feet. I was envious at first of the girls I knew with tiny lotus feet. But then I learned to run, while they remained inside in their deep, quiet oceans," Ma Ma sighed. "I have been blessed by Guanyin in small ways." Her voice floated in the room like smoke from a stick of incense. "The lives of women are calculated, etched in the stars. As women, we have many lives. Daughter, sister, wife, mother. Few that belong to us."

Ma Ma was silent for a minute. Then, she asked, "What are your thoughts on marriage?"

For a moment, Mei Mei worried Ma Ma had somehow discovered the promise she had made, and a feeling of dread welled up inside her.

"Marriage?" Mei Mei asked, drawing her hair around her shoulders.

"Yes, Mei Mei. We can arrange a good marriage, someone to take care of you after we cannot."

"Ma Ma, please." Mei Mei clasped her mother's hands and brought them to her cheeks. "Don't arrange a marriage for me. Not yet."

It was the first time she had ever gone against her mother's wishes. But Mei Mei was determined to keep her promise.

Ma Ma sighed and said nothing more. Mei Mei swore to herself she would marry Haiyang, or no one at all.

What Was Promised

THE NEXT YEAR, the scar on Mei Mei's palm began to hurt again. Perhaps it had never healed completely to begin with, a line of fire in her hand.

In July, the United Front's National Revolutionary Army advanced north across the country in an assault against the warlords. Doctor Sun Yat-sen had died the previous year, and now the army was controlled by a new leader—one Chiang Kai-shek, less of a scholar than his predecessor and more a man of might. Indeed, Chiang Kai-shek's army made its swift advance across Hunan, scarring the land with bullets and fire, and by mid-July occupied Changsha.

The news spread like wildfire among the peasants. Many of Mei Mei's neighbors had relatives in Changsha, who also spoke of what was happening in their letters. One of Ba Ba's patients had a son who gave up working as a cook in the city to join the National Revolutionary Army, as did many peasants, joining in on the fight against the warlords' troops. And Da Ge and Ge Ge, too, Mei Mei learned through their last letter, had decided to put their differences with the Guomindang aside and signed up to fight with the United Front against a common enemy for the sake of the nation, leaving Liying and Fei Fei behind with Liying's family.

Her elder brother had been right. China would change, had already changed. There were days when the world felt like it was ending. Not even dragons could protect them from what was coming.

At night, Mei Mei dreamed of fires. Of rice granaries ransacked, then burnt down. Of parades and protests in the streets. When she woke, she thought of her brothers. Where they walked under the sun. Where they rested their heads in the night. Did they think of her, too, in the spare moments of the days? What new wounds, new scars, had they gathered on their bodies and minds?

In the mornings, Ma Ma gazed deeply into her tea to read the leaves. While the other women talked, she turned her eyes to the road. In the evenings, when Ba Ba returned home, his shoulders were worn like an ox. His weariness was not from the sun.

But they said nothing of their fears to her.

From time to time, her mother brought up the idea of marriage again, but Mei Mei always refused her. The thought of her promise to Haiyang steadied her, a flame in the darkening world.

HER MOTHER AND father were sitting in the lacquered chairs in their common room. When Mei Mei was little, she'd coveted the shining polish of the lacquer. She would slip into the chairs, imagining she was the last empress of a dying dynasty. To a child, even tragedies felt like they were full of power. Now, she saw how Ma Ma's hands trembled as she brought the teacup to her lips. She saw the stiffness in Ba Ba's shoulders. The grayness in his hair. They seemed, suddenly, terribly old.

"What is it? Is it—" Mei Mei broke off. "Did something happen to Da Ge and Ge Ge?"

"No, no," Ma Ma rushed to say. "It's not about your brothers."

"Then what?"

Ma Ma and Ba Ba exchanged a glance. Ba Ba was the first to speak. "A matchmaker has approached us on behalf of Lord Tan with an interesting proposition. A marriage between you and Lord Tan's youngest son. The stars, she says, foretold of the young master being rescued by a young woman with the eight characters of your exact birth time, and they foretell, too, of the harmony between him and that young woman."

Mei Mei's eyes widened as her father spoke. The feeling inside her was not burning anymore, only shining, and the shining took the form of long, white wings. So Haiyang had delivered what he had promised her.

"Although he is the youngest son," Ba Ba continued, "his family's wealth will bring you security. You'll live in a large compound. Your children will grow up in the cool darkness of the house, in the placid green of the fields, without want—"

"However, if you are truly against it—" Ma Ma began.

"No, Ma Ma!" Mei Mei said. She paused at their startled gazes. "I agree."

Her parents were silent. In Ma Ma's eyes, a hint of sadness.

"Are you certain?" her mother asked softly. "Our situation hasn't been easy lately, but marriage is not something to be entered into lightly."

The wings in Mei Mei's blood were beating now. Already carrying her far away. "Ma Ma," she said, "he is everything I could have wished for."

Ma Ma arched her brow. A look of surprise crossed her face, and Mei Mei averted her eyes under the scrutiny. She felt as though Ma Ma could see all that had passed between her and Haiyang. When she looked up again, her mother was smiling. A smile full and unreserved.

"Then, my daughter," Ma Ma said, "joy will come to you soon."

THE GIFTS FROM Haiyang's family arrived, one after another. A tea set, bolts of silk, a silver bowl. Mei Mei lifted the teacups from their padded case. She stroked the silk, brightly woven with peonies and butterflies. But it was the jade bracelet Haiyang had given her that Mei Mei treasured most of all. After both their families agreed on an engagement, Mei Mei wore the bracelet every day, passing it off as one of the gifts she had been sent by his family. Everywhere she went, eyes lingered on the intricate, carved jade. When she washed clothes in the river, the bracelet caught the light running beneath the water.

The matchmaker had spoken of the stars. She had spoken of their paired destinies, like the birds that traveled with the seasons, always together. Mei Mei knew that it was all made up, that Haiyang had bribed the matchmaker to ensure they were together, but she believed it all the same.

The matchmaker set an auspicious date for their marriage in September of the next year. Mei Mei dreamed of the day's arrival.

Once, she had seen a new wife traveling in the street. Her red veiled face behind the curtain of the carriage. Layer after layer she was hidden away. And, behind the last layer, what might Mei Mei uncover? The face of a young woman, filled with hope? The face that might be her own?

Would Da Ge smile when he heard news of her engagement, knowing it was for love? Would Ge Ge compose another song? Mei Mei convinced her father to send a letter she wrote to Liying's address in Changsha.

IN APRIL THE next year, the United Front collapsed. Their shared fight against the warlords could not prevent the power struggles between the Guomindang and the Communists from resurfacing. Each side wanted control of the country. Each believed in their own vision of the future. Indeed, the enmity between the two sides seemed to burn all the brighter for having been forcibly dampened during their brief alliance. Under Chiang Kai-shek's direction, the Guomindang carried out massacres of Communists in Shanghai, Guangzhou, and Changsha. Day after day, Mei Mei heard of the many Communists killed in the purge by the Guomindang. The White Terror, they called it. Wherever Ba Ba went, he spoke to strangers his sons' names, asking for news that never came. Had they been captured by the Guomindang? Had they been imprisoned—or worse? Or had they gone on the run? Were they now in hiding, even from their family?

The coming autumn held her together, the cooling winds after the violent summer heat. A month before her wedding, a star streaked across the sky, shifting the heavens, the old plotted destinies. What had been auspicious was no longer so. The matchmaker, making her new calculations, moved up the wedding by three days.

A week before the new wedding date, Mei Mei helped Ma Ma pack up her dowry, which was to be sent over to Lord Tan's residence before the wedding. Her mother carefully wiped down the zitan trunk one last time and rubbed oil on the outside, then placed her grandmother's blanket, carefully folded, at the bottom. On top of that went the silver tea set given to them years ago, jars of the highest quality ginseng and other assorted medicines, a silk bedding set, a brand-new sewing kit, and a pair of shining scissors.

The night before her wedding, Mei Mei peered at her face in the mirror. She saw a young woman looking back at her with eyes full of hope—and a little bit of fear. Her mother stood behind her, combing out her hair with long patient strokes.

"Tonight is the last night I'll have you all to myself," Ma Ma said. She put the ox-horn comb down on the table and lowered her face to Mei Mei's, and the two women stared at one another in the mirror. Mei Mei looked into her mother's eyes, filled with tenderness and sorrow. She reached up to touch her mother's cheek, but Ma Ma caught her hand and brought it instead to her chest. There, Mei Mei could feel the beating of her mother's heart, just as fast as her own.

THE NEXT MORNING, Haiyang came to fetch her on a shining black horse. Though Mei Mei couldn't see the details of his face through her red veil, he cut an imposing figure dressed in his red wedding robes. And the procession that accompanied him was like nothing she had ever seen. Four strong men bore a bridal sedan chair, and a dozen musicians played raucous music to announce their arrival.

Before Mei Mei stepped into the bridal sedan chair, she glanced back one last time. Through her veil, she could just make out her mother and father standing in the doorway. Ma Ma's mouth was moving. But amidst the din of gongs and firecrackers, Mei Mei had no hope of hearing her voice. And in the next instant, she was inside the sedan.

The curtains swayed with every step of the men bearing her weight. Mei Mei took off her veil in the stifling heat and darkness. Closing her eyes, she tried to calm her heart. She traced the scar across her palm. By nightfall, she would be married to the one she had always wanted. She would have a new name, new father, new mother, new family. Even her ancestors would be new ones now.

AS THEY LEFT their village and headed northeast along the Liuyang River toward Xijiang, Mei Mei pulled aside a corner of the curtain. Outside, there were long stretches of rice fields, glimmering with water under the sun. The peasants toiling in the fields looked up as the procession passed. The women shaded their eyes. Under the brim of their hats, their faces were hidden in shadow.

The children pointed in her direction. One ran over to chase the sedan. Over the raucous music of the wedding procession, Mei Mei could hear him crying out for her to throw some candy. Mei Mei, however, did not have any candy with her. It was not an oversight. Weeks before, Ba Ba had ordered from a famed candy shop in Changsha, but the shop owner had suddenly gone missing. Some said he was on the run from the Guomindang.

One of the men carrying the sedan kicked the child aside.

"Wait!" Mei Mei cried out, though no one seemed to hear her. She fell against the side of the sedan as she was jostled about, then caught her balance and sat back in her seat. Why hadn't Haiyang made the men stop the sedan? Did he see what had happened? Da Ge would have been filled with fury at how they treated the child.

Suddenly, the heat and darkness of the sedan felt stifling. Mei Mei pulled off her veil. She had the urge to open the curtain again, but something stopped her: it wouldn't be proper for her to do so as a new bride. And Mei Mei wanted to be good, as her father had always advised her to be. Haiyang, though, always seemed to think she was good enough as she was.

By the time she looked out the window again, the peasants were nowhere in sight.

At last, the bridal sedan chair came to a stop. Mei Mei felt herself being lowered to the ground, and she drew the veil over her face again. The curtain covering the doorway was pushed aside, and an arm reached inside, uncurling a white hand. Mei Mei looked at the hand that was being offered to her. The red sleeve with its rich, golden threads. The fingers that trembled ever so slightly. Seeing them tremble set her at ease and she smiled. Feeling daring, she brushed her lips over his fingertips, before giving him her hand.

As she emerged into the sunlight, firecrackers sparked noisily in the air. Through her veil, Mei Mei could only make out dark, blurry shapes and indistinct figures. Calls of welcome and merriment filled her ears. Haiyang stepped close to her, supporting her by the elbow. The two of them walked carefully over the threshold of the large manor.

Red bows, golden ribbons. Smoke trailed up from the incense on the long table covered with steaming platters of food: buns and little cakes dotted with red, slices of pork and chicken, sticky lotus root in syrup. A feast for the living relatives who now swarmed around them and greeted Mei Mei's arrival, as well as the dead who looked on as spirits.

Mei Mei and Haiyang knelt for the three bows of marriage. Mei Mei trembled at the first bow—the one to Heaven and Earth. This one was for the invisible ones—those who came before and those who were always watching.

Next, they bowed to his parents, who were now her own. Lord Tan and his wife sat before them in a pair of lacquered chairs that glittered with mother-of-pearl inlay. Slowly, Mei Mei touched her veiled forehead to the ground. As she raised her head, she caught a glimpse of her new mother's black silk shoes, delicate things, embroidered with flowers. Each bound foot was smaller than her hand. They said a new wife's happiness depended on the smiles of her mother-in-law. Did her new mother approve? Would she see her as her own?

Mei Mei and Haiyang lowered their heads to one another. Their last and final bow. As Mei Mei raised her head, she felt the heat of his face against her skin. And when they rose, they performed the crossing of the wine cups. Haiyang's arm over hers. The wine was sweet and bitter and lingered on her tongue. She was both less and more than what she was before, one part of a greater whole.

Then, they were guided into the nuptial chamber while the family banqueted. The chamber was a sudden, cool darkness. A relief.

Hands finally lifted the veil on her face. Haiyang's face was revealed to hers and hers to his. Mei Mei drew her gaze across his smooth, pale forehead, the slender bridge of his nose, and the refined arch of his lips. Then, she looked into his eyes. The light that filled them.

"Yunhong," he said, smiling down at her.

MEI MEI WOKE at dawn to soft, rustling footsteps and a murmuring voice. Slowly opening her eyes, she reached over to touch Haiyang, but he wasn't there. She sat up in bed and glanced, embarrassed and wary, at the serving girl who came to wash her face with a steaming towel.

"There's no need," Mei Mei said. She tried to take the towel from the girl's hands. "I can do it myself."

The girl bowed her head in acknowledgment of the words but refused to let go of the towel. After a few more tugs, Mei Mei submitted. The girl patted Mei Mei's face dry, then took out a cloisonné container filled with a white cream. Dipping her fingers into the cream, she massaged it gently onto Mei Mei's skin. The cream smelled faintly of jasmine and citrus.

"What's your name?" Mei Mei asked, studying the girl curiously. The girl, around fourteen or so, had a wide, square face with red, sunburned cheeks. Her hair lay across one shoulder in a thick braid, as thick as Mei Mei's wrist. The girl looked up at her through her bangs but didn't reply.

In silence, the girl helped her out of bed and dressed her in a new tunic and skirt of heavy cotton, then led Mei Mei to a vanity table and sat her down on a finely lacquered stool. The girl began brushing out her hair with a white ivory comb. If Mei Mei closed her eyes, she could almost imagine it was her mother combing her hair.

After arranging her hair into a bun, the girl gestured for Mei Mei to follow her out of the bedroom and led her through the courtyard, still draped in red ribbons and bows, to the ancestral shrine at the back of the house.

Haiyang was already there, lighting the incense in his hand.

"Good morning," Mei Mei said, making her way over.

Haiyang turned, smiling at her voice. He raised his arm and drew her to him. Mei Mei wondered how long he had been standing there, feeling out the world in its dim, half-lit state. She pressed herself against him.

"Here," he said, dividing the incense in his hands. They bowed toward the shrine, paying their respects to ancestral spirits.

When they were finished, Haiyang turned to her. "Prepare yourself," he said, with a grin.

"For what?" Mei Mei asked.

"To be formally introduced to the family."

Mei Mei laughed and followed him to the courtyard, where breakfast was being served. Faces she half-recognized surrounded her. Haiyang introduced the elders in the family, his uncles and aunts, his brothers, his sisters, and then all the clamoring children. Mei Mei bowed deeply to each one. Hands touched her hands. She was gifted with little trinkets—bracelets, hair sticks, figurines of children. Mei Mei smiled in relief.

"Come, let's eat," Lord Tan swept his arms toward the many circular tables set up around the courtyard. The blue and white porcelain bowls were already laid out, and the dishes were still steaming.

People began to sit down, settling into their old, familiar seats. Mei Mei looked around for Haiyang and spotted him talking to his elder brother. She stepped toward him, but a hand tugged at hers. Mei Mei looked back.

A little girl with her hair up in two round buns was holding onto Mei Mei's hand, pulling her toward a table. "Come," she said, "sit with us."

"Alright," Mei Mei said, laughing a little. She let herself be pulled along. "What's your name?" she asked as she sat down.

"Xiao Hao," the girl said.

Across the courtyard, Haiyang was being dragged to another table. They caught one another's eyes, and Haiyang shrugged helplessly. Mei Mei shook her head with a smile and picked up her chopsticks. She began placing the fattiest slices of pork belly and juiciest pieces of cabbage in Xiao Hao's bowl.

"Let Xiao Hao do it herself," another girl said, furrowing her brows. "She's already seven years old." Older than Xiao Hao, she wore her hair in two braids.

Xiao Hao's mouth acquired a sullen set to it. Swiftly, Mei Mei turned to the second girl. Mei Mei guessed she was around ten.

"What's your name?" Mei Mei asked.

"I'm Yuelu," the girl said. "And beside me is Yuesu."

Around their table, the ten seats were now completely filled by young women. From the way they wore their hair, Mei Mei could tell they were all unmarried. All except for her.

"Why do you have feet like the servants?" Xiao Hao asked.

Mei Mei looked down at her feet. "Like the servants?"

Xiao Hao nodded.

"Don't ask her that," Yuesu hissed.

"Why not?"

"She'll be embarrassed."

"Oh," Xiao Hao said. Her eyes blinked rapidly.

Mei Mei tucked her feet under her seat.

"It's alright," Yuesu said sympathetically. "If she and Ge Ge have a little girl, her feet will be like ours."

Xiao Hao looked relieved.

"Don't say such things," Yuelu said, jumping in. "They'll have sons for sure."

"Yes, of course. Sons first," Yuesu amended. "Then, if there's space, perhaps a little girl."

Mei Mei's eyes darted between the three of them. When they turned to look at her, she couldn't help but smile back. Beneath her seat, her toes curled and flexed against the confines of her shoes.

Mei Mei looked toward Haiyang's table. He wasn't there. She scanned the courtyard anxiously.

A hand fell upon her shoulder, and with it she felt a surge of relief. She knew at once that it belonged to her husband and reached up to interlace her fingers with his. "Yunhong," Haiyang said. He was smiling. "Shall we?"

Mei Mei looked at the others still eating, but Haiyang was already pulling her up by the hand, excusing them from the table. Furtive smiles and muffled giggles trailed behind them.

"Is it alright to leave like this?" Mei Mei whispered, staring at their intertwined fingers.

"Of course," Haiyang said. "They won't begrudge us our first day together." He smiled. "There's so much I want to show you."

THEY PASSED THE kitchens and the reception rooms. They passed the quarters for the children and unmarried young women. At last, they ended up in the library, beside Lord Tan's study.

Mei Mei looked around her at the books that lined the walls. "I've never seen so many books," she said. Ba Ba's collection of medicinal texts was only a fraction of the size of the collection that spread out before her.

"You're welcome to borrow any of the books here," Haiyang said.

"Really?"

"Of course. You're my wife now, aren't you?"

Mei Mei couldn't stop the smile that spread over her face. She picked a book off the shelf. It was bound in thicker paper than the rest and had a rich blue cover. As she flipped through the pages, she could tell—even to her untrained eyes—that the writing was masterfully done.

"What's this?"

"It's our family's generation poem." Haiyang cast his gaze over the other books in the series. "Well, one volume of many," he added, amusedly. "In them are recorded all the names of the members of our family."

Mei Mei had heard of other families having generation poems, though her own did not. Each generation—from the main to minor branches—had in their names a word drawn from an existing poem. The names of the first generation would all include the first word of the poem, while the second generation would include the second word. And so on. Haiyang's generation all had the word *hai*, meaning "ocean," her husband explained to her.

"My generation is the eighth word of the poem. It is the last word of the second line, which expresses hope that the glory of the family will be as high as the mountains, and the virtues as deep as the ocean. My eldest brother's name is Haijun, with *jun* meaning 'eminent' and 'talented.' My second brother's name is Haijia, with *jia* meaning 'auspicious.' And then there's me, of course," Haiyang said, smiling. He paused, then added, shyly, "Our children will be the ninth generation."

Mei Mei could feel her face flushing even more. "What word will that be?"

"*Yue*," he said, pointing to the beginning of the third line. *Yue* was the moon, which was, like the ocean, everlasting. But, while the ocean was deep and dark in its contemplations, the moon burned with a white brilliance.

WHEN MEI MEI looked back, she remembered the day like a dream. The most beautiful dream she had ever dreamt. Years later, she could still feel his hand moving hers, tracing calligraphy across a scroll. Later, his chest against her back as he helped her pull the string of a kite high in the air. Walking beside him through the loquat trees, beneath the leafy shadows. Both of them were children again.

But the matchmaker must have known. She had calculated their lives, their destinies. She had seen their fates written in the stars. Perhaps she had wanted to give them one day together. One perfect day.

NIGHT WAS WHEN it came. The sound of firecrackers. The smell of smoke. Mei Mei opened her eyes with an effort. Her head was still swimming from the wine she had shared with Haiyang. They had retired early to play weiqi in their room and had never made it to bed. Instead, they had fallen asleep at the table. On the board, the black and white stones were in the midst of advancing and retreating. Haiyang rubbed his eyes and stood up, frowning.

"Stay here," he said. "I'll go see what's going on."

Mei Mei blinked at him, watching as he left the room. The smell of smoke was growing more pungent.

Someone let off another round of firecrackers. Someone screamed.

Mei Mei stood up. Something was wrong. She could feel it. But before she could step toward the door, it opened.

"Haiyang—" Mei Mei began. But the man who turned around was not her husband. It was her elder brother.

STANDING IN THE doorway, Da Ge regarded Mei Mei under dark, solemn brows.

"Mei Mei?" He strode over, reaching for her.

She shrunk back, frightened by his appearance, by the wildness in his eyes. She thought of the stories of spirits and demons, of how they took on the appearances of loved ones who came to lead us away from ourselves. Was it really her elder brother? The one who wore such stained clothes? The one with shadows etched into his face?

His cold arms tightened around her body.

"What's going on?" she asked into his chest. The smell of smoke was filling the room. A clash of firecrackers, amidst the rising din. Haiyang— he should have been back by now. There was a feeling of dread slowly pooling in the pit of her stomach.

Through the open doorway, Mei Mei heard the sound of shattering porcelain, heavy footsteps storming the house, angry voices, and the firecrackers again.

No. Not firecrackers.

Gunfire.

Da Ge sprung into motion. He grabbed her arm, dragging her out of the room. Mei Mei fought against his hold, but his hand was unrelenting.

"Wait," she said, pulling at his fingers. "What about Haiyang? My husband."

Da Ge didn't seem to hear her. Mei Mei tore again at his hand as he pulled her through the courtyard. It felt as if the scar along her palm would split open.

"Where are you taking her?" A voice rang out. It was Lord Tan, standing in the courtyard with blood dripping down his arm and a rifle in his hands.

"This is my elder brother," Mei Mei said.

"Your elder brother?" Lord Tan asked disbelievingly. Then, his expression changed. "So it was you who brought disaster upon our house." He looked at her with hatred in his eyes.

"Let's go," Da Ge said.

"Have you seen Haiyang?" Mei Mei asked Lord Tan. She resisted Da Ge's insistent grip.

"You have no right to say his name," Lord Tan said. "Not when he's dead because of you." He hoisted the rifle and aimed at Da Ge.

Mei Mei leapt in front of him.

There was a crack of gunshot, and Lord Tan crumpled to the ground.

"Do you know how much grain we've found stored away, Yunli," a man's voice drawled. "Like rats they are." The man came into view through the smoke. He had a thin, gaunt face and hair cut short like Da Ge. He stopped at the sight of Mei Mei.

"Who is this?" the man asked.

Mei Mei was staring at Lord Tan, lying motionless in the dirt. A pool of blood gathered beneath his chest.

"No one," Da Ge said. "I'll be taking her with me."

The man laughed. "Will you now?" he asked with a leer. "So be it." He began to head toward the main gate. "I'd get her out before the place burns down."

Thick smoke gathered at their heels. Da Ge pulled her with him through the main gate, and then the night was all around them.

The One Who Brought Disaster

WHEN MEI MEI woke, her mother was staring down at her. She was stroking her hair so gently, Mei Mei could barely feel it.

"Ma Ma," she tried to say. But her voice was not a voice. Only a hoarse moan.

"Don't speak," her mother murmured. She supported her head and brought a cup to her lips. The liquid was sharp bitterness on her tongue—medicine Ba Ba must have made. Mei Mei coughed and turned her head away.

Ma Ma laid Mei Mei's head back down on the pillow. "I'll go get Ba Ba," she said, standing up.

Mei Mei shook her head. She reached out and grasped her mother's wrist. "Da Ge?" she whispered. "Haiyang?"

Ma Ma looked at her without speaking. Mei Mei wanted to hide from her eyes, from the pity she saw moving through them. "Da Ge is fine," she said at last. She did not mention Haiyang. What use was there, after all? Mei Mei already knew he was dead.

"Rest, Mei Mei," her mother said.

But she wasn't Mei Mei anymore. The one who had once been loved, the one who had loved in return. Now, she was Yunhong, a hungry ghost risen out of death. Now, she was the clouds that were red from rage.

YUNHONG'S DAYS PASSED before her as if seen through a veil. The bracelet around her arm was now a shackle, so she pulled it off and hid it beneath her bed. Sometimes she dreamed of Haiyang. Of his soul, rising from earth. His soul leaped like a shadow puppet toward the heavens, jumping from cloud to cloud. And there, up in the heavens, souls lived on forever. Families of souls, generation after generation— never to be parted again. There was no choosing between two names, two families.

But could she be thought of as Haiyang's family? She, whose blood had betrayed him. His name was rooted in the blue expanse of water, while hers contained the flame.

Other times, she dreamed of Da Ge—no, Yunli now, to her. In her dreams, Yunli paced back and forth, begging first for forgiveness then shouting her into silence. Yunhong tried to explain, explain that it was the stars, but the groove he wore into the floor could never be repaired. His light pierced her. She was made of paper, after all. All of them were: paper burning like the most beautiful of houses.

YUNHONG TURNED TO her embroidery, but the colors came out all wrong. The stitches were no longer perfect, but crisscrossed like scars. Ma Ma tried to coax her outside, but Yunhong refused.

"She's fine," Ma Ma said to those who came to look at her daughter. "Our eldest son went and brought her back before they were married. They never even completed the three bows before Heaven and Earth."

And, once, another time:

"It was only a frivolous promise between her father and Lord Tan. Casually made. Easily broken."

A HUNGRY GHOST knew only rage.

OFTEN, HER MIND returned to the scissors. The way they had glinted under the moonlight so many years ago. How powerful she had felt holding them in her hand. That day, Yunli had denied that he was cutting himself away from them. But Yunhong knew now of his lie. That was the first step he had taken to separate himself from the rest of them. To unburden himself of his ties to his family so he could do as he wished. So he could be free of the past.

One night, she crept into the kitchen and picked up a pair of scissors lying on the counter. She twisted her hair together in one hand. With the other, she cut.

It was as easy as it had been—that day with Yunli. She wanted to reject Yunli as he had rejected all of them. She, too, wanted to be free of her ties to her family. If only she could cut her heart out of her chest. Cut the pain from her bones. She wished to cut the world into pieces. She went outside and threw her hair to the wind.

AT FIRST, the peasants were victorious in their rebellion against the land-lords in Hunan. They coordinated like they never had before. Overnight, all the landlords' mansions across the land seemed to burn. Under Mao Zedong, the peasants considered themselves Communists and rebelled against the Guomindang, too. At first, they seemed unstoppable. But the Guomindang had rallied and crushed them, killing hundreds of thousands. Now, most were on the run, fleeing with Mao Zedong into the Jinggang Mountains. Yunhong wondered if Yunli and Yunjun were among them, running into the darkness.

Ma Ma and Ba Ba did not press her to go out, receive visitors, or smile as she used to. They did not speak to her of her brothers anymore. They did not speak to her of marriage. They did not speak to her of her short hair. Instead, they treated her as if she were a child again, with soft voices, gentle touches.

But Yunhong couldn't fool herself. She saw the lines on her mother's face. The hunch of her father's back. And her own body, too, was changing. Not just the birthmark on her chest, which darkened with her rage. Overnight, she seemed to gather new aches, new shapes within herself. She watched her feet swell, then her ankles, then her stomach. All of it telling her: see how you have been changed by love.

Alone, hidden away, Yunhong wrapped her arms around herself. If it was her sorrow, she could bear it. It would grow inside her, like something made of knife edges and red fire. She wouldn't be afraid. She might even be happy, trusting that eventually it would leave her. But a child? The thought of a child terrified her.

When Ba Ba returned home from one of his trips, he placed a glass jar on her bedside table, which smelled earthy and wild. The smell of dried deer musk. Yunhong was only three months along. All she needed to do was swallow a couple of dark grains. Then she could be rid of this little shard of the past, could pretend it had all been just a dream.

"A child now will only bring shame," Ba Ba said.

Yunhong knew it was true. How could she raise her baby as a single mother, as the wife of a dead landlord's son? With a child in tow, it would be impossible for her to make another favorable match. Without a child, some things could be ignored. Some histories rewritten.

"Open your mouth," Ma Ma said.

"What are you waiting for?" Ba Ba said.

It would be easier to forget, to move on from what had happened. But a child was also a piece of him forever. The one he had hoped for and named.

"I can't betray him," Yunhong said. "Not again."

ON THE FIRST day of June, Yunhong's daughter was born. Yunhong felt a swelling, moaning pain, a tugging deep inside her. Something wanting to be free that would tear her in half for the sake of its own freedom.

When it was finally over, Yunhong looked at the baby—wet and red and wrinkly—squirming in her mother's hands. She was pained to see the birthmark on her daughter's chest and reached for her. Those who saw the mark they shared would know instantly where her daughter came from and who she belonged to.

Yun gave her the second character of Xin, "dawn," for the star that the matchmaker had seen, passing through the sky. The star had been so bright, people said, it had seemed as if the day was already dawning.

Her first character, of course, was Yue—as Haiyang had foretold.

There were no festivities to announce their new fortune. No killing of the sows. No dyeing the eggs red. And why should they celebrate? Officially, she was not a child of their family, but the child of a distant cousin who passed away in childbirth. That was the story Ma Ma and Ba Ba told to hide the truth of who her father was and salvage some of Yunhong's honor. And the part of Yunhong that wanted to believe the lie, that wanted to rewrite history, took a knife to Yuexin's birthmark in the hopes that the skin that regrew would be clear and blank. For weeks afterward, Yuexin screamed whenever Yunhong tried to hold her again. And when the skin grew back thick and toughened, the birthmark reappeared as well. As if it were saying that the blood they shared between them could never be denied.

She remembered the legend Ma Ma had told her about the birthmark. Now, it felt more like a curse than a blessing. A reminder of the past.

Yunhong did not know what she wanted for herself. She only knew she wanted tenderness for her daughter. Yuexin had been born into a violent world, one built by the hands of her brothers and her own.

Yuexin wailed insistently all through the night, and Yunhong knew that her daughter was the sorrow, after all. She nursed and rocked her in the darkness, but Yuexin never settled easily. Often, she only cried harder, as if to say, *You are not the one I want, you are not the one I am missing.*

AT FIVE MONTHS, Yunhong had no more milk to give. Her body ached more than she ever knew it could. It had started aching, painful tugs deep in her belly, ever since the birth. And so, Ba Ba brought back a ewe for Yuexin to drink from instead. The ewe was small and white, with a mouth that curled up at the edges. Often, when she was finished milking, Yunhong would rest her cheek against the ewe's coarse warm fur and listen to her drawn-out bleating. Neither of them was what the other wanted. In this, they were the same.

WHEN YUEXIN TURNED two, Yunhong heard a soft knocking at the front door of her parents' house. Ba Ba was away on business, while Ma Ma was in the kitchen. It was only Yunhong, playing in the courtyard with Yuexin, who heard the knock. As a child, Yunhong would have run to the door, eager and curious to greet their visitors. But now, as a young woman—albeit one who still lived in her childhood home—she was more timid than she had ever been. She was afraid of meeting a stranger's gaze—of seeing the judgment in their eyes.

A voice from behind the door called her name. The voice was familiar, and made Yunhong leap to her feet. When she opened the door, Liying stood before her, out of the bloom of spring.

"Hello, Mei Mei," Liying said, shading her face with one hand. Holding her other hand was a young girl, looking up with Yunli's eyes.

"Liying," Yunhong whispered. So many times she had imagined her reunion with Yunli, the fury that would possess her. But now, it wasn't him—only Liying and her daughter, Fei Fei.

"Can we come inside?" Liying asked. There was a hesitation in her voice that Yunhong didn't remember.

She led Liying and her daughter through the courtyard, where Yuexin was playing with dolls on the floor.

Liying drew in a breath at the sight of Yuexin. She was silent for a few moments. Then, she turned toward Yunhong. "Yours?"

Yunhong looked into her sister-in-law's eyes and shook her head. "A cousin's daughter."

"I see," Liying said, though her gaze was knowing.

Yunhong flushed and looked away. She always took care to dress Yuexin in clothing that hid her birthmark, which, though scarred, was undeniable proof of her lineage. But still, she felt at times that everyone could see the truth.

The two of them watched as Fei Fei crouched down beside Yuexin. Fei Fei picked up one of the dolls and moved it closer to her cousin, but Yuexin drew back and turned her face away. She was a shy and wary girl, and so fearful that Yunhong wondered if a part of her remembered the circumstances of her conception. And what did Liying see when she looked at Yunhong's daughter? Did she see the echo of Yunli's eyes in Yuexin's eyes? Did she see the shape of her mother's mouth in her mouth?

LIYING HAD TRAVELED for a day, a night. On the water, on the road. She had crouched in the grass to relieve herself and her daughter. She had rested in the shade of a bamboo grove.

Yunhong felt herself growing angry as Liying spoke. She didn't want to see that look of sympathy in Liying's eyes, the tentative smiles. What did Liying understand, after all?

"Has something happened to Yunli?" Ma Ma asked, bracing herself with a hand on the doorway.

"I don't know." Liying looked down. "I thought you might know where he was."

Yunhong's nails dug into her palms. Was he not satisfied with the pain he had already brought her? She couldn't bear losing him, too.

"I haven't seen him for years," Liying added, smiling sorrowfully at Ma Ma's touch. "I used to believe just as fervently as them. I used to make speeches. We were all equal then." Liying paused. "But now, with Fei Fei, things have changed." She looked again at Yunhong. "You understand," she said, softly, tentatively, "don't you?"

Yunhong turned away.

"Don't worry," Ma Ma said to Liying. "Don't cry."

Fei Fei stood in the doorway as her mother cried, watching her with her father's eyes.

The Brother Who Returned Home

WHEN YUEXIN TURNED seven, Yunhong took her for the first time to the ancestral tombs for Qingming: Tomb-Sweeping Day.

"Before we celebrate the spring, we honor our ancestors," Yunhong told her, facing the graves. "To be forgotten, Yuexin, is a second death." Crowned with light, Yunhong bent down to touch the tombstone with her left hand. Smoke curled from the bundle of incense she placed onto the ground.

"Jie Jie, can I burn some incense for my mother and father?" Yuexin asked.

Yunhong looked down at the girl by her side. The one who called her Big Sister. Her bundle of sorrow had grown into a girl. A little girl with wide, downturned eyes and two long braids and a scarred birthmark on her chest.

When they finished paying their respects, Yunhong picked Yuexin up in her arms. "Soon, you will be too big for me to carry."

Yuexin rested her head against Yunhong's shoulder as they left the cemetery. They passed by other families, husbands and wives, sons and daughters.

Now, the part of the day set aside for remembering was over, and in the fields, other children were flying kites, birds and butterflies and fish. In Yunhong's hand, she carried a kite painted like an opera mask, a pair of eyes drawn like wings against a dark red face.

She handed Yuexin the roll of string before walking backward, slowly, downwind, farther and farther away. At last, Yunhong stopped. As the wind came, she threw the kite up into the sky.

Yuexin tugged at the string, reeling it in. The kite went higher and higher, joining the others in the clouds. Then, the string slipped from her palm, and the kite was no longer a face but a small red star. Then, it was gone, a sacrifice to the other world.

Yunhong looked at the sky in dismay before crouching down. Her hands touched Yuexin's face in consolation. "Don't cry."

"The kite flew away," Yuexin cried out. She stared up hopelessly.

Once, Yunhong had been a child, too. She had trusted in the dragon that curled around the mountains. She had dreamed of a China transformed and full of quiet, lush rice fields. The burning had been there, yes, but it had been filled, too, with light. Now, Yunhong was frightened of dreaming. Of wanting. Of her birthmark darkening across her chest like slow flames.

"Everyone has lost a kite before," Yunhong said. "Now you are one of many. Now you are just like me."

THEN, SWEPT BACK by the autumn wind, Yunjun finally returned, after so many years away.

"Hello, Yunhong." Her big brother's smile was strained as he stood in front of the door, bearing his erhu on his back. His body, stocky in his youth, had become thinner and harder like the trunk of a peach tree after a long winter. His arms were wiry and corded with muscle. A long scar ran across his left cheek. He was no longer the boy she remembered.

There were so many questions Yunhong wanted to ask and press upon him. The brother who had not betrayed her like the other. Instead, she pressed the back of her hand to his cheek, wind-bitten and red.

"I haven't brought anything with me," Yunjun said, spreading out his empty hands. "Not a single gift. Only my smile."

Yunhong pulled him into the house. She called for their parents. Ma Ma and Ba Ba came at her call, startling at the sight of him. Ma Ma grabbed his shoulders, embracing him. Ba Ba squeezed his arm with tears in his eyes. The world had borrowed his life from them. The one who carried their name out into the world. Now he was folded again into their arms. Son. Brother. Uncle.

Yuexin came over and stared at him with wide eyes. She ducked behind Yunhong when Yunjun glanced over at her.

"Who is this?" Yunjun asked, crouching down to meet Yuexin's eyes.

"This is—" Yunhong began.

"—the daughter of a distant cousin," Ma Ma said, cutting in.

Yunjun smiled at Yuexin and touched her hair. He murmured a few quiet words to her, too quietly for Yunhong to hear. Then, he held out his arms. Shyly, Yuexin shuffled forward into his embrace before squirming away.

At the table, he lifted the bowl of soup with his hands. He smiled as he held Yuexin in his lap. Then he fell upon his food like a hungry wolf.

"Ba Ba, Ma Ma, I will not stay long." He said nothing of where he had been.

"And what of Yunli?" Ma Ma asked.

Yunjun glanced at Yunhong then, before answering her. "Yunli is well," he said. "He misses you all. He keeps you in his thoughts."

"Where is he now?" Ma Ma pressed.

But Yunjun would not say. "The less you know, the better."

He finished eating and walked around the house, looking at the rooms he had lived in as a child. He examined the contents of each room carefully, rattled the drum Yunli had once given him. He ran his hands over Yuexin's old toys. Wherever he went, Ma Ma turned.

When he was finished, they all went to the courtyard. Yunjun sat down and took out his erhu from its case. It was the same erhu Ba Ba had bought him, all those years ago, although now its wooden neck was scratched and its python skin was faded. The starlight touched the lenses of Ba Ba's glasses, the gray in Ma Ma's hair. Yunhong sat with Yuexin on the floor, holding her in her arms.

Yunjun's silhouette was framed against the window, ringed with light. The song he played was unfamiliar to Yunhong, something more stirring and strident than the tunes of their childhood.

It was late, but they wanted to hear the long, drawn-out notes pulled out from somewhere deep inside him.

Would he leave in the night, or did he still sleep beyond the wall between their rooms? In Yunhong's dreams, she didn't know.

In the morning, Yunjun was there still. Yunhong touched his arm at the breakfast table. Her relief surprised her. The old ache of affection, too. Yunjun helped Ma Ma lay out the dishes. He fed Yuexin with a spoon. Each day he stayed, he played Yuexin a story on his erhu that was half-song, half-dream.

On the first day, he told the story of a second oldest prince who lived in a vast and beautiful empire. "He grew up inside the imperial palace with his Ma Ma and Ba Ba and Mei Mei and Da Ge," Yunjun said, winking at Yunhong. "A divine dragon protected the boundaries of their country and watched over them."

Yuexin was looking up at Yunjun with wide eyes, her food left forgotten on her plate.

"Ba Ba was a great emperor and beloved by the people. All who came to pay their respects were cured of their illnesses," Yunjun said. "Ma Ma, too, was kind and patient. But they were the strictest with their eldest son, the prince, the heir to the throne. The crown prince wanted to be a good son, but he had heard rumors of a beast terrorizing the people." Yunjun formed his hands into claws and growled at Yuexin until she dissolved into laughter.

"One day," Yunjun continued, "the crown prince snuck out of the palace and went in search of the beast. Months passed, and their parents were filled with worry. When the prince returned, he returned with a woman he called his wife. The crown prince revealed that he had traveled far and met her on his journey. Together, they finally tracked down the beast. But it was not the beast they had imagined. It was the dragon."

"What did the dragon look like?" Yuexin demanded.

"A gold ribbon of scales swimming through the air," Yunjun said. "Isn't that right, Mei Mei?" he asked, looking at Yunhong.

"Like the ridges of a mountain," Yunhong corrected. She was frowning, irked by Yunjun's roundabout way of bringing up the past.

"Did the prince kill the dragon?" Yuexin asked.

"He hadn't yet," Yunjun said. "But he wanted to. His father, however, was furious. How could he say it was the dragon? The dragon was the one who protected them from harm. The dragon was the one who guided them. He refused to believe it. From then on, the crown prince was cast out of the family—"

"Was he?" Yunhong interrupted.

"It felt like it, to him," Yunjun said. "The second prince and his younger sister crouched at the window and watched their brother depart, hand-in-hand, with the woman. Their brother's back was tall and straight. He was no longer a prince. Just a man." He hesitated for a moment before continuing. "Now, the second prince was expected to inherit the throne. He threw himself into his studies, not wanting to disappoint his parents.

He did not want to end up like his brother—cast out into the cold. He studied day and night in his own separate palace. When his sister came to visit him, he turned her away." Yunjun glanced at Yunhong, before looking away. "In his mind, she was only a girl. What did she know of the pressures he felt? For in his heart, they were not the same. Later—many years later—lying in the dark on the wild mountains, he would see— would see he had been wrong." Yunjun paused. "He would wish they had been closer."

Yunhong stood up and began to clear the table. "Finish your breakfast," she told Yuexin.

"What about the beast?" Yuexin asked.

"Well," Yunjun said, "the second prince learned that his brother had been right. It was the dragon after all. So the second prince also cast off his title in search of his brother and the dragon, leaving behind his sister to inherit the empire of their innocence."

Was that what he thought, Yunhong wondered. That she had inherited an empire of innocence? That she had remained a child while they had been gone? Maybe they could never truly understand one another, no matter how much they tried. No matter how much Yunjun was trying now.

YUNJUN TOLD THE second story the next night, while putting Yuexin to bed. It surprised Yunhong how tenderly he treated Yuexin. He never seemed to hold much fondness for children before. He never seemed to want children of his own. But now, he was pulling the blankets up to Yuexin's chin with as much attention and care as a father might. As Haiyang might have once.

"Will you tell me another story?" Yuexin asked expectantly.

"Another one?"

Yuexin nodded. "About the dragon and the princes?"

Yunjun considered her request. "How about I tell you a different one? A story about a young man?"

Yuexin nodded.

"In the mountains," Yunjun began, "the young man ran with his friends, hiding in caves from the Guomindang. Over the winter, they made peace with the local bandits and trained with them as brothers. It was then they learned to use the blueness of the trees and the tall grass to their advantage. But the German rifles of the Guomindang found them all the same. So they climbed higher up the mountain, higher and higher, until the land was so cold that only tigers dwelled there."

Yunhong lingered in the doorway of Yuexin's bedroom, which was her brothers' childhood room. Despite how angered his first story had left her, she couldn't help but listen. It seemed, in the intervening years during his departure from home and return, he had gained Yunli's mastery in storytelling. He had always been able to entrance his audience with his music, but now, his words, too, felt like a song.

"The young man's unit made camp for two years," Yunjun said. "At night, across the small, human fires, the young man watched her—the famed female rebel of the Communists. The one who lived like a man among men. The one who they called He Xiang."

"A woman rebel?" Yuexin asked with wonder in her eyes.

Yunjun nodded. "The most brave and beautiful of them all. Everyone who saw her fell a little bit in love with her, and the young man was no exception." There was a pain and sorrow in his gaze. The same pain and sorrow Yunhong saw in her own face in the mirror.

But Yunjun rallied again and continued on with his story. "In the mornings, between the tents, the rebels discovered tiger tracks."

"I've heard that tigers eat men," Yuexin said.

"Where did you hear that from?" Yunhong asked.

"Don't worry," Yunjun said. "They don't eat little girls. But it's true they can be just as ferocious as a dragon. The rebels wondered how the tigers could have slipped so soundlessly—unseen—between them. When he laid in bed at night, the young man sometimes thought he heard the tigers, circling the coals."

Yuexin brought the covers up to her eyes. When she was younger, she had often had night terrors of being hunted by some monster in the flames. She would come running into Yunhong's room, crying out for her big sister. Yunhong hoped that Yunjun's stories wouldn't inspire new ones, and she shot Yunjun a sharp look.

But Yunjun seemed to be lost in his own story. "By the second winter, He Xiang was pregnant with the young man's child. For seven hours, she labored on the rock. When she finally gave birth, it was to a silent child. As the others wrapped the baby in bandages, she begged them to tell her whether it was a boy or a girl. 'What does it matter,' they asked." There was an edge of bitterness in Yunjun's voice, and recrimination. "And did the young man look for their child? Did he go outside to the place where they had left the small, unmoving bundle? He only thought of going." His voice broke, and he fell silent.

Yuexin didn't seem to know what to do with the story she had just been given. She pulled the covers back down. "But what about the dragon?" she asked. "And the crown prince? Did he save the baby?"

Yunjun was silent.

"If the baby was a boy, he must have died that night in the cold. But if the baby was a girl, perhaps she lived," Yunhong jumped in. She looked at Yuexin. "Girls live as discarded things. By morning, the bundle would have disappeared, carried away in the mouth of a striped thing to be raised as a tiger. That is the only way girls can survive."

BUT THE STORY that hurt Yunhong the most was his last and final story. The three of them—Yunhong, Yuexin, and Yunjun—were outside by the pond. Yunjun was on his belly, showing Yuexin how to catch fish with his bare hands. Yunhong had to admit it seemed like magic how the flashing carp kept appearing in his hands. She wondered if it was Yunli who had taught him, or if he had learned all on his own. She wondered when he might have caught fish, in the wilderness, in the mountain streams. If he had needed to rely on the skill to feed himself or others.

"What happened to the crown prince?" Yuexin asked. "Did he defeat the dragon?"

"Well," Yunjun began, "the eldest brother gathered with others to fight for their country. But the beast—that terrible dragon—kept on escaping them. They didn't know where it was or where it would go next. Perhaps, they suspected, it could take on different forms. Perhaps it was hiding amongst them even now." His hands were empty now of any fish. He cupped his hands and let the water pool there slowly instead.

"People had fear in their hearts," Yunjun continued, "and they turned on one another in their fear. Everyone just wanted to live. By now, the young man had joined his eldest brother and his wife and child. They fled with a few others to the mountains, climbing so high they climbed above the clouds. They raced across the fields and valleys. Often, they thought of their parents and little sister."

"Did they?" Yunhong challenged.

A look of shame flashed across Yunjun's face. He sat up and looked at Yuexin. "One day, the brothers heard news that their sister was getting married. It would have been joyous news but for the man she was marrying. His family had ties to the dragon. An enemy of the people. And the people wanted revenge."

"Revenge," Yuexin echoed. Fascinated, she crept closer.

"The brothers knew their sister was in danger," Yunjun said. "The eldest brother said he would go save her and asked his younger brother to look after his family. On the long journey back, he thought of how to prevent his sister's disaster. But when he arrived, she was already married. Men were burning down the palace of her husband. So the eldest brother pulled her out of the fire—her and her alone. He brought his sister to the door of their parents, leaving without waiting for her to wake. For he was afraid of what she would say, of how she might look at him."

"Like a coward," Yunhong said.

Yunjun paused for a moment before continuing. "He walked through the darkness and the cold and the hissing rain. In the forests, he was stalked by a tiger. At last, he made it back—back to the arms of his wife and daughter. But he thought often of his sister whom he loved. He wondered if she loved him still. For hers was no longer the life he wanted for her, but it was all he could give her."

"So they defeated the dragon in the end?" Yuexin asked.

Neither Yunhong nor Yunjun had an answer for her.

AND AT NIGHT, sleeping beside Yunhong, Yuexin recounted all the stories Yunjun told her. From each word bloomed an image. Each image, a dream. And the dreams were as real and solid to Yuexin as the erhu Yunjun played. But Yunhong knew better. They were all just lies. Lies to smooth over the pain of the past.

ON THE EVENING of the fourth day, Ma Ma rushed into the room, distraught. "A man is at the door asking to buy a pig. He refuses to leave. He says he knows the song you play."

Yunjun startled but soon began to laugh. He set aside the erhu he had been playing. "No need to worry. I know him. He is the one I have been waiting for."

Yunhong pulled Yuexin away from Yunjun. So, his songs hadn't been for them after all, just a signal for someone else.

Ma Ma understood immediately. "You are going to leave again." She stood in the doorway, blocking him.

Will you never return again, Yunhong asked him with her eyes. She gathered Yuexin in her arms. The line of her brother's shoulders was the shape of leaving.

THAT NIGHT, YUEXIN cried all through the darkness, the way she used to do as an infant. Yunhong stroked her hair with sweeping, tender gestures. She hushed and rocked her in her arms, but the girl only cried harder, her tears relentless and violent.

"He promised," Yuexin said, turning her face into the bed. The blades of her shoulders rose and fell.

"Promised what?"

Yuexin turned to look at her. "To tell me about the tigers."

"I can tell you stories about the tigers."

"They aren't stories," Yuexin said, a defiant set to her mouth. "They're real. And I was born from one of them."

Yunhong sat up, filled with a sudden fire. She began to tremble from what burned through her. "Is that what he told you?"

Yuexin raised her chin. "I am the daughter of a tiger," she said, "who lives high up on a mountain."

"You are not."

"I am," Yuexin said, pushing herself up. Her hands were clenched now into little fists.

"He lied to you," Yunhong said, her voice steely. "He's always been a liar. The both of them."

"He didn't—!"

Yunhong threw her hand over Yuexin's mouth. She wished she could press down the words that were rising up in Yuexin's throat, wished she could press down the words she herself was about to say. Instead, she lowered her face and brought it close. "Listen to me," she said. "Your mother is dead."

SOON AFTER YUNJUN's erhu notes faded, winter came again. For the first time in many years, it snowed, and Yunhong stood outside with Yuexin to stare at the sky in wonder. Yuexin caught snowflakes in her hand. Yunhong tilted her face toward the sky and closed her eyes. At times,

Yunhong dreamed of following the Communists' Long March—their flight across the country from the Guomindang. In some dreams, she was a tiger on the hunt, her arms striped, her teeth fanged. In others, she was a deity of protection, her long white robes trailing in the wind. When she woke, she didn't know which one she wanted to be. She only knew her desire to follow them. She watched them from the shadows as they walked for weeks, months, a year. She heard reports of how more and more died from the cold and hunger. Though their numbers dwindled, Yunhong wanted to believe her brothers still marched on.

THEN ONE NIGHT, a clamor of voices broke through her dreams. Pounding footsteps. Yunhong's eyes flew open. She groped for Yuexin, stirring beside her. From beyond, somewhere in the darkness, her mother was crying. Yunhong scrambled out of bed and pushed open her door. Men—soldiers—were dragging Ma Ma and Ba Ba across the courtyard.

"What are you doing?" Yunhong grasped at her mother, her father, but she was held back. She fought desperately against the hands holding her. It was too late. Her mother and father were gone, absorbed into the darkness of the night.

The One Who Could
Never Return Again

INSIDE THE WINDOWLESS room in the jailhouse, the warden sat behind a gleaming desk. A lamp illuminated the curl of his mustache and the stack of papers he was signing. Papers passed through his hands, one after another. Yunhong caught glimpses of names and dates. Lives marked down then cast aside.

"What do you want?" The warden didn't raise his head.

"Master," Yunhong said, bowing deeply. "I am here on behalf of my parents—Zhang Fulong and Zhang Yufang."

"Zhang Fulong?" At this, a hint of interest entered the warden's eyes. "Doctor Zhang?"

Yunhong nodded cautiously.

The warden put down his pen and looked at her.

"Soldiers took my parents here several days ago. They haven't done anything wrong. My father is only a doctor." Yunhong watched the warden closely, but his face gave nothing away. His face was impassive as an idol in its wooden niche. Removed from human matters.

The warden frowned. He shuffled through the pile of papers on his desk and ran his finger down a list of characters. His frown grew.

"They've been accused of being sympathetic to the Communists," he said. "I see here you have two brothers?"

Yunhong knelt down before him and slipped the jade bracelet off her wrist. The one she had once treasured and had kept hidden under her bed for so long. Its delicate carvings seemed to glitter in the lamplight—each carving coming alive. Yunhong offered it up with both hands. "Please, I beg you to review their case again." The jade was cold in her palm.

The warden stared at her for several long moments. "You look a little like him," he finally said.

Yunhong's eyes widened in surprise. "You know my father?" she asked.

He didn't answer her question. Instead, he asked one of his own. "How often do you speak to your brothers?"

"We haven't seen them in years," Yunhong said. It was true. Of Yunli, at least. "They live their lives separately from ours," she added desperately. "And their choices are their own."

"Their choices are their families," the warden said.

"They have their own families now," Yunhong said.

"But the blood that runs through them, runs through you all."

She knew it was true. Her birthmark was proof enough of it.

The warden regarded her for several long moments. "After my wife gave birth, she fell ill with a persistent cough," he said. "We spent a fortune inviting doctors from the city to treat her. None of their medicines seemed to work. And then we heard of a doctor who, they said, could bring those even on the brink of death back to life. Your father took one look at my wife and said he couldn't help her. All he could do was give her something to ease her pain. And when I went to her the next morning, she had already passed in her sleep."

Was this his means of refusal? Would the failures of the past haunt them forever? Yunhong slowly lowered her hands.

"Although your father couldn't heal her, he was merciful," he said. "And I suppose some fates cannot be avoided." The warden reached into his drawers and pulled out a document. "If your parents sign this, I'll let them go."

"Thank you," said Yunhong, rising and bowing deeply. The warden's eyes flicked to her hands. She quickly laid the jade bracelet down on his desk and took the paper in return. The paper was cheap and thin. It could so easily tear apart in her hands.

"Ba Ba. Ma Ma." Yunhong took in the sight of her father and mother, standing weary and defeated before her in the cell. Ma Ma grasped her hands through the bar. But when she passed the document to them, they passed it back, shook their heads. Yunhong knew what it said—that signing meant they renounced their brothers and had no more claim to them because of their crimes.

"But what if there is no other way?" Yunhong looked at them in disbelief. "You would rather die? Rather leave Yuexin and me behind for their sake?" Yunhong's entire body trembled. Ba Ba and Ma Ma turned their faces away. They cast their eyes to the floor, resigned to their fate.

But Yunhong wasn't. She stood before her parents and signed their names on the paper, just as Yunli had once taught her. His hand had clasped over hers, guiding each mark.

"What are you doing?" Ba Ba demanded.

"You yourself once turned away from Yunli," Yunhong said. "For years, you refused to see him or Liying."

Ba Ba closed his eyes. "I've come to regret my choices," he said. "All I want is them to be alive and well."

"We can't turn away from them now," Ma Ma said.

Despite their pleas, Yunhong's hand didn't tremble. It didn't waver as the burning burst through her.

AFTER THEY RETURNED home, Ma Ma no longer touched her as she used to. Not with the same tenderness. Ba Ba didn't meet her eyes. Only Yuexin approached her with the same innocent trust, asking to be held, asking to be loved.

But Yunhong knew what she had done. She had renounced her brothers. Renounced the bonds of family, the past, and all the old traditions.

THEN A FEW days after the New Year, Yunli appeared. Yunhong saw him standing outside, looking up at the house with a lost expression on his face. A spirit summoned from her darkest dreams.

Yunhong stepped through the doorway. He looked older, so much older than Yunhong remembered. In her dreams, he towered over her, but now, he seemed thin and frail. Yunhong's eyes traced the scar on the underside of his jaw. Only his eyes remained the same. Gentle and solemn. He bowed his head before their parents, who had now also come out to meet him.

"Yunli," Ma Ma cried out. She reached for him, but he drew back.

"My son," said Ba Ba quietly. The years of uncertainty had softened his gaze.

Yunli closed his eyes. He was trembling when he opened them again. "Ma Ma. Ba Ba. Mei Mei," he said. "Yunjun is dead."

YUNHONG CHASED AFTER Yunli down the path outside the house. Don't go, she wanted to say. She felt as if she were a child again, chasing after her older brother. But another part of her—the part that remembered how they had betrayed one another—wanted him to vanish.

They passed the bend in the road, the cracked stone.

He stopped when she caught up to him, touched his hand.

"Before," Yunli said, tears gathering in his eyes, "I thought the future was you, Yunjun, me. We were the ones who could change the world. For whom the world could change. I wanted it to change, Yunhong. For you. All for you."

In the distance, the mountains rose and fell. Once, they had been the ridges of a dragon's back.

"I know I have done terrible things, Yunhong," Yunli said. "All for a dream. But still, the dream is beautiful to me." He paused, then went on. "China needs saving. Now, against the Japanese. So I will continue to fight."

After everything, he was still the one leaving them.

"Goodbye, Yunli," she said, turning away.

WHEN MA MA told her of Diyu, the underworld, she said it was gray and dark and deep under the earth. It was a city like a human city, but with roads that turned without end. There, souls wandered for decades, centuries, until they could be reborn again.

But without his body getting a proper burial, Yunjun would not be joining the ancestral home. While other souls carried the offerings their living had burned for them, Yunjun would wander through the courts and layers of hell, without even a name. No longer theirs, no longer hers. Something else entirely.

THE NEXT YEAR, the Japanese invaded China. They, too, could smell the woundedness of the country. At the end of the year, Yunhong heard news of the Japanese at Nanjing, 800 kilometers away. The massacre. The people whispered how when the Japanese came, the river ran red with blood. Even the reeds along the banks turned red. And the new reeds that sprouted up were also red. One for every lost soul.

To FIGHT AGAINST the Japanese invasion, the Guomindang and the Communists joined together once more in an uneasy alliance. A Second United Front. But both sides were still weakened from the civil war between them and full of distrust. And the wounds of the past—of Chiang Kai-shek's betrayal of the Communists during the First United Front—were too deep to forget. Ill equipped and badly organized, the

Second United Front could not pull off a swift defeat. Instead, they hoped to wear down the invading army until they gave up.

Two years later, when the Japanese attacked Changsha from the east and occupied Hunan in the north, Yunhong fled with her mother and father and Yuexin and the other villagers into the mountains. They were all terrified of what the Japanese soldiers might do to civilians should they capture the region. Better to leave everything behind than to be killed—or worse.

It was cold and heavy with mist as they walked through the bamboo groves. Carrying food and blankets on their backs, the four of them hiked in silence with the other villagers. China was finally changing. It was not the dream her brothers had dreamed of, not the dream she had dreamed of either. Who could say who had been right?

"Jie Jie, I'm scared," Yuexin whispered when they had stopped for a rest on the overgrown mountain path. She sat down on the ground and wrapped her arms around herself. Yuexin's braids were coming undone. They were falling out of their ties.

"Get up," Yunhong said. Ma Ma and Ba Ba were walking on ahead.

Yuexin began to cry. "I want my mother."

Yunhong crouched down and took her hand. She had wanted Yuexin to be free of the past, free of it all. But she had survived. And Yuexin had as well, despite all her fears. The stars had determined Yuexin's fate, but the stars, too, were in constant motion, filling the universe with their divine fires. Perhaps it was time for Yuexin to know who they really were and what they meant to one another. That is, mother and daughter.

"Don't be afraid, Yuexin," Yunhong said. "And I'll tell you a secret."

PART TWO

NANJING

1967–1979

The Bell That Calls the Dead

LIKE ALL NINE year olds, Yonghong and Hongxing were loyal members of the Little Red Guard and knew the party slogans by heart.

"DOWN WITH THE OLD IDEAS, OLD CULTURE, OLD HABITS, OLD CUSTOMS," the students chanted as loudly as they could on their morning march to school, Little Red Books in hand.

"REVOLUTION IS THE END," Yonghong shouted, loudest of all. "REVOLUTION IS NO CRIME."

"REBELLION IS JUSTIFIED," Leap Forward called out, joining the sisters on their way to school. Leap Forward was named after the Great Leap Forward, and he was Yonghong's best friend, and his mother was Ma's best friend, too. He was the tallest student in their class—as tall as a middle schooler—which meant that he was great at keeping the other students in line.

And then they all joined in on Yonghong's favorite:

"DARE TO THINK. DARE TO ACT."

The walk from their apartments to the elementary school was long enough for two chants—three on a good day. Usually, it was Yonghong who decided what they would chant and when. Sometimes, she took inspiration from the newest slogans painted on the walls that lined the streets to the school. Sometimes, she made up slogans of her own. Often, she wished she could paint the slogans she came up with on the wall— but only the older students were allowed to paint. It was the duty of the younger students, they were told, to bolster the revolutionary spirit of the community through their voices.

Leap Forward and Yonghong were always at the front of the line of students—sometimes walking even farther ahead than Teacher Wu, their language teacher, who came to fetch them in the mornings. The two of them were natural leaders of the next generation, they were told. It was not only in their blood, but their names. Leap Forward. Forever Red. The perfect match.

Hongxing usually lingered in the rear. She wasn't fond of shouting the slogans that Yonghong and Leap Forward loved so much. "Loyalty to Chairman Mao," she would declare, her voice flat. "Loyalty to his thought. Loyalty to his revolutionary line." She liked to save her energy for singing and dancing.

Hongxing was known for her loyalty dance performances at party meetings and commemorative events. While dancing, her hands and face would be turned toward the sky in a show of reverence. She'd leap from side to side like a little bird. Those watching could never look away.

At first, Ma and Ba had tried to get Yonghong to sing and dance as well. Wai Po had even sewn matching dresses made of special cotton cloth that Great-Uncle had mailed them from Beijing, where he worked in the Ministry of Health. Decorative flourishes like the ones that Wai Po embroidered along the collar and hem of the dress belonged to the old world—but sometimes exceptions could be made. Especially if they were made in service of the Party.

Wai Po was masterful with a needle and thread. Their grandmother could embroider anything that Yonghong or her sister requested—from blue-winged birds to yellow magnolia flowers to mythical beasts with scales and claws. But the ones Yonghong most liked were her swirling red clouds, which were a reference to Wai Po's given name—Yunhong.

However, despite being dressed for the part, Yonghong could never sing as well as her sister. When she sang, there was something strident in her tone that made the lyrics of the songs sound more threatening than pleasing to the ear. From Ma's furrowed brows during her first ever performance, Yonghong knew she was wondering how twins could sing and dance so differently.

Yonghong had practiced with Hongxing for weeks after class, copying her leaps and twirls exactly. One of the cooks at the cafeteria who used to be a music teacher had even taught them how to harmonize together. But these efforts were to no avail. Where Hongxing's song inspired the clapping and beating of the feet, Yonghong's efforts resulted in an uneasy silence.

"Why can't you be more like your sister?" Ma had scolded Yonghong after that first performance. She looked at Yonghong with disappointment in her eyes, a look that was never present when Hongxing was around.

"Let them be children," Wai Po said.

Her words, however, did not appease Ma. Instead, Ma turned away from the both of them to fuss over Hongxing. No one would ever be able to criticize Hongxing, Ma always said. She was the perfect daughter.

After that performance, all seemed in agreement that Hongxing would perform by herself in the future. Yonghong didn't mind. In fact, she was relieved she no longer had to attend weekly practices. She had no desire to sing or dance for others—no matter how beautiful the dress was, or the song. No, she wanted to shout, to march, to stand at the front of the line. She'd leave the singing to Hongxing.

As ONE OF two class monitors—along with Leap Forward—Yonghong had a list of duties in addition to making sure that all twenty-five students of their third grade class made it safely to school in the morning. She was also responsible for leading everyone from their math class to language class—and then from language back to their families' on-campus apartments during the midday lunch break. After their hour-long break, Yonghong and Leap Forward once again lined up all the students to return to school for their last, and most important, class of the day—Chairman Mao's Revolutionary Thought.

Chairman Mao's Revolutionary Thought was not only the most important class but also—in Yonghong's opinion—the most enjoyable. During each class, Teacher Huang had them carefully study the latest essay that Chairman Mao had disseminated to the people. Often, Teacher Huang had Yonghong stand up and read it aloud. This was where Yonghong shined the most—in declarations and announcements. The words gripped her, rushing out of her mouth in a way that seemed out of her control. It was thrilling—the idea that the words inside her had once belonged to the great and honorable Chairman Mao. But no matter how carried away she felt, Yonghong made sure to carefully enunciate each word. It wouldn't do for his message to get lost in the speaking of it.

Her efforts were recognized by Teacher Huang, who always nodded approvingly when she finished. Her other classmates, too, respected Yonghong for her delivery, and they all listened with rapt attention. It was perhaps the real reason why she was the de facto leader of their class—not simply just because of her title as class monitor. And why they usually looked to her for instruction, instead of Leap Forward.

After school was over, all the classmates gathered around the plum blossom tree in the yard behind the school. Everyone liked to play under its far-spreading branches, which provided welcome shade under the hot sun. It was an ancient tree, with a broad, gnarled trunk that gave off the impression of a human body. Its roots were a thick multitude, rippling the earth around the tree. It wasn't uncommon for Yonghong—or anyone else, for that matter—to trip over one of its roots. The tree had caused many a child to scrape a knee or bruise the palm of their hands. Leap Forward even had a long scar down his forearm from when he had tripped and split his skin open on a rock. But whatever physical wounds the tree might have inflicted on them, Yonghong and her classmates never held toward it any ill will.

The tree occupied a special place in their hearts—a place of reverence that should have been reserved for the murals or slogans painted on the wall that enclosed the apartments where they lived. Perhaps it was because the splendor of its pink blooms in the spring was reminiscent of the glory in the murals that depicted Chairman Mao looking triumphantly into the distance, the rising sun at his back. Perhaps some might have thought—if such a thought could be admitted—that the sight of the tree in bloom was even more glorious. But of course, such a thought could never be thought at all.

If the tree was not as glorious as Chairman Mao, it was at least as glorious as firecrackers bursting in the street on New Year's Eve or dishes piled high with caramelized squares of roasted pork belly.

And such a tree naturally came with an equally enchanting ghost. Yonghong had long forgotten who had told her about the ghost or when she had first heard of her. Perhaps it was an older student who had told Leap Forward, who had then told her. Or perhaps he had told Hongxing first, and by extension her. Or maybe it wasn't Leap Forward at all. Maybe it was the tree itself.

When the Communist party took over, they had cleared out both the landlords and the poisons they were peddling. Unlike the Guomindang, who used the sale of such drugs to fund their army, the Communists wanted to cure the country of its illnesses. They gathered the people in city centers and village squares to impart to them the necessity of rooting out decay.

Denounce him, the Communists had told the third—or was it the second?—wife of the landlord who used to own the lands where everyone was now standing.

Denounce him, Yonghong's classmates shouted as they reenacted the scene around the plum blossom tree.

The third—or was it the second?—wife, played by Hongxing in their schoolyard plays, stood up before a large crowd of Communist brothers and sisters and shouted that she had been sold to her husband's—no, the Landlord's—family as a servant when she was just a young girl. Her family had been poor peasants who needed the money in order to pay for their only son's wedding. Her entry into the Landlord's household had been, therefore, an act of filial piety. She had done it for her most beloved aging parents, as any of them might have done so. Later on, when she was a little older, the Landlord had decided to make her one of his wives. But it had been a marriage by force—a sham, really. Either way, she had been unhappy. He had been a cruel master, and an even crueler husband. And here, Hongxing might touch the corner of her eye or press her face against the trunk of the plum blossom tree. And if the wind happened to blow a little, bringing with it the smell of spring, the blossoms on the tree might shake and scatter a pink cloud of silky petals upon their heads.

She was a great actress. Hongxing, that is.

Later, after the trial was over and the Landlord had been executed, the third—or was it the second?—wife was said to have often been seen lingering by the plum blossom tree. Was it because she regretted what she had said? Perhaps she had made it all up, as Hongxing did—each time changing the story. Perhaps the tree as it blossomed had been a welcome and longed-for sight for her during the long and miserable years. And that was enough of a reason for her ghost to make an appearance from time to time in the shadows of the branches. Or perhaps it was none of those reasons at all. The past was full of questions, most of them unanswerable. But the existence of the ghost couldn't be denied.

Yonghong and Hongxing had seen her. They had sighted the ghost during last year's Mid-Autumn Festival, after Leap Forward had convinced them to go cricket hunting. The crickets were the luckiest, Leap Forward had told them, in mid-autumn. If you caught one, all your wishes would come true.

Yonghong had been determined to catch a pair of them for luck—for that was the year that Ma had shut all the curtains in the apartment, plunging them all into a state of perpetual darkness, and refused to open them again. "I like it better this way," she said, when they asked her why she had done so.

"What nonsense," Ba scoffed.

At first, it had seemed exciting to Yonghong and Hongxing. They pretended they were living in a cave in the wilderness. And it kept the rooms cool in the summertime. But the darkness soon took its toll on them, day after day. And when summer turned to fall, and fall to winter, the shut curtains became a never-ending source of contention and shame.

Every time Ba tried to open the curtains, she would push him aside. "Don't you dare take this away from me," she snapped. Not even Wai Po could convince her.

"You call yourself my mother now?" Ma would snap harshly. "Well it's too late to make up for the past." Sometimes, there was an anger to Ma's voice when she spoke to Wai Po that made Yonghong shirk away. Once, she had heard Ma yell at Wai Po, "Why would I ever want a mother like you? Why don't you go back to pretending?"

But when Yonghong and Hongxing questioned their mother about the curtains, her response was softer, and more pained. "They're watching me. They're judging me. I can't bear it anymore. I've never been good enough. Not for anyone." She had held them close then and apologized.

Yonghong and Hongxing hadn't been able to catch any crickets, but they discovered the ghost behind the school instead. She had worn a long white robe, and her hair was a streak of starlight down her back. The moon was hanging bright and full in the sky, but the ghost had seemed even more luminescent in the night. No one but the two of them had seen her—not even Leap Forward, who had followed close behind. By the time Leap Forward appeared, the ghost had disappeared—like petals swept away by the wind.

IT WAS SAID that the Granary Technical School had been built on lands formerly owned by the Landlord. As their parents worked for the technical college, Yonghong and Hongxing lived on the school grounds along with most of their other classmates, including Leap Forward. Ma and Leap Forward's mother worked as nurses for the college, while Leap Forward's father taught ways to measure and weigh grain. However, since Chairman Mao's proclamation in the *People's Daily* the year before, colleges like the Granary Technical School had stopped all classes in accordance with his orders.

Ba was a foreman at the automobile manufacturing plant across the railroad tracks. He held an elevated position as a worker of the people, and Yonghong always felt a sense of pride at the way everyone looked up to him. He was often called upon to settle personal disputes between the factory workers and was widely praised for looking after them as if they were his own family. He was the very model of a revolutionary man— courageous and generous and hardworking.

Leap Forward's family and Yonghong's family shared a unit on the second floor of the green apartment building. Every apartment building—white, red, and green—had three floors with eight units on each floor. Every unit was comprised of two large rooms and one or two small rooms, along with a communal kitchen and bathroom. Most units were split up between two families, who divided the large and small rooms according to the number of people in each respective family. Only very large families—like Principal Liang's—had an entire unit to themselves.

In the unit that Yonghong and Hongxing lived in, Ma and Ba lived in the small room, while she, Hongxing, and Wai Po lived in one of the large rooms. Their room contained both the bed that all three of them slept in and a dining table and living room area. Yonghong didn't mind sleeping in one bed with Hongxing and Wai Po. In fact, she enjoyed falling asleep to the sound of Wai Po's soft snores and Hongxing's still back.

She wasn't like their father, who preferred his peace and quiet. The thin walls that separated each of the rooms often frustrated Ba, who had grown up in the countryside with its stretches of open fields and hours of silence. Through the walls, they could hear the sounds of Leap Forward's family as they went about their day: Leap Forward's mother complaining about her bad knee, which had been fractured when she was a child and never healed right; Leap Forward's father as he coughed and sneezed; Leap Forward's brother, Kangmei—"Resist America"—who walked around with a slight limp; and Leap Forward himself, who sometimes spoke to Yonghong directly through the wall.

It was easiest to hear him if Yonghong sat beneath the dining table and pressed her ear into one particular divot in the wall—though Ba was irritated whenever he caught her doing so. "You can't fart without the neighbors knowing about it," her father would say, before leaving again.

There was only one person Yonghong knew of who lived in a room all by herself, and that was Teacher Wu—who lived in the apartment building by the elementary school. It hadn't always been that way, Yonghong knew. When she had first moved to Nanjing from the countryside, Teacher Wu had brought with her a young husband—three years younger than her. But he had been sickly ever since the day they first moved in. He had been assigned to work in the automobile manufacturing plant, but his health had only allowed him a few months of work. After that, he retired back home and rarely left their apartment. In fact, Yonghong had only seen him once or twice, standing in the yard behind the school, gazing up at the plum blossom tree when it was in bloom. Ba had made frequent trips to their house, bringing them food and packages. But by the time Yonghong was made a class monitor, Teacher Wu's husband had already been two years dead.

THE SCHOOL GROUNDS, which were encircled by a tall cement wall, included ten school buildings, three apartment buildings, two administrative buildings, one cafeteria, one athletic field, one pond, and one gigantic billboard, upon which a larger-than-life mural of Chairman Mao was painted.

The latest iteration of Chairman Mao, Yonghong thought, was the best one so far. In this one, the sky was awash in light oranges. The clouds swirled—looking more like flames. There was the faintest trace of blue mountains in the distance, stirring the imagination. In front of this landscape, the people were marching—a great many of them—a mass. Their figures were nondescript—almost anonymous—but the clothing they wore was clean and of good quality. One could tell, even at a distance, that they were healthy and well taken care of and full of passion. And the flags they waved in the air were painted in the most beautiful of reds. The flags rippled across the mural, proudly displaying the party slogans that had been carefully painted on them.

And in front of all of this stood Chairman Mao, in his modest green uniform. He stood on the right side of the mural, and his body was slightly angled toward the left. His expression as he looked out of the mural was content and benevolent. His eyes were slightly squinted against the light that illuminated him.

The sun did not appear within the boundaries of the mural. It did not need to make an appearance. The people were the soil, Chairman Mao the sun.

FROM WHAT YONGHONG had gathered, the Landlord had made his fortune by selling poisons to his own countrymen. In those days, it was a common practice, Yonghong and Hongxing learned in school. Foreigners would sell these poisons to the landlords, who would then sell them to the common people. A single puff of smoke was enough to get you hooked forever, Wai Po always said. Her own father had ended up succumbing to it in the end, after the death of her Ge Ge.

Wai Po told them that, when she was younger, she would help her father collect herbs from the mountains that surrounded their home. Sometimes, it would rain—a light rain that kissed the top of her forehead, her cheekbones, the nape of her neck, as she bent down to pick the plants or gather the clean moss that, once dried, would be perfect for dressings. Often, it was cold. Through the mist, she would follow her father's back as he wove between the bamboo groves and boulders that shaped the landscape. The mountains then were alive. Now, she said, the people think they can shape the earth to do their bidding.

He had been a brilliant doctor. Patients came from kilometers away to be treated by him. Coughs, fevers, unexplained chills, irregular heartbeats. But not even he was able to cure himself of his sorrow.

"There are some heartaches that can never be cured," Wai Po added.

"But the poison—it made him feel better?" Yonghong wondered aloud.

"For a time," Wai Po said.

YONGHONG AND HONGXING both wondered about the smoke that would get you hooked forever. How it might rise from the pipes in strange, seductive shapes. Yonghong imagined a dragon, wings stirring the air of the dens where the common people gathered to indulge in the poison. Hongxing imagined a woman, rising from the plumes.

The wealthy masters of China hadn't cared if they destroyed their own people or their country for the sake of profit, their teachers told them. That was what life was like before the great and glorious Chairman Mao. Before the establishment of social harmony.

That was what Yonghong thought about whenever she looked upon the mural, and the plum blossom tree as well—which was why she almost didn't notice the snake until she was right upon it.

The snake was curled up in a small hole at the roots of the tree. As long as her arm, it was greener than the peels of candied limes Great-Uncle had once mailed them. Although the snake hissed and flicked out its small, pink tongue when she crouched down to inspect it, it hadn't made any move to bite her. Yonghong grabbed it in her fist and held it in the air, triumphantly, to show the other kids.

"Look! Look what I found!"

"That's disgusting!"

"Let it go!"

"What is that?"

"It's mine," Yonghong answered them.

"Let me see," Leap Forward said, holding out his hand.

Yonghong handed the snake over to him.

Leap Forward must have held on to the snake tightly—more tightly than her—for it suddenly squirmed and went taut. In a flash, its fangs bit into his hand. He yelped and flung it down.

"Where did it go?" . . . "Get it away from me!" . . . "There! There!" The children clamored in excitement.

"Don't hurt it!" Yonghong shouted.

BY THE TIME the children stopped moving, the snake was silent and motionless. Its head had been partially crushed into the dirt, and its mouth was open, revealing a glint of its fangs. It almost appeared to be warning Yonghong not to come any closer, but she approached anyway.

"Who did this?" Yonghong said, kneeling down beside the dead snake. Its skin was no longer a bright vibrant green but dulled by dirt. She picked it up by its tail, then let it flop to the ground.

"It wasn't me."

"I didn't even touch it."

"It was an accident," said Leap Forward, holding onto his wounded hand.

"I gave it to you," Yonghong said, accusatorily.

Leap Forward broke her gaze—but only for a moment. "Look what it did to me," he said. Blood oozed from two points on the back of his left hand, between his thumb and index finger.

"Why did you have to kill it?" Yonghong asked him and the others. "You could have let it go."

"It was an accident," Leap Forward said again—or maybe it was one of the other boys. Yonghong wasn't listening anymore. She gathered the snake into a coil and held it in her hands. A snake was a little dragon on Earth, Wai Po had always said. In her palms, it looked even smaller. Yonghong would have to give it a proper burial, lest she call down the disapproval of the Heavens.

That evening, Yonghong returned to the hole at the base of the plum blossom tree. She placed the snake in the shadows on the ground and began to dig at the hole with her bare hands. She dug until her fingernails ached and felt raw. Her anger fueled her through the sunset in all its deepening oranges and reds. Then, when the sky began to darken, Hongxing came out to find her.

"Have you gone crazy?" Hongxing said, staring disapprovingly down at her. "Ma says it's time for dinner."

"In a little bit," Yonghong said, reaching down into the hole. She dislodged a rock and pulled it out. Her nails were dark with dirt. She flicked away a little white grub that was stuck to the back of her knuckle.

On the wind came the voice of their mother, calling both their names.

"Let's go," Hongxing said impatiently, tugging at her arm. "Ma's waiting."

Yonghong tried to shrug her off, but Hongxing gripped her tightly—so tightly it began to hurt. But Yonghong only felt the most minor of annoyances, for any pain she felt or inflicted was shared between them. They were twins, after all.

"Come on," Hongxing said.

Yonghong got up reluctantly, but not before placing the body of the snake inside the hole. She threw some soil loosely over it, silently promising to return to perform the proper rites. She would do so the next day, as promises had to be kept—particularly to the dead.

WHEN YONGHONG RETURNED to the plum blossom tree the next morning, however, the snake was gone. The layer of soil she had thrown over the hole had been moved to the side. Yonghong felt around carefully, but the hole was empty. Did some animal with coarse fur and low haunches paw at the soil in the darkness until green scales were revealed to the night? Or did the snake shake the soil off its own body and emerge anew—revived? A dragon on Earth, after all.

Yonghong reached inside again, just to be sure. This time, the tips of her fingers touched something at the bottom. She frowned and reached down again. Yes, there was something there, at the bottom. Smooth and cold. She pulled out her arm and peered in. There was a flash of white in the depths.

Yonghong returned to the apartment and rummaged through the little chest at the foot of the bed she shared with her sister and Wai Po. She pushed aside the mound of folded winter blankets, but the left corner of the chest was empty.

"Try the right corner," Hongxing said from the bed. One arm was thrown across her eyes.

Yonghong looked in the other corner. It was there—the shard of pottery she had found by the railroad tracks near the school. There were still faint markings left on the outside of the pottery. Rows of waves in black scratched into terracotta clay. Whole, it would have been beautiful, Yonghong thought. Now it was a perfect tool for scraping away the dirt.

Oftentimes, she and the other children would find fragments of the past, buried beneath the soil around the apartments and schoolyard. Not just shards of pottery, but tiny pieces of black lacquered wood and mother-of-pearl inlay. Once, Hongxing had found a carved pipe in perfect condition. But Wai Po had whisked it away when she saw them playing with it, and the two had never seen it again. That was what happened to things from the old world—the world that came before the dawning of a new China. They had to be taken away and burned or hidden in the bottom of a chest. They were evidence of the Four Olds after all. The four olds that Yonghong and all loyal countrymen hated: old ideas, old culture, old customs, and old habits. These were things like temples and bound feet and classical paintings and marrying multiple wives. But although Yonghong rejected the Four Olds with all her heart, just as she had been taught, she still couldn't help but be curious about the artifacts she found.

Yonghong didn't ask Hongxing if she wanted to dig with her at the base of the plum blossom tree. From the sound of her breathing, Yonghong could tell her twin was slipping into dreams. And in dreams, one could travel the farthest.

"Where have you been running off to all day?" Ma asked her in the evening. She told the sisters to go wash their hands and sit down at the dinner table, where Wai Po was already waiting.

"Yonghong was digging a hole," Hongxing tattled.

Yonghong shot her twin a displeased glance, then reached over to try to wipe her hands on Hongxing's dark blue dress. Hongxing evaded her, but Yonghong thought she might have been able to get a few smudges of dirt on her. It was hard to tell, with the room so dark as usual. The past few days, Yonghong had spent her time beneath the plum blossom tree after school. Neither Hongxing nor Leap Forward had been helping her. Leap Forward, in fact, had taken to ignoring her on their marches to and from school. Yonghong tried often to coax a word or two out of him, to ask him how his hand was doing, but he was staunch in his refusal to speak to her. Even when she crawled beneath the dining table and knocked on the wall between their two rooms, she received only silence back.

"Just like your father," Ma said, "running off all day long."

It was true that Yonghong spent most of her days outside the apartment ever since Ma had begun keeping the dark red curtains drawn. She didn't like to sit within the stifling darkness, the only reprieve being the balcony that was attached to their apartment. Instead, Yonghong much preferred feeling the sun on her face and the wind at her heels.

"The ice pops are almost melted." Ma pointed to the ice pops on the table. One in each cup.

Yonghong grabbed one of the cups and squinted down at it. The ice pop—the color of pale cream—was already mostly liquid. Yonghong drank it down. It was thick and syrupy and tasted faintly of milk, as it always did.

"Eating cold treats so close to autumn is harmful to one's health," Wai Po said from across the table. She was a strong believer in traditional medicines.

Ma sighed and said what she always did—which was that the pops were given as nutritional supplements to sickly children. If anything, Ma added, they would help Yonghong and Hongxing grow up stout and strong—strong enough to live through anything.

Yonghong wanted to grow up strong—even stronger than Ba, who could carry both her and Hongxing under each arm. But for now, she would settle for being stronger than Hongxing at the very least.

Hongxing was both her twin and her mei mei—"younger sister"—all at once. While Yonghong had come out of their mother red-faced and crying before even opening her eyes, Hongxing had come out cold and blue. Wai Po had to hit her three times on the chest before Hongxing decided to take her first breath. Although both twins' chests bore a red bruise at first, Hongxing's eventually faded while Yonghong's mark remained.

The birthmark was not the only feature that differentiated the two. Wai Po said that one took all the fire, and the other, the ice.

"Xing Xing! Come tame your sister's fire," Ma would always say. But it rarely worked. For though Hongxing was quieter and more reserved, she would often go along with whatever Yonghong was up to. Keeping watch while Yonghong snuck into the cafeteria after hours. Boosting her over windows in the darkness. Less the ice than another type of fire.

Yonghong took her last bite of the ice pop. The sweetness almost allowed her to forget about the trials of the day before. The way the snake had almost seemed to shudder one last time in her hands, before going limp. The way Leap Forward had stared at her, angry and hurt. All of it was melting away under the sugar on her tongue.

"Is digging holes better than ice pops?" Ma asked.

Yonghong could make out the disapproval on her mother's face, even in the darkness. She curled her tongue around the remaining traces of syrup on the stick. Across the table, Hongxing was doing the same. In that moment, Yonghong felt, nothing was better.

BA DIDN'T COME home until after Ma had wiped Yonghong and Hongxing down with a washcloth dipped into a basin of hot water and put them both to bed. Yonghong heard him enter the apartment as she drifted between wakefulness and sleep. Beside her, Hongxing was turned away.

What was the object Yonghong had touched at the very bottom? The one that felt cool and slippery on her fingers? The one that seemed to send a little shock up her arm as she had touched it? It had felt, almost, like a flash of lightning had run through her veins. Her digging had so far failed to uncover it again.

"You're close," Hongxing seemed to murmur beside her.

"Are you awake?" Yonghong asked.

"Do you think there really is a hungry ghost wandering the yard?" Hongxing asked.

"We've both seen her, haven't we?"

Hongxing didn't say anything. Yonghong scooted closer, then rested her chin on Hongxing's arm. When she closed her eyes, she could imagine what her twin was seeing—remembering all over again.

"But did we really see her?"

"Of course," Yonghong said, reassuringly. "Who else could it have been?"

"She didn't look like a landlord's wife."

"Then what did she look like?"

"Someone familiar," Hongxing said.

"How familiar?" Yonghong asked over the indecipherable murmur of their father's voice.

"Like someone we might know by name."

It was true. Yonghong had felt as if she, too, could call out to the ghost circling the plum blossom tree. But neither of them had called out. Instead, clouds had drifted over the moon, plunging them in darkness. By the time the clouds had passed, the woman was gone.

CLOSE TO WHAT, exactly? Yonghong wasn't certain, but she had her suspicions.

IT TOOK YONGHONG a few days' digging before she discovered the answer.

It was an old skull, yellowed and with a sheen to it like ivory. Yonghong didn't know for certain where it came from or who it had belonged to. But she suspected—hoped—that it belonged to the woman who appeared in the darkest parts of the night to wander the yard. And now, Yonghong held it close to her chest, staring with distrust at Leap Forward, who stood in front of her.

"Won't you let me see it?" he asked again. It was the first they had spoken to one another after the death of the snake.

Yonghong was relieved and annoyed all at once. "No," she said, shaking her head. It was hers to give away or to keep. She was the one who had spent days returning to the tree, digging into the sandy soil. She was the one who had clutched the shard so tightly that it cut into her skin.

"Why not?" Leap Forward reached for the skull again.

Yonghong jerked it away and looked at him pointedly. Had he forgotten about the snake already?

When he grew frustrated and tried to wrest it out of her hands, she shoved him to the ground. From where he had fallen, Leap Forward stared up at her.

"I'm going to tell my brother," he said.

Yonghong wasn't afraid. How could she be, with a revolutionary hero as her father?

Blood was beginning to well up from the scrapes on Leap Forward's left arm. His brows drew together, and his lip trembled. Yonghong knew he was waiting for her to comfort him and pull him up, but instead, she only held the skull closer and turned slightly away.

Once, the skull had belonged to another. But now, it was hers.

THE NIGHT AFTER Yonghong unearthed the skull, the hungry ghost visited her in her dreams. She came to her dressed in white, as all ghosts were, with a length of white silk wrapped around her neck. The other end of the strip of silk was tied around a branch of the plum blossom tree, and as she walked, the silk fabric wound around the trunk of the tree. The ghost was pacing around in circles, her head turned so that Yonghong couldn't make out her face, even illuminated as everything else was under the moon—which was full and bright. Still, Yonghong could hear her weeping . . . weeping . . . weeping . . .

When she woke, Yonghong could still hear her. It was dark. Beside her, Hongxing was turning restlessly in her sleep. And beyond Hongxing, Wai Po was snoring away.

"Do you hear that?" Yonghong whispered to her sister.

The sound of a woman weeping seemed almost louder now, as if it were getting closer. As if it were almost right outside. Frightened, Yonghong tried to nudge her sister again. But Hongxing was still, her breathing slow and steady.

It couldn't be the ghost, Yonghong reasoned to herself. The ghost only made her appearances by the plum blossom tree. She couldn't stray far from its branches. She couldn't possibly be looking for her skull, which was now hidden in the chest at the foot of the twins' bed.

The sisters knew that Wai Po's own big brother, Ge Ge, had returned as a hungry ghost, to the home where he had grown up as a child. The Guomindang had killed him during the Long March, and his body had been lost to the mountains. He had died far from home, and the family had not been able to perform the proper rites for his funeral. They had tried the best they could without a body—burning offerings of rice paper. A little paper house and a paper suitcase full of paper clothes. Her father had hired a priest, too, to help send his spirit off to the afterlife. Still, it wasn't surprising, Wai Po had said to them one cold night as they were laying in bed before sleep, that his ghost should return—restless and unhappy. He had not been properly laid to rest. He had not been at peace. There was so much he had left unfinished.

When his ghost came back, she continued, he had haunted their father—appearing to him in dreams at night or in the thick fog that covered the mountains in the early mornings. Then her father began to see his son everywhere—out of the corner of his eye or even standing right in front of him. For the first few years, her father tried to pretend it wasn't happening. But ghosts have a way of changing you, Wai Po said. Eventually, the haunting began to take a toll. And the day her father began talking back to Big Brother Ghost was the day that she knew the end was near.

After his death, in 1944, Wai Po and her mother tried the best they could to survive on their own while taking care of Ma, who was sixteen then. Great-Uncle, still climbing the ranks of the Party, sent them money every month to help them out.

But eventually, the ghost caught up to them. Or rather, to Wai Po's mother. Overnight, it seemed, her hair turned white, and she began to be more forgetful—aging ahead of her time. She was seventy-two then, and soon she was stooped and her back rounded. The more her mother saw the ghost of Ge Ge, the more her eyes seemed to dull and the black of her iris fade to blue. Wai Po was determined not to let her mother succumb to Brother Ghost as her father had, so for three days and three nights, she made offerings without rest. In return, the monks gave her a charm to cure their haunting.

The charm was a little bronze bell that hung from a braided loop made of red silk. Wai Po had only showed it to Yonghong and Hongxing once, but the two of them had never forgotten the sight of it. When Wai Po had taken it out of her little lacquered box, the bell rang. The sound the bell made was startling—two tones seemed to sound at once. Yonghong had never heard anything like it.

Wai Po quickly covered it with one hand to silence the sound. Then, she showed it to them carefully, making sure it would not ring again. The bell was made of a special kind of metal that the monks at the temple had forged themselves. The bowl of the bell was double-layered, Wai Po explained, and had a hollow core. But the real magic, she explained, was in the spells and prayers the monks had infused it with. Even the fires it was forged in were divine.

And how had Wai Po gotten rid of the haunting? She had stayed up the very night she received the bell, waiting for Brother Ghost to come after her mother had been soothed into an uneasy, restless sleep. She had rung the bell, standing by a fire she lit in the field behind their house. The night smelled of rain and the cold, and stars spun around her. That year, Wai Po remembered, it rained as if it would never stop. As if the country wanted to wash away memories of the past.

Wai Po had known the bell would call her brother in a manner he wouldn't be able to resist. Maybe it would sound like the voice of the woman he loved. The woman he had met in the mountains. Or maybe it would sound like her own: his sister's, who always loved him—despite all the ways they had hurt one another.

Across Wai Po's lap that night lay an erhu whose soundboard was made of python skin that was by then worn and faded: the erhu he had played on as a child. It was the last gift she would give her brother, she decided. Once, he had played it on the earth when he was alive. Once, she had heard the sound of its voice emerging from her brother's hands.

In the fire, the snakeskin seemed to writhe. It wasn't an erhu at all, but a little dragon—like the dragon of the mountains that surrounded her. That was what she was burning. What they were all burning. The memory of the past—no matter how much love it might have once held.

The erhu took all night to burn. The rain lingered heavily in the air, dampening the flames. But when dawn arrived, all that was left was a pile of ash. Wai Po rang the bell once more. This time, it signaled farewell.

After the burning of the erhu, Ge Ge never returned again.

PERHAPS THE OTHERS also sensed the presence of a ghost, encroaching upon them. In the morning at school the next day, Leap Forward maintained his rigid silence, and even Teacher Wu seemed distracted. Teacher Wu's eyes kept glancing up at the windows of the apartment buildings and offices, as if she were wary of someone watching her. Maybe it was just the weather, which was now slowly turning colder and colder with the coming of autumn.

Before the start of class, the elementary school principal came out and began his morning address.

Overhead, there was a rumble of thunder. Leap Forward, standing beside Yonghong, turned his head toward the sky. In front of them, Teacher Wu's hands tensed into fists before relaxing again. Principal Liang continued his speech as if he hadn't heard a thing.

"Each and every one of you is a child of Mao. You are all a reflection of his love, which is greater than the heavens and deeper than the sea."

Little droplets of rain were darkening the courtyard dirt. The sky turned gray. Teacher Wu sneezed, and Principal Liang began to talk a little faster.

The entire school must make preparations, Principal Liang announced, to put on a glorious welcoming ceremony during the Mid-Autumn Festival for a group of newly elected government officials. Their school, as a model of learning under new revolutionary values, would allow the officials to witness for themselves the progress that was being made. The welcoming ceremony would not only represent the spirit of the school, but also the hopes and dreams of an entire nation. As such, the visit would be extensive—lasting three full days—and filled with festivities.

As a class monitor, Yonghong knew she would be expected to take on more duties in the month leading up to the visit. The news, however, did not agitate her. She felt a great sense of responsibility. She had known already of the impending visit to the school. Indeed, her great-uncle had written of the visit in one of his letters, though he would not be coming himself. Lately, his letters came more and more frequently. And whenever they did, Wai Po's eyes looked worn and tired.

SOMETIMES, Yonghong and her sister asked Wai Po to tell her stories of their respected and powerful great-uncle, who had often sent them gifts from the capital. He had fought both the Japanese and the Guomindang in his youth, Yonghong knew. He had even gone to the same school—First

Normal School in Changsha—as Chairman Mao and learned from the same teachers. He was also the one who had made arrangements for Ma's education and medical training in Beijing. There, Ma had met Ba, who had been a junior officer working under Great-Uncle.

"Without my elder brother's doing, you might never have existed," Wai Po would say sometimes to Yonghong or Hongxing. Her tone was not wonderment, but something more puzzled—almost bewildered.

"What was Great-Uncle like when you were little?" Hongxing would ask, though Wai Po was usually reluctant to answer. Hongxing liked to learn about the beginnings—of people, of places. She was always asking how things got started—perhaps because she had not been conscious for her own start into the world. Yonghong, on the other hand, was more concerned with how things would end, maybe due to the mark on her chest that she shared with Ma and Wai Po. Sometimes, Yonghong was ashamed of the mark, as the difference with her sister was always compounded when she looked at it. Why couldn't she have unblemished skin like Hongxing?

But Yonghong's birthmark was also different from the one on Ma's chest, and Wai Po's, too. Wai Po's mark was dark in color, a deep, rich red. Ma's was twisted and scarred.

Wai Po had always told her it was a mark borne from her bloodline—a mark of the women in the family—but Yonghong remained unconvinced. If what Wai Po said was true, then why was Hongxing missing hers? What did it say about all of them? If they were marked from birth, then how would each of their lives end? Would Hongxing's have a happy ending? Would Yonghong's have a sad one? Or would there be perfect harmony—as everyone was always promising?

"Be proud of this mark, Yonghong," Wai Po insisted. "For it is a mark of your legacy. Proof of where you came from, and your history. Remember this whenever you're afraid."

"What about me?" Hongxing asked.

"You're the version of me that was born without a mark," Ma said, frowning. "The better one that Wai Po wished for."

Wai Po's mouth tightened, and her eyes were sad—but she didn't refute Ma's words.

AT LUNCH, Leap Forward sat with the boys from Teacher Bing's class beneath the plum blossom tree. Teacher Bing had been suspended while he was being investigated, so the students in his class had joined theirs until the school could find a replacement—though teachers were becoming rarer and rarer these days. Months ago, Yonghong and Hongxing had both watched as the students forced Teacher Bing to kneel on the ground before the mural of Chairman Mao and press his forehead into the dirt. Yonghong heard that he had been disloyal to Chairman Mao and said something critical of his policies. Hongxing heard that he had been embezzling funds. Either way, he was now assigned to sweep the streets, shunned by all.

It was the first time Leap Forward had sat with the boys from the other class despite being a class monitor. Leap Forward never took his duties seriously, and Yonghong knew the change in his seating arrangement at lunch meant that he was still angry with her. He was, she concluded, shunning her.

Beside her, Hongxing slowly chewed her steamed bun.

Perched on the stoop, Teacher Wu was spitting out seeds into a handkerchief. She was known for spitting out the seeds of cucumbers that were a little overripe, or even the seeds of grapes—small as they were. Her prim eating habits had earned her the moniker of Miss Wu or, at times, Lady Wu—though no one ever called her that to her face. To be called a class traitor was a serious accusation, after all.

"Miss Wu" suited her, Yonghong thought. In her early twenties, Teacher Wu was the youngest teacher at the school despite her widowed status—the youngest and the prettiest. Her eyes were wide-set and large, and her hair, worn always in two long braids, shone with a captivating luster. Although she was one of the few women who still wore her hair long and not in a revolutionary bob, her family background was impeccable. She was descended from a long line of peasants and revolutionary fighters. There was not a single drop of power or wealth in her bloodline.

But there was something unsettling in her manner. It wasn't just in the way she carried herself—quiet and solemn—but something in the way she spoke as well. She chose each word carefully, as if they might cost her something. And whenever someone talked to her, she listened intently—with an indecipherable smile on her lips.

As Yonghong looked at Teacher Wu, she was reminded of the visitation she received in her dreams. She turned to her sister and told her of what she had seen.

"We need to catch her," Yonghong said to Hongxing.

Hongxing nodded.

They knew they needed to capture their own ghost before she could cause havoc like Wai Po's big brother had caused. They knew what could happen when ghosts were filled with resentment, when they were uneasy and restless and filled with the desire for retribution. The vengeance of a hungry ghost could be the worst vengeance in the world.

In the afternoon, it began to rain in full force. Large drops drummed against the roofs and streets in a heavy torrent. In Nanjing, the storms came down hard and fast. Sometimes, they continued for weeks. Other times, like today, they passed in a flash. There was one last strike of lightning, and then the storm was gone, leaving behind droplets of rain that clung to the trees.

When the twins arrived home, making their way past the shared kitchen and into the big room, there was a tense silence in the air in the apartment. Ma's face was drawn and pale. Ba was there, too, which was unusual. He often came home only when they were all fast asleep. Usually, Ma waited up for him, pacing back and forth in front of the windows.

But today, everyone was home. Under the watchful gaze of their father, the twins dutifully studied and completed their homework. After what felt like an eternity, it was time to eat dinner together. Wai Po had cooked pea sprouts and little pieces of beltfish caramelized to a deep rich brown. Each piece had a crisp exterior with delicate white flakes inside, which melted on the tongue. The dish was a rare treat that Wai Po only made for special occasions.

"One of the neighbors gave me some as thanks," Wai Po said when Ma asked where the fish was from. Wai Po was often helping their neighbors out—mending clothing or advising them on medical matters of the body and the heart. Their neighbor, Wai Po, explained, was suffering from a terrible migraine, and Wai Po had advised her husband on what soups to brew for her to replenish her vitamins.

"She's lucky to have such a devoted husband," Ma said, shooting a luck at Ba.

"He's a good-for-nothing husband," Ba said, frowning. "He barely does any work."

"While you're quite the dedicated worker for the country, aren't you?" Ma said, scathingly. Ma's mood could turn as quickly as a flash of lightning.

LAST SUMMER, Yonghong and Hongxing had returned from dance practice to the sound of their mother crying in their apartment.

"Should we go in?" Hongxing had asked uncertainly. The twins stood in the kitchen outside the door to the big room, listening in.

"The pain will pass soon," they had heard Wai Po say to Ma from within the apartment. "You'll be alright."

By the time Hongxing and Yonghong finally mustered up the courage to enter the apartment, it was dark and Ma had stopped crying. For several days afterward, their mother had laid in bed, moaning in pain. Clumps of blood appeared between her legs. Wai Po went in and out of Ma's room with bowls of steaming soup. And when Yonghong entered the room to lay on Ma's chest, all she could smell was a thick, animal scent. The scent of Ma's sadness, and the baby they had all hoped for.

The curtains hadn't opened since.

THAT NIGHT, as Wai Po slept, Yonghong crept out of bed and lay flat on the floor. She reached out her right arm and pulled the lacquered box out from beneath the bed. The box was inlaid with mother-of-pearl that shone in the moonlight. Yonghong could feel Hongxing's eyes peering down at her as she carefully unlatched the lid and felt inside. There was a folded letter, an ox-bone comb, and some tiny photographs with scalloped edges. Then—finally—her fingers touched cold metal.

A shiver of excitement ran down her back, but Yonghong forced her arm to remain still. Wai Po had never let them touch the bell, believing that touch was invitation enough for its blessings to start working. If what Wai Po believed were true, then it was calling out even now to the hungry ghost in the voice of someone she loved.

The One Who Cries

"THE GREAT DISASTER is coming! The Great Disaster is coming!"

Yonghong's eyes snapped open. Her heart was beating fast, and her hands were clenched into tight fists. Outside, the sky was just beginning to lighten. She fumbled beneath her pillow and felt for the bell, which she had hidden there.

"The Great Disaster is coming!" The shout came again—louder this time. A gong rang three times.

On the other side of the bed, Wai Po was beginning to stir.

"The Great Disaster is coming!" The gong rang again.

Yonghong startled. The cry sounded as if it were right beside them. The door to Ma and Ba's room flew open. Wai Po sat up in bed.

"You girls stay where you are," Ba directed, as he always had ever since the cry first began one year ago.

No one it seemed quite knew what the Great Disaster was, exactly. Some said the Great Disaster was the name of a group of rebels turned bandits who now roamed the country, plundering and pillaging. After last winter, all thought the cry would never return. The group had, most likely, not been able to survive the winter. But the cry had returned, again and again.

Ba, Ma, and Wai Po carried the dining table over to the door, then they stacked chairs on top of it to strengthen the barricade. From the sounds that Yonghong could hear through the wall, she could tell that Leap Forward's family were doing the same.

Yonghong slipped out of bed and crawled over to the spot where she and Leap Forward liked to speak to one another. She knocked three times and waited.

Soon, her knocks were returned.

Yonghong smiled and scooted closer to the wall. "Leap Forward," she whispered. "Are you scared?"

"No."

Yonghong grinned. Despite his bravado, she knew that he was. He wasn't scared of much, not of heights nor of American bombs—only the Great Disaster, and occasionally his older brother who was able to see through his lies in an instant.

Secretly, the twins had wanted the Great Disaster to return because that meant being able to get another glimpse of the man who warned them all so diligently with his gong. The man whom they had named the One Who Cries. They had seen him one day while out playing by the train tracks. They hadn't realized he was the the One Who Cries— not at first. He was a slim man with cropped hair and stood only two heads taller than Leap Forward. He had been wearing the nondescript uniform of a blue shirt and trousers that the workers of the manufacturing plants were given. That was who Yonghong had thought he was at first—just another worker. But then she caught sight of the gong in his hand.

She knew Hongxing had noticed it, too, for she felt her twin stiffen beside her. They stopped playing with their dolls and watched the man as he walked in the direction of the school's gated entrance. He walked slowly but steadily, with a kind of resignation to his steps. The top of his spine was slightly stooped. It was almost as if he had no choice but to continue walking toward the school. His gait reminded Yonghong of the time she had seen a row of prisoners walking on the road lead-ing to the city center. All the prisoners wore a sign around their necks stating their names and the crimes they had committed. Some were thieves; others were murderers. But for the most part, they were the worst of all—the antirevolutionaries. Ma had tried to usher Yonghong and Hongxing back inside, away from the scene of the prisoners. She had told them it wasn't a sight for little girls, though Yonghong knew it was because Ma was afraid of the ghost. Ghosts were attracted to misery, after all.

That was how the the One Who Cries was walking that day—like one miserable and condemned.

Yonghong couldn't tell how old he was. She had caught only a partial glimpse of his face and the distance prevented her seeing clearly.

Yonghong stood up from where she had been crouching and began to walk toward the the One Who Cries.

"Where are you going?" Hongxing asked.

"Don't you want to see?" Yonghong said. She couldn't imagine how such a man could be the one with a great booming voice. How such a man could sound the gong in his hand like thunder crashing down from the Heavens. She had to know how he did it.

Hongxing got up and began following him, too. They kept a safe dis-tance—giving themselves enough space to escape should the man turn into the monster they had always imagined.

And what a performance it was! The second the man entered the gates of the school, his entire demeanor changed. His back straightened until it seemed as straight as a wooden board. He grew taller and taller until he was the tallest man they had ever seen. His strides, too, lengthened, until Yonghong and Hongxing were running to keep up with him. Vigorously, he banged three times on the gong in his hand. The sound was fearsome—like the braying of a mule. Once the gong rang in the air, those who had been outside disappeared in a flash.

"The Great Disaster is coming! The Great Disaster is coming! The Great Disaster is coming!"

For the first time in her life, Yonghong could see the the One Who Cries in action. As close as she was, she realized that it wasn't his gong that sounded like thunder, but his voice.

DESPITE THE EXCITEMENT of the morning, Yonghong and her classmates still lined up in time for their morning march to school. Leap Forward offered her a smile when he saw her—the first sign of any acknowledgement from him in days. Yonghong smiled back. She never held grudges like Hongxing.

More high schoolers were out and about than usual, wearing their red armbands. They were standing guard against the Great Disaster. As a Little Red Guard, Yonghong dreamed of one day joining the Red Guards in their fight against foreign influence, invasion, and other violences. She dreamed of one day becoming the leader of a unit in her own right.

Yonghong tried to channel the power of the the One Who Cries into her slogan chants. She shouted them loudly—thunder and lightning escaping from her lips. She thought it might have worked, considering everyone seemed to walk more briskly on the way to school. Even Teacher Wu, who often appeared to glide rather than walk, kicked up her heels a little higher.

Yonghong had brought the bell with her on their way to school. It rested safely inside the inner pocket of her jacket, wrapped in a strip of cloth. Hongxing was the one who had wrapped it that morning. Neither of them wanted the bell to ring accidentally.

During lunch, Yonghong explained to Leap Forward how they would catch the ghost that night. She knew he would want to help them—not just because of their friendship, but out of a sense of duty as well. Hongxing, however, bristled at the idea.

"Who said you could come with us?" Hongxing asked.

"Leap Forward has already said he's sorry," Yonghong lied.

Leap Forward nodded eagerly. "I am sorry."

Hongxing kicked up some sand in his direction, then dragged Yonghong with her toward their apartment, where Wai Po would be waiting with lunch.

"Sneak out of your apartment and meet us in our unit's kitchen!" Yonghong called out, looking back at Leap Forward. "Midnight!"

YONGHONG AND HONGXING could tell when Wai Po's sleep was the deepest by the rhythm of her breaths. Wai Po was a sound sleeper—never waking until dawn. She had not always slept so well, Wai Po once told them. As a young girl, she often woke during the night—restless and full of worries. But later—after she had experienced what sorrow truly felt like—she learned how to fall into the deepest of sleeps. She spent many of her days sleeping, and consequently had become a master of it.

And so, with Wai Po asleep and their parents in the other room, Yonghong and Hongxing slipped out of bed and crept over to the locked door. Hongxing was the one who knew how to turn the lock in the quietest manner. She pressed her cheek against the door and used both hands to turn it. Yonghong waited patiently beside her.

The twins had only ever snuck out for important reasons—like hunting down the crickets with Leap Forward. But that was the only time they had ever been caught—walking back from the fields on the night of the Mid-Autumn Festival. They had almost made it back home when they felt hands descend upon them and grip their shoulders. They were practically hauled into the air with how roughly they were gripped. There was a scream caught in Yonghong's throat, and then, just as she was about to release it, she realized it was Ba holding her.

But was it their father? This one was furious. This one slapped them both hard on the cheeks. It was the first time Yonghong had ever experienced her father's fury. He dragged them back to the apartment and woke up Wai Po with how he slammed the door open—then shut.

"What were you doing?" their mother had asked them the next morning. "What did you see?" She peered at them intently.

"They were just fooling around as children do," Ba interjected brusquely.

Later, after Ba had left for work, Ma had summoned Yonghong and Hongxing into her room.

"Did you see her?" their mother had whispered to them with a desperate look in her eyes. She crouched down and placed her hands on their shoulders.

Yonghong realized that Ma meant the hungry ghost, whom they had both seen. It explained why Ma had shut the curtains—she had been afraid of seeing the ghost through the windows. Yonghong didn't want to frighten her further, so she shook her head. The sisters let their mother hold them tight without their usual protests. Yonghong pressed her ear against Ma's chest and listened until her heart beat slow and steady.

"Don't worry," Wai Po had told Yonghong and Hongxing that night before sleep. "Your mother's strong—stronger than she knows. She came from me, after all. All of you did."

If Yonghong got rid of the hungry ghost once and for all, her mother would never have to be afraid again.

BY THE TIME the twins slipped out of their apartment, Leap Forward was already waiting for them in the kitchen. He motioned for them to be quiet, and the three of them snuck out of their unit. They made their way down the stairs of their building. Yonghong's heart pounded. She was afraid that Ba might catch them again. They walked close together as they trekked over to the elementary school. The darkness made the familiar walk unfamiliar. Paths seemed to appear out of nowhere, leading in mysterious directions. Lights flickered in the distance.

In the night, the plum blossom tree seemed to shine like a star. Its branches gleamed as they twisted toward the heavens. Yonghong brought out the bell from her pocket and carefully unwound the strip of cloth wrapped around it. Before long, the bell was shining in her palm.

"That's it?" Leap Forward asked doubtfully.

Yonghong held up the bell and rang it. The bell produced its strange, double-toned note like it did in Wai Po's hands. There was a sudden gust of wind, and the night darkened. All three held their breaths.

Hongxing held the skull out in her arms. "Is this what you've been looking for?" Hongxing's voice said to the ghost in the night. "Come and take it back."

They waited. Then waited some more. The clouds shifted across the sky, and the night brightened again. Still, the ghost did not appear.

The Ones in Love

The east is red. The sun rises.
From China emerges one Mao Zedong.
He seeks the happiness of the people.
Hurrah, he is the great savior of the people!

YONGHONG AND THE others gathered in front of the apartments to sing along to the song pouring out of the loudspeakers in their complex.

Everyone knew the song by heart. Today, everyone was striving to sing it louder than they ever had before. Beside her, Leap Forward nearly shouting, drawing in deep breaths between each line. His older brother, Resist America, was trying his best, too, though his weak health prevented him from achieving much volume. There was an excitement in the air—so tangible it seemed to shimmer between them.

It was the day before the government officials would arrive on their tour of inspection, after all.

Many said that it was the most beautiful song they had ever heard. But despite her dedication to Mao, Yonghong didn't think so. The most beautiful song she had ever heard was one the loudspeakers had played many years ago. Her entire family had been eating dinner—rice with tomatoes and eggs, Yonghong remembered—inside the apartment when it came on. Hongxing had been sitting to her left, Wai Po to her right. She could see the sun setting outside their window.

One clear, sustained note on the erhu. A sudden silence. Then, the music started up again. It swooped then rose higher and higher. Hongxing had jumped in her seat. Ma had put down her chopsticks. Across the table, Ba stopped chewing. There was a slight frown between his brows. Wai Po had begun to weep.

It was the sound of Wai Po's weeping that Yonghong remembered the most vividly. Her tears bonding with the erhu itself, echoing across the sky.

Later that night, Wai Po had said, "My ge ge used to play that song." And that was all.

The loudspeakers never played the song again. Older now, Yonghong could barely remember the melody, though sometimes she thought she heard it in her dreams.

Now, as Yonghong sang along to the second-best song, she watched several Red Guards at work on the mural of Chairman Mao. They repainted the oranges and reds that swirled across the billboard. Some of the Red Guards were crouched on the ground as they touched up small details. Others stood at the tops of unsteady-looking ladders. Last year, the Red Guards had acquired a set of new brushes for the purpose of beautifying the complex. They came in shiny plastic packaging, and their bristles were straight and glossy. Yonghong had been told that Chairman Mao himself personally sent a set of brushes to every neighborhood across the nation.

The care and maintenance of the brushes for her community had been given over to Zhu Wenliu. Wenliu was the tallest of the Red Guards and very thin. His figure was in fact not dissimilar to the handle of a paintbrush. There was something very rigid about the way he held himself—and the way he spoke as well. He would have been in his second year of college, had colleges still been accepting new students. Instead, after high school, he had gone to work for a year at their province's Publicity Bureau, where he received training on mural and slogan painting. During his time there, he had written an art manual that was distributed to all the districts in their province. He was particularly proud of the section on how to capture Chairman Mao's features and expressions. Everything was considered—from the color of his attire to the shape of his eyebrows.

As the de facto leader of everything related to official art within their complex and the surrounding neighborhood, Wenliu could often be heard dispensing the wisdom of the manual to the other Red Guards. "Let the paint dry a little more before applying another layer," he might say, or "More red! More red!"

Other Red Guards were at work constructing a stage around the mural—nailing in the last planks, sanding down the rough corners. In a few hours, Yonghong and the other children in her class would have their last rehearsal before the performance the next evening to welcome the officials. They would sing. They would dance. All for the glory of Chairman Mao.

Although Yonghong did not have a solo part like Hongxing, she still had a prominent role in the dance performance. She, along with eleven other girls, would carry red fans with a shimmery fringe. All of the girls had made their fans at school, while the boys had made military costumes for their mock parade.

"It'll look just like it does in the movies," said Teacher Lu with delight as she supervised their work. Teacher Lu was the newly-hired replacement for Teacher Bing, who would play no part at all in the festivities. Two days ago, Teacher Bing was gone from school, and no one explained to them exactly why. Principal Liang only said he had not been loyal. Teacher Bing had been stripped of his membership in the party and, therefore, his employment, housing, stipend, and whatever comforts the party provided. Yonghong had watched his family leave their former apartment with the clothes on their backs and a few heavy bags scraping along the pavement behind them.

"Good riddance," his neighbors had said. No one wanted anything to go wrong—or anyone wrong. The show had to be perfect. Everyone agreed with that. And that was why Yonghong knew that she and Hongxing and Leap Forward had to try to capture the ghost again that night.

THE MOON THAT night was not bright and full, but a dark, flat disk. Still, Yonghong could just make out the gleam of Chairman Mao's eyes on the billboard as he watched them exit through the college gates.

Yonghong, Hongxing, and Leap Forward slowly approached the tree, but stopped when they were still a distance away. The three of them crouched behind one of the walls of the schoolhouse.

Hongxing inched forward and raised the bell in her hand. She rang it once, and the note seemed to hang in the air, before fading away.

"How long are we going to wait?" Leap Forward asked after a few moments of silence.

Hongxing glared at him. "As long as we need to."

Leap Forward clutched the skull tighter and sighed. Yonghong sat back on her heels to settle in. She had the feeling it would be a long night. Despite the darkness, the plum blossom tree still shone—as if illuminated from within. Tonight, red strips of paper hung from its branches. On each strip, there was a slogan.

OUR LOVE FOR CHAIRMAN MAO IS EVERLASTING.

HIS LOVE SHINES UPON US LIKE THE SUN.

YOUR LOVE FOR YOUR FELLOW COMRADE BRINGS HARMONY
TO OUR NATION.

LOVE. LOVE. LOVE.

Yonghong suddenly opened her eyes. She didn't know when she had closed them, but Hongxing's grip on her arm had woken her.

"She's here," Leap Forward whispered.

Indeed, the hungry ghost appeared as she did in Yonghong's dream. Her face was turned away, and though the wind lifted up her hair, it never revealed anything in the lifting. There was something wild about her hair—black as ink. It seemed more like an ocean wave—endless—than hair that had once belonged to a living person.

The robe she wore, Yonghong saw, wasn't a robe at all, but a jacket and a pair of paints. And she wasn't barefoot as Yonghong always imagined. Rather, she had on dark cloth shoes.

And she had a voice, too. A voice that sounded living and warm when it called out:

"Are you here?"

Yonghong, Hongxing, and Leap Forward froze. Before Yonghong could react, someone else answered:

"I am."

The one who answered was a man. A man, who now stepped out and swept the hungry ghost up in his arms. And—standing there beneath the plum blossom tree—they bent their heads toward one another and pressed their lips together. Their arms were wrapped around each other, and they seemed as tangled up as the twisting branches of the tree that sheltered them. When the wind blew through the yard, the strips of red paper trembled and rustled in the night. It looked, for a moment, like a wedding scene.

Yonghong couldn't look away. She knew her twin felt the same way. Leap Forward's breath seemed to quicken.

Though there was no moon hanging in the sky to reveal the lovers, the light of the tree illuminated them all the same. But Yonghong didn't need to see the man to know him. She had already recognized him by his voice alone. It was Ba who was kissing the hungry ghost.

But then the two turned, and no, it wasn't a ghost who was kissing their father, it was the face of someone much more familiar, her long hair now as distinct and recognizable as her manner. Miss Wu.

WAS IT REALLY their father they had seen? Maybe it was just a dream that both Yonghong and Hongxing had dreamed. It wouldn't have been the first time they shared a dream.

But in the morning, the heel of Yonghong's right shoe was dark with mud—proof of their outing.

"Why do you look so wan?" Ma asked Yonghong as she brushed her hair. "You're not coming down with anything, are you?" She pressed her lips together. "You need to look your best today."

Yonghong had been looking forward to the inspection tour, but now her thoughts were overshadowed.

"He's gone early to work," Ma said when Hongxing asked where Ba was. Then, their mother went off to work, too.

Wai Po began tidying up the apartment.

"The party leaders that are coming to visit us today are newly elected ones," Wai Po said as she wiped down the dinner table. She had heard they had little experience in leadership or administration. They had been plucked right out of the factory line and put in positions of power in the Ministry of Education. That was what was happening all over China. The new guard replacing the old. "It's happening in the Ministry of Health, too, where your great-uncle works," she said.

"He said he wished he could see me—all of us—again," Wai Po added. "It reminds me of how little time we have to spend with one another— why not enjoy ourselves while we can?" Wai Po went over to the window. She raised her hand to the curtains. It seemed, for a moment, that she might open them. But then, Wai Po dropped her hand.

"Won't you open them?" Yonghong pleaded. She and Hongxing knew better than to even touch them. After Ma had started crying the last time they did so many months ago now, they had never tried again.

Wai Po sighed. "I want to," she admitted. "But it should be your mother's choice to do so. She's the one who needs them closed. Out of shame, she says." She shook her head. "How can I take that away from her?"

"THE COMMUNIST PARTY is like the sun!" Hongxing sang into the microphone. Dressed in the uniform of a Red Guard, Hongxing stood at the front of the stage. Behind Hongxing, Miss Wu led Yonghong and the other girls in a choreographed dance around the stage. The faces of the audience intimidated Yonghong, but she felt emboldened by the knowledge of Chairman Mao's smile on the billboard behind them—which served as a kind of backdrop to the stage. All the performers were dressed in military-inspired costumes: a solemn green shirt and pants. The only concession to the celebratory nature of the performance was the spectacle of the shimmering red fans of the dancers.

Music rang out from the loudspeakers, so loudly Yonghong was certain others beyond even the train tracks could hear it. It was the last dance of the evening, and the audience was on their feet. It seemed as if everyone she knew was there that evening. And who wouldn't want to be present to bask in the light of Chairman Mao?

From where she was dancing, Yonghong could easily see Ma, Ba, and Wai Po. They were always given good spots for any performance due to

Ba's position at the factory. Ma was smiling as she mouthed along to the words that Hongxing sang. She had that proud look on her face as she always did whenever Hongxing performed. That was always when she seemed the happiest, and now Yonghong had an inkling of why. One could get lost—could forget everything else—listening to Hongxing's song.

Hongxing sang passionately—"with love," as their singing teacher had advised. In their lessons in class, love always seemed simple and easy. Love for Chairman Mao would bring harmony across the land. It would make the fields bountiful with wheat and rice. It would keep the people well-fed and warm during the winters. It would bring glory upon the country.

Now, however, Yonghong knew of a different kind of love, one that was furtive and secret. And yet, at the same time, it seemed as expansive and all-encompassing as the cries of the One Who Cries. And, like the One Who Cries, it inspired fear and curiosity.

Yonghong raised her fan in the air and formed a circle with the other girls. The tassels of their fans trembled and shimmered, catching the sun. They spun around, then lowered their fans and knelt on the ground. Miss Wu slowly rose out of the center of the circle. She was smiling. Her face was flushed. She looked like a comrade who would inspire the masses. But, as Yonghong looked at her, she felt only a rising anger in her chest.

"Wherever the Communist Party is . . ."

Miss Wu saluted the audience, and the circle of girls straightened out. Yonghong found herself standing to the right of Miss Wu—just as they had practiced before in rehearsals. In front of them, Hongxing held the final high note of the song—suspending it in the air.

". . . the people are liberated!"

With a shove of her elbow, Yonghong pushed Miss Wu toward the billboard. Stumbling, Miss Wu put out a hand to steady herself, smearing the still-wet paint of the mural with her palm. The music came to an end. The dancers froze in their final positions.

Across the shirt of the great and venerable Chairman Mao, there was the ghost of a handprint.

"How could you be so clumsy?" Ba hissed at her, gripping Yonghong's arm on the way home.

"It was an accident," Wai Po said, walking close behind.

"I can't believe I raised a girl like you," Ba spit out. He took a deep breath, as if to release a torrent of words, but then Miss Wu passed them.

"Teacher Wu," he called out.

Miss Wu did not look back. Instead, she hid her face, which was flushed with humiliation.

At bathtime, Ma was quiet as she poured cups of water on Yonghong's head. Standing in a basin, Yonghong closed her eyes against the sting of the soapy water trickling down her face.

"Why did you push Teacher Wu?" her mother asked.

"It was an accident."

Ma wrung out the towel. Her knuckles turned white with effort. "Don't lie to me, Yonghong."

"She's mean."

"To you?" Ma asked.

"To you!" Yonghong couldn't hide the secret anymore.

Her mother was quiet for a long time. She put down the washcloth and studied Yonghong's face. "Did you see her and Ba together?" she finally asked.

"I hate him," Yonghong said, and she was surprised to find that she really meant it.

"The harmony of a marriage is like that of a nation," Ma said. "It's not easy to achieve."

Without Ma sponging her with the hot water, she was growing cold. Yonghong began to shiver. "Don't you hate Ba?" Yonghong asked. "And her, too?"

"How can I hate him," Ma asked, "when he was the first one who ever loved me without being ashamed of it? When my own mother couldn't even accept me as her daughter?" Her tone was filled with weariness. She began wiping her down again. Her belly, then her thighs. But the water was no longer warm. When Ma was finished, she handed Yonghong a dry towel. "You're old enough now, Yonghong, to dry yourself," Ma said. Her words were not angry, but matter-of-fact. Then, her mother stood and walked out of the room—leaving Yonghong in the cold and stagnant water.

What Was Confessed

"Who among us will now confess?"

There was silence in the classroom. Then: "I will."

Yonghong climbed onto her desk and stood up. Hands on her hips, she surveyed the nine faces that looked back at her—including Hongxing and Leap Forward. All of them stared at her with rapt attention.

"I have something to confess to the revolution," Yonghong began as she always did. The room was silent with anticipation. The light shining through the window seemed to dim in response to the hush. "This week," she said, "I noticed that the leg of a table was a little bit wobbly. But instead of taking the time to fix the wooden leg, I decided to ignore the problem." A brown sparrow alighted on the windowsill. "I thought to myself that it wasn't my problem—and that someone else would fix it." Yonghong shook her head emphatically.

In the last year, she had picked up many tricks and tips from Hongxing—who was, undeniably, the best at confession. Recently, Hongxing had been invited to join the Literature and Art Propaganda Club at their school and there, under the tutelage of Lan Suhai, one of the parent leaders who used to be a Yue opera singer, had improved her acting and singing by leaps and bounds. For National Day on October 1, Suhai had even decided that Hongxing would take the starring role in the performance.

"But," Yonghong continued, rocking the desk she was standing on, "as my great-uncle once told me, even a wobbly wooden leg is my problem. And he, as you might know, met Chairman Mao himself. As every table and desk and chair belongs to the nation, a wobbly wooden leg is a national problem. And a national problem is my problem." Yonghong pressed her hand against her chest and looked into the distance. The sparrow flew off.

Everyone was allotted ten minutes and encouraged to fill those minutes to the brim. If they fell short of time, then a process of interrogation would begin.

"Is there anything else you want to confess?" the other students would ask. "No thought is too insignificant."

If nothing was offered, they would continue to prod. "How did you feel listening to the loudspeaker this morning? Yesterday? What did you think of when hearing Chairman Mao's latest decree?"

Or: "What do you think of the state of the nation? What do you think of the party leadership?" And also: "Who do you love the most?"

But rarely did her peers need so much questioning, Yonghong thought with no small amount of pride. They were a responsible and disciplined group—not only making sure to keep themselves in line, but others, too. She and her peers often shadowed the older middle school and high school students while they went about attending to official Red Guard business. Many of them wanted to follow the college students around, too, but the college students were more impatient and less inclined to instruct them. Read Chairman Mao's *Little Red Book*, the college students would say to them. That has everything you'll need to know.

Well, her fourth grade class didn't need them, Yonghong thought uncharitably (which could be her confession for the following week). They were a good enough group on their own.

And now that Yonghong had finished her ten minutes, it was her turn to say the words that signaled the next person to go:

"Who among us will confess?"

"I'll go," said 716, who had so renamed himself the year before, honoring Chairman Mao's heroic swim across the Yangzi River on July 16. 716 was always encouraging his fellow classmates to rename themselves with names more closely aligned with Chairman Mao. "Reject the names given to you by your parents. Now your father is Chairman Mao, and your mother is China," 716 would say from time to time, and Yonghong would try not to roll her eyes.

"Yesterday, as I was sitting in the air raid shelter, I thought about how crowded and dirty it was. I was angry at having been woken up in the middle of the night by the alarms and wanted to curse whoever operated them. Why did they always send out false alarms? We've never had a single real strike come down from the skies." 716 frowned angrily. "But then, I realized it was wrong of me to think that way. I should be grateful that no American bombs fell from the sky. It is evidence our Air Force is so good at protecting us that we never see nor hear a single bomb."

Everyone listening nodded gravely. They had all heard of the atomic bombs that the United States had dropped on Japan. There had been stories of entire cities that had been decimated in the aftermath. No survivors. Just empty buildings where there had once been families living together and the sound of children playing. Not even the birds had been spared.

But that was to be expected from a country as wicked as America.

CONFESSION WAS NOT just reserved for Yonghong's fourth grade class. After Chairman Mao had announced the Great Proletarian Cultural Revolution two years earlier at the Eleventh Plenum of the Eighth Central Committee, the art of confession spread across the country. Now, everyone had to do it—from little children to elderly grandparents—especially anyone who felt the slightest longing for the old ways. And besides, it was cleansing for the spirit, and for the nation.

In the mornings, Red Guards within their complex marched out the college principal and deans from the apartments to stand in front of the mural of Chairman Mao. There, they were forced to bow or ketou to the portrait—depending on the mood of the Red Guard who held them. Then, they were left to kneel and reflect on their antirevolutionary thoughts all through morning exercises.

If someone could be classified under the Nine Black Categories, they deserved punishment and instruction until they could be reformed. Yonghong, who had studied the list carefully with the other students, remembered the ranking well:

Landlords
Wealthy farmers
Antirevolutionaries
Bad elements
Right-wingers
Traitors
Spies
Capitalist roaders
Intellectuals

Even grade school teachers—like Miss Wu—weren't safe from being labeled intellectuals. In the last year, what was once an occasional moniker now became the name that most called her by: Miss Wu, rather than

Teacher Wu. Although she came from a long line of peasants and farmers—and not wealthy ones at that—her relatives had gained positions of
power in the years leading up to the Cultural Revolution. Since then,
however, many of them had been removed from their positions.

So Miss Wu had been Miss Wu now for some time. It wasn't only
Yonghong who thought of her that way. And people still brought up what
had happened during the performance. It was hard not to, what with
the permanent stain that had been left on her hand from where she had
pressed it against the paint on the mural. The paint of Chairman Mao's
shirt had been a vigorous, revolutionary green. And it was that same
color that covered most of her palm.

Many thought the stain was a fitting punishment for what Miss Wu
had done. A sign from above. Hadn't she messed up the performance?
Hadn't it been on purpose?

Sometimes, Yonghong felt guilty. How could she not, whenever she
met Miss Wu's quiet eyes? When they crossed paths, Yonghong averted
her gaze.

Yet not a word of reproach crossed Miss Wu's lips, though the others
had reproached her so at the last struggle session. Even Ba had stood up
and spoke against Miss Wu.

But struggle sessions were common all across China. It was necessary
for the remaking of the nation. Those who were brought onto stage in
public halls and deemed guilty by the crowds might be stripped of their
offices, kicked out of their housing, or sent to the countryside for reedu-
cation. Even Great-Uncle seemed to hint in his letters at his own falling
out of favor. Whenever Wai Po read his letters out loud, there was always
a furrow in her brow, and now, in the autumn, it had grown as deep and
dark as the reds of the leaves.

ONE EVENING, WENLIU and two other Red Guards knocked on the door
of their apartment.

"How can I help you, comrades?" Ma asked.

"We've gotten complaints about your closed curtains," Wenliu said.

"From who?" Ma asked.

"It doesn't matter who," one of the Red Guards said. "All that matters is the fact that your closed curtains are disturbing the harmony of the neighborhood."

"In what way?" Wai Po said.

"Why hide behind curtains?" Wenliu asked. "Why not enjoy the bounty of the sun as everyone else does?"

"We're loyal comrades of Chairman Mao," Ma said. "We have nothing to hide."

"Don't you?" Wenliu asked. "But who was your father?" He turned to Wai Po. "Your husband?"

"Don't speak to my mother that way," Ma said, her face cold with fury. "Who was the one who cured you of your fevers when you were a child?" she asked. She strode over to the windows and flung the curtains open. Wenliu squinted against the sudden light and raised his hand to his eyes.

It was a perfect day, the sky blue and cloudless.

"Are you happy now?" Ma demanded.

The sun was shining on all their faces.

"Get out," Ma said.

IT WAS ONLY a few days later that another visitor unexpectedly appeared at their apartment complex. But Miss Wu didn't come to their door. Instead, she stood outside the building, looking up in silence. Tears were falling from her eyes.

Hongxing, by the window, spotted her first. She called Yonghong over and pointed down at their former teacher. "What do you think she's doing?" she whispered to Yonghong.

They watched as one of their neighbors went outside and approached

Miss Wu. He seemed to be asking if she was alright, but Miss Wu ignored him and continued weeping.

"What's the matter down there?" someone called out from the second floor.

"What are you looking at, Miss Wu?" questioned another.

Soon, the spectacle of Miss Wu attracted the attention of everyone in the building. Some went down to try to talk to her or lead her away— but she refused to budge or speak to anyone. Others gathered at their windows and craned their heads, too, to look at the sky. Did she see an American aircraft careening toward them? A bomb falling from the sky?

Leap Forward's mother came knocking at their door. "Did you see what's happening?" she asked Ma with no small amount of delight. "What's wrong with Miss Wu? She's acting crazy."

Ma said nothing. She called Yonghong and Hongxing away from the window to sit down for dinner. Ma, as she usually did, scolded Yonghong for her posture and placed food in Wai Po's bowl. In the past, Ma might have drawn the curtains, but now she paid no mind to the windows.

Ba, too, continued to eat his dinner.

Why didn't he go to Miss Wu as he had that night in the light of the plum blossom tree? When Yonghong finished dinner and was finally allowed to leave the table, she and Hongxing rushed over to the balcony. It was too late. Miss Wu was already gone.

In the morning, Miss Wu was discovered by some schoolchildren hanging by a white silk scarf from the plum blossom tree. The hanging itself wasn't a surprise. No, it was the white silk scarf hand-painted with peonies and birds that mystified those who lay their eyes upon it. How did she manage to possess such a thing—when silk was so hard to come by? No teacher could afford such a thing. It was a symbol of the old world—the world of landlords and emperors and the bourgeoisie. Strangely enough, it remained white even after they cut her down from the tree, without a speck of dirt on it.

THE FOLLOWING SPRING, the plum blossom tree bloomed the most beautifully it had ever bloomed. Its blossoms opened in a cloud of pink. When the blooms fell, the schoolchildren gathered the petals in their arms and threw them up into the air. The petals drifted down, again and again, like the most heavenly rains.

BUT, AFTER THAT, the tree never bloomed again.

Sent Down to the Countryside

As a high schooler, Resist America was now facing the prospect of being sent down to the countryside. It was an honorable prospect, to be sure. Rather than remain in the city or attend college, these urban youth would go to the countryside to live and work among the people. As Chairman Mao put it, "The countryside is a vast world where you can accomplish much."

Of course, in a household with multiple children, one child was allowed to remain in the city to look after their parents. The choice, then, was up to the parents. Which of your children would you keep? Which would you be able to let go?

Resist America was an exemplary Red Guard in every aspect, but he had not volunteered to go down to the countryside. He had always been sickly since birth. Every winter, he acquired a persistent, rattling cough that lasted through to spring—to say nothing of the limp he had developed at the age of ten. And so, it was finally decided that Resist America would remain at home and Leap Forward would serve for his family once he graduated high school—which was still seven years away. As Resist America was of age to be eligible, their decision to volunteer Leap Forward instead had to be reported to the authorities and recorded down for the future.

"I'M SCARED," Leap Forward said as they sat on the stoop of the school.

Yonghong offered him a bite of her baozi. "Of what?"

Leap Forward chewed for a long time. "What do you think it's like in the countryside?" he asked.

"Like how it is in the murals," Yonghong said, thinking of endless fields of wheat and rice and clear, blue skies.

Leap Forward rested his chin on his knees.

Yonghong nudged her shoulder against his. "Chairman Mao wants the best for us. And for the nation."

Leap Forward sighed. "But look at Teacher Qian."

Teacher Qian had been recruited directly from the countryside. He was a stern-looking man, with broad shoulders and a missing big toe. It was said he had been the head of the farmer's collective in his youth, leading the collective to new heights of production. Now, in his fifties, he had taken up the call to educate the next generation of youth. Everyone hated Teacher Qian for his rough manners and stubborn attitude.

"Don't worry so much," Yonghong said. "And besides, we'll both be going together." She knew she would be the one in their family to go down to the countryside when the time came. She had never spoken of it with Hongxing, but there was a silent understanding between them. Yonghong knew she could survive—maybe even thrive—in the countryside or near the wild borders of the country. Hongxing, on the other hand, flourished under appreciation and praise. But who would praise her artistic talents in the country as they did in the city?

From where Leap Forward and Yonghong sat, they could see Hongxing rehearsing in the schoolyard. She circled the barren plum blossom tree with leaps and twirls. The other children clapped and sang along to the song she was singing. Teacher Suhai had been coaching Hongxing on breathing and enunciation techniques common in Yue opera. Now, Hongxing's voice had a richness and depth to it. She could be heard from a far distance.

Using her new voice, Hongxing had sung a song to Yonghong the other day—a song whose meaning had been transformed from a love song to one about Chairman Mao.

"I'll sing just for you," Hongxing said on the balcony of their apartment. Although she kept the new words, no one who heard the way she sang could imagine it was anything other than a love song. Neighbors stood on their own balconies to hum along. Others paused in the road below to listen to her sing. In the sky, even the birds quieted.

AT THE BEGINNING of August, Great-Uncle sent another letter. He'd be shipping them a large trunk for safekeeping. It would only be temporary, he wrote, but he would appreciate it if they could keep it safe.

Wai Po had frowned when she read his letter. She sat by the window, picking apart a piece of her embroidery that she claimed was untidy and needed to be redone. Yonghong watched as the embroidered birds were disassembled, thread by thread. First, it was the beak that went—back into a tangle of brown, black, and silver threads. Then, it was the head—blue and lively. The neck and body were taken care of in quick succession. Then the feet—clawed and sharp. The wings, however, went slowly. They were the last. Wai Po teased out each thread with her needle, pausing often to hold the fabric up to the window. As Wai Po squinted her eyes against the light, they seemed to water. Eventually, the wings, too, disappeared.

THE TRUNK THAT arrived at the end of the month was made of dark, heavy zitan wood. It was plain on the outside, almost nondescript. Wai Po stared at it and ran her hands over the latch.

"I thought it burned in the fire," she said to herself, over and over again. "He's returned it to me."

"What fire?" Ma asked.

"He must have gone back for it," Wai Po said under her breath. "Maybe he went back for him."

When the trunk was open, the first thing that caught Yonghong's eye was its bright-red silk lining. The silk was glossy and embroidered with clouds in a darker, contrasting red. In that moment, it was even more beautiful than the strip of white silk that once belonged to Miss Wu. Yonghong ran her hands back and forth over the slippery cloth while Wai Po and Ma went through the contents of the trunk.

Inside, there was an embroidered pillow. A blue blanket. Some jade bracelets. A gold ring. Another letter. All that and more. A life's little treasures.

A look of understanding was dawning on Wai Po's face as she examined each object. She opened the letter that was addressed to her. After a while, she pressed a hand to her forehead.

"What is it, Ma Ma?" Ma asked.

Wai Po's hand dropped away. "My elder brother is being sent to the countryside," she said.

Great-Uncle and his family were being sent to the countryside outside of Beijing—a lighter sentence compared to some of his other coworkers who had been sent to remote locations around the country.

Ma expressed her relief at his proximity to the city, as that meant his living conditions would be better than most. "He'll have some access to medical care at least," she said.

It was true that Yonghong had heard of some sent-down youths dying in the countryside—from famine or illness. The ordeal was a test of the mind and the body.

"At his age," Wai Po said, "there's no telling what might happen." Her face was colorless.

THAT NIGHT, Yonghong dreamed of a strip of white silk, turning red. When she woke, it was to Hongxing's scream.

Hongxing was looking down at Wai Po curled over the trunk. Wai Po's hair was undone and draped over her face. At first, Yonghong thought Wai Po was simply in a deep sleep, dreaming one of her dreams. But when Hongxing shook her, she didn't wake.

Then, Ma was there—placing her hand gently on Wai Po's shoulder.

"Ma Ma?" she called out fearfully. Then her eyes filled with tears—just as they had after Miss Wu's death.

THAT MORNING, snow fell gently from the sky, slowing the arrival of the men the funeral home sent over. Wai Po had died of a heart attack. She was sixty-two that year.

After the funeral home took Wai Po away, the apartment was quiet. There were no more tears, just as there was no more Wai Po. Yonghong felt her absence pressing her into a little corner. She wanted to lie down but couldn't move. She could only stare at Hongxing, who was buried in Ma's arms.

For days afterward, Hongxing refused to sleep in the big room. She clung to Ma when bedtime neared and insisted on sleeping in the twin bed that Ma shared with Ba. Ma tried compromising with her—perhaps Yonghong and Hongxing could sleep in the small room while Ma and Ba slept in the big room? Or maybe Ma could join Yonghong and Hongxing in the big room? Hongxing refused all options.

Yonghong didn't understand why she was so insistent about joining Ma and Ba in the little room. She had thought Ba would protest, but—to her surprise—he was silent. Miss Wu's death had changed him. There was an air of resignation about him that added a softness to his words and gaze. When Hongxing insisted and stomped her feet, he simply shrugged and said, "Let her do what she wants."

So, Yonghong slept alone in the bed by herself where once there had been three. She tried to call out silently to Hongxing at night but never received an answer. It was the first time she had ever been ignored by Hongxing. Yonghong curled in on herself and covered her face with her hair.

THE FUNERAL HOME returned the ashes three days after Wai Po's death. She wasn't buried with the traditional rites of burning paper money, hiring professional mourners, and dressing in white. Those rites belonged to the Four Olds, as Chairman Mao had decreed. She didn't have a funeral at all. Instead, Ma and Ba brought her to the cemetery where they were assigned a plot.

Her tombstone was the same as all others—a simple pale-gray granite marker carved with her name—Zhang Yunhong—and the dates of her birth and death.

"Will I be buried next to her when I'm dead?" Hongxing asked.

"No," Ma said.

"Why not?"

Ma was silent for a time. "There's just enough space in one plot for a husband and a wife. Maybe a small child, too."

"Where will I be buried then?" Hongxing asked.

"In whatever plot is next available, with your husband," Ma said. "But that won't be for a long time."

"We'll all be separated from each other?" Hongxing asked.

"Don't worry," Ma said.

"I don't want to be buried all by myself," Hongxing said. "I want to be with Wai Po." Her eyes filled with tears. "She must be lonely all by herself."

"Don't be such a crybaby," Yonghong snapped. Didn't she realize how lonely Yonghong had been feeling at night?

As their mother turned and began to comfort Hongxing, Yonghong felt a sense of growing anger. It was always she who was treated this way, while Hongxing was coddled and comforted. "I hate you!" she yelled at them all and ran through the cemetery.

What was this new feeling growing inside her? It belonged to the old world, she knew—where landlords hoarded wealth and the emperor married a thousand women. Jealousy.

"It isn't for forever," Ma said one night—after Hongxing had started sleeping again with Yonghong in the big room. "My mother always told me that she would wait for me in the underworld—just like my father would. She'll wait for you both." There was a measured certainty in her voice. Ma had changed after Wai Po's death in ways that Yonghong didn't quite understand. There was a toughness to her that hadn't existed before, like a newly-formed bark wrapped around her. Or perhaps it was just the knowledge that she had no one left to lean on.

"Then we'll be together forever?" Hongxing asked.

"Until you drink from Meng Po's cup," Ma said, repeating the story that Wai Po had told her: "After wandering for some time in the underworld and enduring various trials according to your sins, your soul will make its way to the Bridge of Forgetfulness. There, Meng Po waits for you with a bowl in her hands. She wants you to drink what she offers. She has brewed it just for you—and for all souls. Take her bowl and drink what is inside. Once you drink it, you will forget all the details of the life you once lived. Then, you will cross the bridge over a dark and fast-moving water to emerge into your next life."

Ways to Accompany the Dead

SPRING ARRIVED, BUT few of the flowers bloomed as they had in previous years. Something had changed them, just like the plum blossom tree. Summer came and went, then autumn blew in with its chilly winds. Winter heralded the passing of the migratory geese.

The next spring, the geese returned, and 716 declared his love for Hongxing. He had loved her ever since he heard her singing on the balcony, he told all who cared to listen.

"Ridiculous," Hongxing said, before disappearing for hours to rehearse again.

Yonghong could tell their parents were relieved Hongxing did not return his affections. 716's parents fought so loudly that they could be sometimes heard in the streets. Some even suspected they might be considering a divorce, which was unheard of. A marriage reflected the harmony of a nation, after all, and those who were not able to maintain a state of harmony were often demoted, shunned, or—the worst of all— stripped of party membership.

But Hongxing's head was not filled with matters of love. She dreamed of joining an art troupe in the People's Liberation Army to perform her dances and songs for the nation. It was hard to be selected as one of the members of an art troupe. One not only needed talent and skill, but also—in many cases—a connection or two.

Hongxing hoped she would catch the eye of a recruiter. Suhai had hinted she might have a connection to a more local art troupe, but Hongxing wasn't quite ready yet. She still needed time to practice, practice, practice . . .

While Hongxing's head was filled with posture and pirouettes and perfect pitch, Yonghong's was filled with Leap Forward. After her thirteenth birthday, he had given her a kiss on the cheek—not like one between brother and sister. He liked her, he confessed. Did she like him, too?

Of course she liked him, she replied, elbowing him in the side.

But did she want to be with him forever? he asked.

Yonghong didn't reply, but the answer, she knew, was yes. She couldn't imagine life without him. Even when he was angry at her and refused to speak, she was still reassured by the thought that they would always— eventually—find one another.

Nothing really changed between them after that. Occasionally, the smile they shared held something more secretive. At night, when Yonghong thought of him smiling back, her birthmark seemed to burn— just like Wai Po had told her it did when she had first fallen in love.

TWO YEARS LATER, news arrived from their Great-Uncle, who had been released from the countryside and was considered officially "rehabilitated" at last. There in the countryside, he and his family had labored in the fields for three years, working alongside the sent-down youths and peasants. Weekly, they had attended classes, organized by the peasants and youths, on correct ways of thinking about Chairman Mao, China, and themselves. The experience was both a punishment and a blessing, he said—a duality that sometimes troubled Yonghong.

Won't you all come visit us? Great-Uncle wrote.

After some discussion, Ma and Ba decided to send Yonghong and Hongxing to visit him and his family in Beijing. And so, a few days before the Lunar New Year, they sent the twins off on a train, along with the belongings he had sent to them in the trunk two years ago.

When Yonghong and Hongxing arrived at the station, they saw an old man standing on the platform with hair streaked through with gray. His brows were thick and full—casting a dark shadow over his face—but his eyes were all Wai Po's.

He recognized them at once and beamed. There was a young man standing beside him, and Great-Uncle directed him to help Yonghong and Hongxing with their luggage.

"You must be Yonghong, and you Hongxing," Great-Uncle guessed, correctly. "This is my grandson, Jun," he said with a laugh, gesturing to the young man. "Your cousin, twice removed. You can call him Da Ge."

Great-Uncle was everything Yonghong had imagined from his letters and more. He brought them to a mansion that had once belonged to Empress Cixi's favorite eunuch. Now, it housed the officers of the rehabilitated staff of the Ministry of Health. Nevertheless, there were still remnants of that previous world in the mansion. In the courtyard stood a large peach tree carved from jade. To Yonghong, it was like something out of a story, though her great-uncle looked upon it with disdain.

"It would be too much effort to remove this nonsense," he said, gesturing at the tree. "But, as it stands, it serves as a reminder."

"Of what?" Yonghong asked.

"Of the wealth the eunuchs hoarded while the people starved," he said. "Of how easily money and power corrupts the human heart."

"But that'll never happen again under Chairman Mao," Yonghong said.

Her great-uncle smiled wryly without answering.

Every day, their newfound elder brother took Yonghong and Hongxing out to tour the sights of the capital. He took them to Tiananmen Square, where they saw the portrait of Chairman Mao hanging in the center of the square, staring benevolently over them all. Yonghong and Hongxing fell silent with awe, and Yonghong felt tears prickling at her eyes.

Their new elder brother even took them to parts of the Forbidden City where emperors and empresses once held rule.

"Relics of the past," their da ge said. "To show how far we've progressed."

Yonghong and Hongxing climbed on top of a pair of bronze qilin that guarded one of the entrances inside. Now, there was nothing of the past left to guard.

On the last day of their visit, Great-Uncle took them to a playground on the way to the train station. He sat on the park bench with Yonghong beside him while Hongxing ran off to play.

Great-Uncle took out a cigarette from his pocket. It was a foreign brand—one that only officers could get.

"Have you enjoyed yourself?" Great-Uncle asked.

Yonghong replied that she had.

"I'm glad," he said, lighting his cigarette. "You and your sister must come visit again soon. And bring your parents with you next time." He took a deep drag, then sighed, smoke escaping his lips. "It's hard to believe that your wai po is gone. I almost didn't believe it. Now, I'm the only one left of my siblings. As the eldest, I always thought I would be the first to go."

Great-Uncle was quiet. Yonghong watched as the end of his cigarette flared with light. His eyes—Wai Po's eyes—were filled with sadness.

WHEN SHE TURNED sixteen, Hongxing was recruited into a military arts troupe like she always wanted. Yonghong ran to find Leap Forward, who was painting a slogan that evening on the walls of their complex. It was their first year as high schoolers, and with it came all the privileges.

Leap Forward grinned when he heard the news and picked Yonghong up, spinning her around. Yonghong returned his smile, giddy with happiness. It wasn't only her own happiness she felt, but Hongxing's, too, coursing through her.

The army! Yonghong almost couldn't believe it. There, Hongxing would be guaranteed a job, housing, meals, and special benefits not afforded ordinary civilians.

Leap Forward put her down, and his smile faded.

"What's wrong?" Yonghong asked.

"Now that your sister's going to the army, you'll be the one remaining by your parents," he said.

"I'll volunteer to go to the countryside with you," Yonghong offered. The high schoolers who did so received lavish send-offs and much fanfare. She still remembered the names of the ten high schoolers in a neighboring city who had volunteered to work in the remotest mountains, though she didn't know what happened to them afterward.

"Don't be ridiculous," Leap Forward said, a hint of anger in his voice.

"I'm not being ridiculous. I'll go with you," Yonghong insisted. "We promised each other, didn't we?"

"You can't sacrifice your future for me," Leap Forward snapped. "You think I would be happy to see you suffer?" He was angry and didn't speak for the rest of the night.

TWO YEARS LATER, the dreaded parting finally arrived. After graduating high school, Yonghong had been assigned to work as a secretary in the local manufacturing plant. She was given a room in the dormitories, which she shared with five other women. Leap Forward was assigned a placement in the countryside reserved for the children of those who worked at the college. It wasn't as close to the city as those given to children of factory workers, who took precedence over college staff and faculty. It would take two days of traveling. But at least it wasn't as remote as it could have been, Yonghong told herself.

The night before their parting, Yonghong and Leap Forward met beneath the plum blossom tree, whose branches were now barren. Leap Forward brought his cassette player, which his older brother had given him for his last birthday.

Yonghong rested her head on Leap Forward's shoulder as he held the cassette player up to both their ears. The volume was turned down low, but Yonghong could still hear Teresa Teng's sweet and clear voice threading through the air.

"Smile a little, won't you?" Leap Forward murmured in her ear.

"Can't you look less happy?" Yonghong asked.

"What's the use of looking sad?"

Yonghong frowned and pulled away. She wanted him to look as sad as she felt inside.

"Maybe I'll forget all about you," Yonghong said.

At this, Leap Forward's smile slipped a little—but then it was back. "You won't," he said, holding her tightly.

It wasn't the only parting that came that year. In July, the city of Tangshan fell to a terrible earthquake. The earth split into large fissures, and the soil collapsed in on itself. Buildings fell. People were trapped in the rubble. Hundreds of thousands perished. The shaking, they said, could be felt in the Heavens itself. Though the shaking never reached them, Yonghong was certain she had felt it, too. She and Hongxing were nauseous for days, and they dreamt of being crushed under the rubble.

Ma said the earthquake was a sign of doom. Ba made a speech in front of their apartment commemorating the event. Neighbors placed flowers under the billboard of Chairman Mao. When Chairman Mao died just two months later, many said the dead were meant to accompany Chairman Mao as his retainers in the underworld. His death shocked the nation as much—if not more—than the earthquake.

Yonghong went to the streets to weep, wailing with the rest of them. It felt as if Wai Po was dying all over again. As if no one would ever be able to be happy in the ways they were before.

EVERY DAY, Yonghong wrote letters to Leap Forward and waited for his letters in turn. Leap Forward wrote brightly of his time in the countryside. He had been elected by the villagers to teach a class on communism to the other youths, peasants, and rehabilitees and had accumulated plenty of new slogans to share with her upon his return. Although he enjoyed teaching the others, he missed home. He longed for the days he could sleep soundly at night. Sleeping in a room with nine other snoring youths was like sleeping in a symphony hall. They worked long hours in the fields, but he told her not to worry. He had never been more fit in his life, he joked. He asked her to call on his parents from time to time and check up on them.

Yonghong worried, despite his reassurances. Everyone knew how hard it was to live and work in the countryside. Sometimes, the youths didn't have enough to eat—a thought that pained her.

Winter came, feeling colder than it ever had before. Or maybe it was just the sense of being left behind—by Wai Po, by Hongxing, by Leap Forward, by Chairman Mao.

One day, Yonghong's high school language teacher saw her walking past the school and pulled her aside. "Listen," her teacher said, "I heard that colleges might reopen soon."

"Really?" Yonghong was surprised.

Her teacher nodded. "You'd be better off spending your time studying."

Would colleges really open up again? It had been so long since they last accepted students.

Day and night, Yonghong spent her spare hours studying mathematics, language, composition, science, and more. No one knew what might be on the entrance exams. They only knew the exams could represent a new opportunity—one they had scarcely allowed themselves to dream of before.

THE DAY BEFORE the exams, Hongxing returned home. She arrived with her hair cut in fashionable bangs and curled at the ends. She smiled brightly and gave them all a hug. Hongxing had been sending photographs, and yet her presence in person still caught Yonghong by surprise. There was something changed about her sister in a way that the photographs weren't able to capture. Perhaps they were all just growing up.

The exam itself, taking several hours over three days, seemed to pass in an instant. Yonghong emerged from the testing center on the final day, her hands cramped from all the writing she had done.

Hongxing was waiting with a bottle in her hands. Every day of the exam, she had waited faithfully to accompany Yonghong back home.

"How was it?" she asked, handing Yonghong the bottle.

Yonghong took a sip. There was beef broth inside, still hot and steaming.

"I think I did well," Yonghong said. The adrenaline was only just beginning to drain out of her, leaving her mind muddled and foggy. As they walked back home from the testing center, Yonghong suggested they stop by the post office first.

"It'll be closed by now," Hongxing said.

"I want to send a postcard to Leap Forward," Yonghong said, disappointed. "I last heard from him a month ago." Lately, his letters had been coming less and less—with fewer words each time. She would have worried over it more had her mind not been consumed by her studies.

Hongxing was silent for a long time. The street was filled with other test-takers and their families and friends.

"Yonghong," Hongxing said.

"What is it?"

Hongxing looked at her with sad eyes. "There's something I've been meaning to tell you."

"What?"

"He's gone, Yonghong."

"What do you mean?" Yonghong asked.

"I'm sorry," Hongxing said. She turned her face away, but Yonghong could see that her eyes were glistening with tears.

"I don't believe you," Yonghong said, growing angry.

"It happened a couple of weeks ago," Hongxing said. "Ma and Ba sent me a letter, but we agreed not to say anything until your exams were over."

"I would have known." Yonghong was certain of it. She had heard of others who had died in the countryside—countless others who had been worked to death or fallen ill, but not Leap Forward. Not him. How could such a loss not reverberate across the land? How could it not bring down the Heavens?

"He was a good man." Hongxing brushed away tears from her eyes.

Yonghong's body began to tremble, but she felt as though she were looking down upon it all from a great distance. Her breath came fast, and her fingertips grew numb. It wasn't possible. It just wasn't. "You're lying," she said over and over again. The blue of the sky filled her gaze, and then, the ground.

THAT NIGHT, Yonghong dreamt about Miss Wu—who she hadn't thought of in years. And in her dream, Miss Wu's tears weren't for herself.

They were for the many students who died in the countryside. Millions had been sent away from their homes, and thousands upon thousands, like Leap Forward, never made it back.

It was cold that day in February 1978 when Yonghong went to Nanjing University. She made her way from the station to the college, dragging her bags, which had been carefully packed by Ma. In her inner pocket, there was a roll of money that Ba had pressed into her hands. Her breath blew out in front of her in large white clouds.

At the gates, there was a young man caught in a scuffle with two other students.

"How can they let someone like you in?"

"You should have been reeducated, along with your parents."

The young man remained defiant. "My parents have been rehabilitated," he said.

"Your mother's a no-good—"

At this provocation, the young man leapt forward and tried to throw a punch. Instead, he found himself being pushed back. He stumbled and fell to the ground. When he looked up, his nose was bleeding. The other two ran away at the sight of blood.

Yonghong went up to him and handed him her handkerchief. The young man tried to refuse at first but relented after Yonghong insisted.

"Thanks," he said begrudgingly.

"What's your name?" Yonghong asked.

"Aiguo," the young man said. He pressed Yonghong's handkerchief against his nose. "I'll buy you a new one," he said, not looking at her.

"Don't worry about it," Yonghong said.

There were tears dripping down his face, but he didn't seem sad—only angry. As angry as Yonghong wished she could feel.

"You shouldn't fight so close to the school," Yonghong said.

"What does it matter to you?" he snapped.

Yonghong found herself looking closely at him, turning his face over in her mind. He was handsome, in a way she had never encountered before. He had a sharp jawline and eyes of a bright, startling blue. As Yonghong studied him, she knew he would never be able to remind her of Leap Forward.

"My great-uncle was rehabilitated, too," Yonghong offered.

At this, Aiguo leapt up in a fury. "You don't know anything," he said, before running off, still holding her handkerchief, stained, now, with blood.

A Dance Interlude

Beijing

A YEAR HAD passed since her older sister had entered Nanjing University, and now it was Hongxing's turn to go back to school. She stood outside the exam room, steeling herself. She had studied for this moment, for hours after dance practices, burning the midnight oil, until her shoulders ached and her ankles swelled. She had bigger dreams than the military. She had dreams of performing on stages around the world. She knew that the only way possible to succeed in the new decade was through education. Everyone, she knew, had a strange and winding story that led them to the examination room.

Inside the room, on the table, there was a variety of props for her to choose from. She studied them carefully. A piece of paper, a calligraphy brush, a pair of boots, a tin cup, a porcelain bowl, a man's overcoat, a blunted axe.

"You have five minutes to improvise a performance for us," one of the examiners said.

Hongxing recognized him as he stared at her from across the table. While waiting in line for her exams, she had heard other students speak of him as he passed. He had recently been released from a seven-year stay in the "cowshed" on Beijing University's campus with other intellectual enemies of the state. His crime had been watching Hollywood films—bourgeois films of the enemy. He likely would have gone to jail even if he had been only watching a blank screen. He came from a distinguished lineage of actors and playwrights—the intelligentsia class.

But now the Cultural Revolution was over, and its four ringleaders—the so-called Gang of Four who had been accused of orchestrating the whole thing and committing treason against the country—had been imprisoned or sentenced to death. A purge, so to speak, of the old guard. Chairman Mao was three years dead, and a new star was rising—that of his successor, Premier Hua Guofeng.

So now, the examiner and many others like him were free—free to resume their lives and pretend the past few years had never even happened.

"Are you ready?" the examiner asked.

Hongxing nodded. She hadn't known what she would perform when she first walked in through the door. She hadn't come with different scenarios prepared in her head like the other students who told one another of the props they had heard would be laid out in front of them. But Hongxing knew what she wanted to perform as soon as she laid her eyes on the axe.

She grabbed it in her hand and swung it at an imaginary tree. As she worked, she sang a song about the hopes and dreams of the people and glanced from time to time at the other students she imagined all around her, the other sent-down youths who were also swinging their axes beside her. They were hard at work clearing away the trees for planting rice fields. But, being sent-down students, they were not used to manual labor and were hunched over with fatigue.

Suddenly, Hongxing saw that a large oak several feet away from her was about to fall. The young man who had been hacking away at it stood directly in its path. At the last moment, Hongxing flung her axe aside and pushed him out of the way. The two of them tumbled to the ground. Hongxing clasped her hands over her ears and closed her eyes tightly to protect against the dust that rose in the air. When the dust settled again, she looked at the young man, whose invisible body she curled against.

Hongxing thought of her sister and looked at the invisible boy with the same eyes Yonghong had used to look at Leap Forward. She smiled at him. Both of them were breathless. Both were filled with a growing awareness of one another. The boy stood up first and offered her his hand.

She grabbed his hand and stood up. "I'm glad you're alright," she said, and clasped her arms around him—the boy she had saved.

"Thank you," the examiner said. His words dispelled the vision of the young man, which disappeared like a ghost.

THE FOLLOW-UP EXAM required applicants to write an analysis of a short film that was played for them in the room. In the seat beside Hongxing, there was a young woman named Xiaoyan whom she had befriended over the past few days.

Xiaoyan was from the Hebei province of China and spoke with a heavy Northern accent. She came from a humble background—the best kind of background. Her father was a foreman at the farmer's collective, while her mother worked as a secretary. She had been particularly talented at painting depictions of Chairman Mao around her village. Eventually, she had transitioned to stage design and taking on bit parts of her own in performances. Like Hongxing, Xiaoyan had come from a military arts troupe and had decided to try her luck at auditioning to have a chance at going to college.

Hongxing stood up, the first to finish in the room. She brought her paper over to the proctor who looked at her in surprise.

"You don't want to check over your work?" he asked.

"No."

Hongxing never liked to go back and review her work. It wasn't in her personality to look back. Dancers who lingered over past mistakes had a harder time continuing on with their performance. The present moment, she knew, was all she had.

Hongxing and Xiaoyan were both admitted into the Beijing Film Academy class of '80. They were assigned a dorm with four other women. Hongxing slept on the top bunk above Xiaoyan. In the bunk directly across from them were Guiying and Hongmei.

The other two women didn't like to talk to Hongmei. She had a quiet and serious demeanor and never joked around with them. It almost seemed as if she had been released recently from a stint in the "cow-shed" rather than her mother and father. Her parents had been part of the Beijing intellectual elites before they had been imprisoned, and she had grown up under the care of a distant aunt.

But despite the other women's dislike and Hongmei's unfortunate family background, there was something about her that attracted Hongxing's gaze. In the military and over the years, Hongxing had learned how to blend in. She learned that life was a performance—that it never stopped after leaving the stage. Hongmei didn't seem to understand that fact of life yet. If Hongxing were Yonghong, she might have extended a hand or included her in their conversations. But she wasn't her sister. So she simply watched Hongmei from afar.

Her hair, which shimmered like starlight, had an unusual curl to it. And her lips were always berry-red, as if they had been just bitten. But it was her eyes most of all that drew Hongxing's attention. Her eyes, which curved down at the outer corners. They always looked so depthless, so beseeching.

Hongxing loved studying at the academy, just as she knew she would. It was everything she had dreamed of, and more. During the Cultural Revolution, Chairman Mao's fourth wife, Jiang Qing, a former actress, established a university of the arts in Zhuxin Village. This site, located on the outskirts of the city, was where the Beijing Film Academy had been ordered to move to fulfill Jiang Qing's vision. The Beijing Dance Academy had also relocated to Zhuxin, along with two other art colleges, but managed to maneuver its way back into city. Now, only the Film Academy still remained.

It was out of the abandoned dance studios of the Beijing Dance Academy that Hongxing heard the sound of strings and flutes one afternoon. She paused in the hallway and peered into the room. Inside, Hongmei was dancing, twirling and leaping across the floor as the recording played. A beam of sunlight entered through a gap in the boarded-up window, illuminating her feet. She moved gracefully through the air, looking as if she were on the verge of flying.

She would look beautiful in flight, Hongxing thought.

Hongmei noticed her on one of her turns in the air and stumbled upon landing. Their eyes caught. Something electric passed between them. Something that coursed through Hongxing's entire body. So this was what love felt like, Hongxing thought. A strike of lightning setting her aflame.

Hongxing fled. That night, she snuck glances at Hongmei, sleeping in the top bunk across from her. Hongmei tossed and turned all night, almost as if she were dancing even in her dreams.

A week later, Hongxing returned to the abandoned dance studio, a pair of borrowed ballet shoes in hand. She waited there in silence for what felt like hours. Her heart pounded, and the back of her neck was damp with sweat. When Hongmei finally arrived, Hongxing leapt to her feet with a smile.

"I'm sorry I startled you the other day," she said.

Hongmei stood in the doorway, her eyes wide.

"I started out in my arts troupe as a dancer," Hongxing said. "I've always loved dancing more than acting," she confessed. "But don't tell anyone I said that."

"I won't," Hongmei said with utter seriousness.

"So what do you say?" Hongxing asked. "Can I join you?"

Hongmei nodded cautiously. "If you'd like." She entered the room and set her belongings down. She sat on the floor and put on her pointe shoes. She flexed her feet, then wrapped the ribbons around her ankles.

There was a birthmark, Hongxing noticed, on her ankle, dark and red, just like her sister's. The sight of it made Hongxing's heart thump in her chest. "Where did you learn to dance?" she asked casually, trying to disguise her nervousness.

"My aunt taught me," Hongmei said. "She was trained in Russia."

"Really?" Hongxing said. "Maybe you can teach me some moves."

Hongmei took out her tape recorder and set it in the middle of the studio.

"Weren't you playing *Swan Lake* the other day?" Hongxing asked. She had heard the suite once years ago while she was in the arts troupe. She had never danced to it before—it would have been unpatriotic to dance to another country's music. But the memory of the melodies had resurfaced upon hearing them again.

"Yes," Hongmei said.

"Will you play it again?" Hongxing asked. "For me?"

"Alright," Hongmei said, and pressed Play.

SOON, HONGXING AND Hongmei became known for their choreographed pas de deux, in which the two of them leapt and twirled across the stage. The other students called them the Two Swans of their year, a nickname that made Hongxing blush. Swans, Hongxing knew, danced as a form of courtship and mated for life. Once, Hongxing had seen a pair floating across a lake. They curled their long white necks around each other, as if to prevent anyone from tearing them apart. It was said that the bond between them could only be broken by death.

Hongxing had always had a talent for choreography, for expressing emotions through the movements of the body. But Hongmei's background in Russian ballet and her inclination for improvisation expanded Hongxing's understanding of what a performance could be. When Hongxing performed a pirouette, Hongmei would encourage her to add a subtle flourish of the hands. Hongxing, on the other hand, instructed Hongmei on how to use her eyes to her advantage.

"Like this?" Hongmei asked. She tilted her face down, then raised her eyes coyly to meet Hongxing's gaze.

For the final recital of their first year, Hongmei and Hongxing danced to *Swan Lake*. Hongxing poured her heart into the dance. Every time she spun around, she kept her eyes on Hongmei to ground herself. Every time she arched her arms, she was reaching toward Hongmei. At the end of the performance, they clasped hands and raised them into the air. Applause thundered throughout the performance hall.

Backstage, Hongmei pointed out her parents, who were sitting in the audience.

"They've never asked anything of me. They've always encouraged me to follow my dreams. I dreamed of the day they would be free and watching me on stage," she said to Hongxing. She began to weep. "I thought if I danced well enough—if I became a star—I could somehow set us all free."

"You are free," Hongxing said, clasping her in her arms. Hongmei looked up, then, just as Hongxing had taught her. Standing in the darkness, the two came together in a kiss.

PART THREE

MASSACHUSETTS

2004–2009

The Stranger from China

THERE WAS A mysterious package in the middle of the living room. It was roughly three feet long by two feet wide, and about the same height as the coffee table. The package had been carefully wrapped and padded with layers of foam and coarse brown paper. Emily obediently snipped through the duct tape holding it all together, then wrestled off the outer layer of paper. The package smelled dusty and old—like something that had traveled not only halfway across the world, but across centuries to reach them.

"You shouldn't have gone to so much trouble," Grandma said to the stranger. She wore a pleased smile on her face as she sat down on the couch. Gifts, Emily knew, were important. Emily's family always brought a gift whenever they visited the other Chinese families in town. Sometimes it was baskets of fresh lychee. Other times, boxes of expensive tea from the homeland. The more trouble one went to getting the gift, the more one esteemed the receiver.

Several years back when Grandma went to China by herself, she packed a suitcase full of gifts to give to her relatives. There were bottles of vitamins, stacks of name-brand clothing, and pairs of American-made sneakers. The kinds they can't get so easily in China, Grandma explained to Emily. Even when times were hard and food was scarce, Grandma said, her own mother would give gifts of embroidery to her neighbors. She was masterful with a needle and thread, Grandma always bragged. It was true, even to Emily's untrained eye. Three years ago, on her tenth birthday, Grandma had gifted her a handkerchief embroidered by Emily's great-grandmother. All along the border were swirling red clouds. Her signature, Grandma said.

But Emily had been careless with the handkerchief. She had stained it one day with mud and dirt on her hands. When Grandma saw what she had done, Grandma snatched it back with fury in her eyes.

"I'll be more careful," Emily had promised, apologizing.

"There are some things apologies can't fix," Grandma had said.

Emily never saw the handkerchief again, though she had begged her grandma to give it back to her.

But now, Grandma's face lit up as she gazed upon the stranger. Emily knew that he had come all the way from China, this so-called uncle of hers. Dressed in a sharp gray suit, he appeared rather youthful, though he was, in fact, older than Mom—who kept referring to him as her "older brother." His hair had streaks of gray in it, but his eyebrows—thick and untamed—were still the blackest of blacks.

But, he wasn't actually one of Mom's brothers. He was one of Mom's cousins—once, or maybe it was twice, removed. Emily wasn't entirely certain of the relationship. She hadn't really listened when Grandma explained to her who he was or why he was coming.

"Would you like some more tea?" Mom asked her uncle. She brought over a teapot and placed it on the coffee table.

"Thank you," he said.

"What present did you bring us?" Mom asked. She came over to where Emily was kneeling and peered down at the package.

A smile spread across his face. "A surprise," he said. "I hope you like it."

When Emily peeled away the last layer of foam padding, she revealed before them all a large trunk made of dark purple wood. Grandma drew in a breath. Mom did, too. There was a stricken look on both their faces.

"I nearly forgot about this," Mom said. She bent down to examine it.

Emily ran her hands over the beautiful wood carvings on the surface of the trunk. The carvings were deeply etched into the wood, depicting birds alighting upon branches and flowers in bloom. Some of the carvings were chipped and scratched. Others were broken off partway. Emily tested the weight of the trunk by pushing against it. The trunk didn't budge. Unwrapped, the trunk smelled even more musty. Like the fur of a cave-dwelling animal.

"I didn't realize your family had kept it after all these years," Grandma said. "I thought it might have been lost."

"My grandfather always told us to keep it safe," Uncle said. "He told me it used to be your mother's dowry. Before he passed, he instructed me to return it to your side of the family one day."

There was a tightness around Grandma's eyes. "Emily, come sit next to your uncle." She patted the couch beside her.

"How old is this thing?" Emily asked.

"Come here," Grandma said.

"I can't believe you brought this over," Mom said as she fiddled with the lock of the trunk.

"We can open it later," Grandma said.

But Mom continued her efforts, and the bronze latch finally opened. Mom knelt down and rifled through the contents. The animal smell of the trunk soon filled the entire room as she lifted various objects out, one after another. Bundled scraps of cloth. A packet of letters. She plucked out a photo album and began to flip through it. It was covered with red silk, though the color had dulled and darkened over the years.

A smile spread across her face.

"Look, Ma," she said. Mom brought over the album to show the three of them on the couch. She pointed to a photograph of herself as a child standing next to Grandma and Grandpa, whom Emily had never met. There was Mom's sister, Aunt Hong, the one who had been a dancer and then an actress, in the frame, too.

"You look like the spitting image of your mother when she was young," her uncle said to Emily. He turned to her mother. "Do you remember when you first came to Beijing?"

"Oh yes," Mom said. "How many decades has it been?"

"Too many," her uncle said. "I never could have imagined you would end up in America." He paused, then added, "If anything, I might have guessed that Hongxing would be the one living abroad."

"You know Aunt Hong?" Emily asked, looking up.

"I saw her just last month in Beijing, when she was there shooting a television series," her uncle said.

Grandma pointed to the DVDs on the coffee table. "Your uncle brought over your aunt's latest shows."

"Do you like your aunt's shows?" her uncle asked Emily.

"She loves them," Grandma said with a smile. "She'll watch them for hours." She turned to Emily. "Isn't that right?"

EMILY REMEMBERED CLEARLY the first time she ever saw her aunt on television, watching as Grandma fiddled impatiently with the remote. The people on the screen paused, spoons raised halfway to their mouths, then sped forward through cold rooms, walking stiffly in a blur, then down crowded and tree-lined streets, the hallways of offices, hospitals, into one another's arms, then backward, up the stairs, into smaller rooms, bedrooms, where they touched each other's faces, hair, leaping apart back down the stairs, through doorways, into kitchens, chopping furiously, the pieces of an apple reassembling itself on the wooden board. There! Yes, there.

Grandma paused the tape, played it, rewound. Yes, it was Mom, dressed strangely, her hair curled at the ends. She was cutting up an apple, splitting it back apart into little pieces.

"Mom." Emily pointed at the screen. She had only been three then, full of certainty.

But no, it wasn't Mom, Grandma explained. It was her aunt, whom she had met once before in China. Didn't she remember? Twins, Grandma explained, laughing a little, they were twins.

But how could it not be Mom? The one on the screen who moved her mouth, her shoulders in the same way. The one who was answering the doorbell, smiling at a strange man, picking up another child in her arms. Surely it was her.

When Mom came back home from work, Emily clumsily tugged her over to the television. "It's you," she insisted. "It's you."

Mom didn't laugh. She touched the face on the screen without answering. Then, she turned and crouched down. "It's not me," Mom said gently. "It's my sister. My twin." She pulled Emily in close. "One day, you'll get to meet her."

Emily frowned. "When?" she asked, suspiciously.

Mom sighed. "I don't know," she said, glancing again at the screen. "She's a star, you know." After a few moments, she shook her head and smiled. "But we'll be okay. I have you, Emily. You're my other half now."

Emily liked the sound of that. Liked the thought of being Mom's other half. If she left, Mom would surely miss her terribly. Would never be complete. The thought soothed some of her fear, but she remained unconvinced. Each time Emily saw her aunt on the screen, she was certain it was her mother instead, convinced her mother was living in other cities, other homes. At first, it was thrilling. Then, an awful thought—

Maybe Mom wasn't hers. Maybe she belonged to the other families, the other children. Maybe Mom wasn't a mother after all, but a doll. Not only for her, but for others, too. Emily couldn't stand it. Couldn't stand the thought of Mom loving other children. Loving them, perhaps, more than her. Emily trembled in bed just thinking of it. Thinking of Mom holding the hands of other children. Carrying them in her arms. Brushing their hair. Leading them through the garden, all abloom. Leading a secret life.

"DO YOU THINK I look like Aunt Hong, too?" Emily asked her uncle.

"Yes," he said. "You look like the both of them."

Emily mulled over this information. She didn't know whether to be pleased or not with her uncle's statement. "I don't look like either of them," she finally said, just to be contrarian.

"Oh?" Uncle had a bemused smile on his face.

Emily knew it was a lie. Her birthmark, she couldn't deny, was exactly like her mother's. And it was similar to Grandma's, though hers looked mangled and scarred. It had been an accident, Grandma had told her. Emily wondered what kind of accident, but when she pried, Grandma didn't answer.

Mom flipped through the pages of the album. A photograph fell out and fluttered to the floor. She picked it up and cradled it in her palm. Shock flashed across her face. There was a kind of pain in her eyes. Emily had never seen that look on her mother's face, though she had seen it before on Aunt Hong's face in her television shows. It was the kind of look that appeared when her character was going somewhere far away from home or looking back at a lover who was walking away. Walking down the road and disappearing into the night.

Emily was about to ask her mother what was wrong when Dad entered the room. He apologized for not being able to greet Uncle upon his arrival. He had to stay late for work, he explained. "We're on a tight deadline right now," Dad said.

A few months earlier, the whole family had moved for Dad's new job. The current house—an old colonial built in the fifties—was larger than their previous one. It was large enough for Emily and Grandma to have their own rooms each and had a big yard and plenty of room for Grandma to grow her vegetables, and Mom, her roses.

But Dad didn't seem to appreciate any of this. He didn't seem to notice much of anything. His hours were longer at the new financial management company he was working at. He had to "put in the hours" in order to stay competitive, he was always saying. Mom was away more as well, since the move increased her commute to the pharmacy where she worked behind the counter, doling out pills to customers. For most of the summer, it had just been Grandma and Emily at home by themselves, which Emily didn't mind. In fact, she longed for the days of relative solitude, particularly now that it had been interrupted by her uncle's visit.

Her uncle was thanking them all again for hosting him for a few days.

"We're honored by your visit," Grandma said. "It's hard for me to travel to China in my old age, and it's rare that I'll have the opportunity to meet relatives." From time to time, Grandma expressed the desire to go back to China and see their old apartment in Nanjing, where she raised Mom and Aunt Hong. But the apartment had been torn down long ago, Mom always reminded her, and besides, why would she want to return to the place full of bad memories, the place where she'd made them keep the curtains closed for so many years. Emily had been puzzled by the comment and asked her mother what she meant, but no one explained anything to her—like always.

"You have a wonderful life and family here," Uncle said.

At her uncle's words, Mom's face went blank. Emily watched as her mother slipped the photograph back into the album. Mom gripped the album with both her hands, then she placed it back inside the trunk. The lid closed with a thunk.

THAT NIGHT, after everyone had gone to bed, Emily crept out of her room. The moon was full and bright as it shone through the windows, illuminating her way into the hall, past Grandma's room, the guest room where her uncle was staying, the shared bathroom, and her parents' room. Emily navigated slowly and carefully down the stairs. She wasn't as familiar with all the creaky floorboards of this house. It was still new to her. But it wasn't like she was doing anything wrong, she reasoned. No one had forbidden her from going to look inside the trunk. In fact, for the rest of the evening, both Mom and Grandma seemed to pretend the trunk wasn't there at all.

Emily was simply curious about the photograph that her mother had hidden away. What was it that had caused the expression on her mother's face? She wanted to know what her mother had seen.

In the dark living room, Emily's fingers fumbled for the trunk and touched something freezing. She snatched her hand back, her heart pounding. After a few moments, she realized it was simply the metal latch she had touched. There was nothing to be afraid of.

The lid gave a terrible groan when she pushed it open. Emily winced and listened for the sound of anyone waking up. But there was only silence.

As she peered into the trunk, she seemed to see something move in the darkness. She hesitated, then reached down and felt for the silk cover of the photo album. She had the eerie sense that anything could emerge, provoked by her prodding. A white hand, torn and decayed. A ghostly face, smiling back. But it was none of these that made her scream. It was the feel of hair, unmistakably human, beneath her fingertips.

And a woman's voice at her ear.

"What are you doing?"

It was her mother's voice at her ear. It was her mother's face staring down at her. It took Emily a few moments to realize she wasn't an apparition.

"I couldn't sleep," Emily said. She didn't know how else to explain herself before those disapproving eyes.

"It's time for bed," Mom said. "Not the time to go searching for things in the dark."

Emily slunk off to bed. She often felt frustrated by how carefully her mother watched her. When she was younger, her mother wouldn't let her out of her sight. Once, Emily had gotten lost in the mall, following another woman she mistook for her mother. She must have been about six or seven then, and her sense of certainty had been shaken ever since she found out about her mother's twin. So Emily had followed the woman halfway across the mall before she realized that it wasn't her mother. It was someone she had never seen before in her life. A total stranger.

She could still remember the utter panic that had gripped her. She tried to retrace her steps back to the store, but nothing looked familiar to her then. And the strangeness cast a dizzying sheen on everything.

Then, suddenly, arms wrapped around her.

"I thought I'd lost you," her mother whispered. "I thought I'd lost you." There were tears in her eyes.

Mom always acted as though the moment Emily was out of sight, she'd disappear forever. Now that Emily was older, her mother allowed her to wander the conservation land that bordered the edge of their yard but expected her to be back home on the dot. Emily couldn't imagine how her mother would react if she stayed out later. It was suffocating.

Sometimes, Emily wondered what kind of childhood her mother might have had, and if they would have been friends. Would they have been able to get along growing up together? But her mother was much too fearful—fearful in ways Emily didn't understand.

EMILY WOKE EARLY. She had slept fitfully all night, and her dreams were filled with visions of ghosts with long black hair and white robes floating all around them.

She went down into the living room, where Grandma was already watching a television show.

"Where'd the trunk go?" Emily asked, looking around.

"Come watch your aunt's latest show with me," Grandma said.

Emily peered into the kitchen and the dining room, but she couldn't find any trace of the trunk. She knew her grandmother couldn't have moved it. It was far too heavy for her. But could her mother have moved the trunk all by herself? And where would she have moved such a heavy trunk to, and what was it she didn't want Emily to see?

"Stop scampering about," Grandma said. "Bring me some tea."

Emily did as her grandmother asked. After handing over a cup of tea, Emily sat down on the couch. She'd have to investigate where her mother had hidden the trunk some other time. When no one was watching her.

AUNT HONG'S NEW television show wasn't as good as her previous ones, Emily thought. The plot was too predictable and saccharine. Aunt Hong didn't even have a major role in this one and calling it a supporting role might have also been too generous.

On the television, the camera panned over a Chinese opera house. Her aunt, wearing a silk blue shawl around her shoulders, walked with a businessman into the theater. They settled into their seats. The lights dimmed.

An opera singer with a painted face emerged on stage. Gongs sounded. Cymbals clashed. The singer opened with a wail. It sounded like a sad song, but Emily wasn't sure. She always found it hard to interpret whether Chinese opera songs were meant to be happy or sad. She couldn't pick out the words they were saying or recognize the storylines like Grandma could. At times, the sound of laughter, to her ears, seemed too similar to the sound of sobbing. The singer hid her face behind her sleeve.

Grandma always enjoyed watching Chinese operas whenever they played on TV. During the times when an opera was on, even Dad—who usually scoffed at any sort of television show—would stand in the doorway of the living room and watch. Emily knew his parents had once been performers themselves, putting on plays for the public. But he wouldn't tell her about the plays, whether they were happy or sad, or if he had acted, too.

But even if he had performed as a child, Emily couldn't ever imagine her father in a comedic role. She couldn't see him ever playing the fool. When he picked her up from school, he never cracked jokes or made plans to get together with the other parents. He only ever introduced himself by full name and profession, with a challenge in his voice. No one took himself more seriously than her father. Sometimes, Emily wondered why he couldn't be like the other fathers—the ones she saw on TV who were always laughing. Even his laughter had an edge of anger.

Mom came downstairs just as the television faded to black. "You two are up early," she said.

Emily searched her mother's face, but her mother avoided meeting her eyes. Instead, Mom told them she was taking their guest sightseeing in Boston.

"Let's go together," Mom said. She met Emily's gaze then. Though she smiled, there was that same sadness in them. The one that had appeared when she looked at the photograph. In the daylight, Emily saw it clearer than ever.

DURING THE SUMMER, Boston was full of crowds—tourists and students on break and families visiting for colleges. But once they stepped through the gates of the Granary Burying Ground, the noise of the city seemed to fall away. It was always peaceful in the cemetery, due in part to the buildings that enclosed it on three sides. There was something eerie about the way the tombstones were tilted this way and that, almost as if its occupants belowground had tried to push their way out.

When Emily had been to the cemetery for the very first time, she had thought that all the witches had been buried there. That's what they used to do around here, she knew, hang people for witchcraft. Later, she realized the witches weren't buried here. And, in fact, likely hadn't been witches after all. That's why they were probably ghosts now. Grandma had told her all about the hungry ghosts who wandered the earth, restless and angry. They were the ones who died unjustly, who still had so much left to do. In death, they'd have abilities denied to them in life. They'd be able to cast curses upon their enemies. They'd be able to walk among the living, unseen and unnoticed. Emily hoped she might become one.

Perhaps it was the hair of a hungry ghost she had felt the night before. In the darkness, the trunk had seemed a tomb.

Mom pointed out the famous graves, navigating deftly between the leaning headstones. There was a tour group in the cemetery, too, led by a man dressed in breeches and a tricorn hat.

"Charming," her uncle said, watching the tour guide. He was struck, he explained, by how much of Boston had been preserved throughout history. Not like in China, where so much of the past had been destroyed in the last hundred years. When attempts at preservation failed, construction companies were charged with recreating historic buildings so everyone could have a sense of the past. But attempts at recreation often ended up with buildings and neighborhoods that looked more like they came out of movie sets than history.

"When we were children," Mom said to him, "everyone wanted to forget the past."

"We had all sorts of different ways to do so," Uncle said in agreement. "My father sent me abroad to London, and you came here."

A flash of hurt crossed Mom's face.

"But maybe they were right after all," Uncle said. "Better to look toward the future. Toward progress." He repeated the word *progress* again, and it seemed to energize him. "It's what will keep us from repeating our past mistakes. Don't you agree, Sister?"

Emily looked at her mother, but she had brought a camera up to her face. What stared back at Emily was a lens, dark and gigantic.

IN THE BOSTON Public Garden, the four of them took a swan boat ride around the lagoon. Willows wept along the edges of the water. Grandma gazed out at the lake, but her face had softened, and Emily knew she wasn't really seeing any of it. Neither the glimmering ripples nor the turtles that sunned themselves on the large rock where the shoreline bent. No, Emily knew that look in her grandmother's eyes well. She was thinking of the past.

There was a pond behind the house where she grew up, Grandma had once told her. "The waters there were deep and cool in the summer and froze over in the most beautiful panels of ice in the winter," her Grandma had said. "Some years, the water glittered with the flashing scales of fish. Other years—harder ones—the water was still. But one could always find a fish or two swimming inside, even when the water was low and muddy. Those survivors were my playmates, Emily, when the other children weren't."

"Why didn't they want to play with you?" Emily had asked.

"Well, I was motherless for some time. Before regaining one." Grandma touched the scar on her chest, as if it pained her still.

Emily didn't understand. How could you gain a mother after losing one? Once you lost her, she was gone forever. But her grandmother never explained. It was another mystery Emily couldn't puzzle through.

AS THEY WALKED through the garden, Emily's uncle fell into step beside her.

"So your grandmother tells me you want to be a doctor," Uncle said.

"Not really," Emily said. She knew it was her grandmother's dream for her to go into the medical field. Her own grandfather, Grandma had once explained, had been a respected doctor, and she hoped Emily might follow in his footsteps.

"Wouldn't that be nice?" Grandma had asked.

However, Emily couldn't stand the sight of blood. Once, she had skinned her knee terribly jumping off a swing. The gravel had been embedded so deeply, it felt as if it had cut to the bone. The wound was a mess of red flesh, and Emily had felt like throwing up all the way to the hospital. When the doctor had cleaned her knee and sewn it up, Emily couldn't watch as the needle went in and out of her skin. The thread, the doctor explained, would dissolve by itself.

Emily was repulsed by the whole process. The local anesthetic they had given her made her feel like her body wasn't her own. She had imagined a phantom pain the entire time, and it had lasted long after her knee had healed and the thread dissolved. And by that time, Emily knew she never wanted to set foot in a hospital again—not if she could help it.

"What do you want to be instead?" her uncle asked.

Emily shrugged. "What do you do?" she asked.

"I suppose you could say I'm building a better technological future for China."

"What does that mean?"

Uncle laughed a little and apologized. He was so used to explaining his project to investors and consultants, he said, that he forgot how he sounded at times. "It means I'm working on high speed trains."

Emily had heard about the trains from the Chinese news programs Grandma watched all day long. Their construction would cost billions, Emily knew. Sacrifices had to be made, and land reappropriated from families who had lived on that land for decades and more. But the price was worth it, everyone seemed to agree. "How long will they take to build?" she asked.

"A couple of years," he said. "By the time we're done, people will be able to go from Beijing to Nanjing in a few hours."

"Will they look like regular trains?" Emily asked.

"A little sleeker," he said, "to reduce the friction, but the inside will basically be the same. You'll still have seats and windows you can look out of to watch the world rush by."

It sounded nice to Emily. It sounded almost like how she felt sitting in her makeshift tree house in the woods of the conservation land. She would lie on her stomach and peer over the edge of the platform to watch people on the trails below come and go. But no matter how much she observed them, people never seemed to make much sense to her. What made them love each other with such passion? What made them stay? Once, she had watched a young couple kiss against a tree. They held one another tightly as if they would never let go. The next week, they returned but no longer kissed. Instead, their voices echoed angrily through the woods.

"What did you go to London for?" she asked.

"For college," he answered. "My father was disappointed in many ways by what China had become. What the country had put our family through. He was hoping that I would become a professor. That I would stay there and build a life."

"But you liked China better?"

"I don't know if liking it has anything to do with it," he said. "There's something about one's motherland that makes it hard to stay away." He smiled. "Maybe seeing its flaws is what gives me hope for the future."

As they walked among the roses in the Public Garden, her uncle told her his vision for China. Not only of the trains speeding past like shooting stars, but also of the shiny new apartment buildings that would rise up from sprawling cities. The subways, too, would fly by seamlessly underground. Machines would till the land and harvest truckloads of vegetables and fruits. No one would ever go hungry ever again.

Her uncle's words were so vivid that Emily could see it all in her mind. She liked hearing his stories about the future, maybe even more than her grandma's stories about the past—which always raised more questions than answers. Like the one she had told her the week before. The one about the princess and the dragon.

"Once, there was a land guarded by an ancient dragon," Grandma had said. "Near the mountains of this land, a young, handsome man fell and hurt his leg. He was rescued by the daughter of a famous doctor, who saved him from the brink of death. Over the passing weeks, she cared for him, patient and devoted. When he was well enough, he set off to return to his home. Before he left, he promised he would return to marry her and asked for her to wait for him. She agreed, for they were in love—the kind of love they sing songs about. Days passed, then months. The young woman gave birth to a daughter who brought her joy. Everywhere she went, she'd call her daughter her little tiger. That was how proud she was to be a mother. Her brothers told her to forget about the young man. Her parents wanted to marry her off. Still, she waited for him, trusting in his return—even as the ancient dragon began to stir."

"And then?" Emily asked, after Grandma had fallen silent.

"Then, they were married," Grandma said. "And the three of them were a perfect family. They were happy together, Emily. Believe me."

"What about the dragon?" Emily asked much later—after it had occurred to her.

But of the dragon, Grandma said nothing more.

Forever Red

Two DAYS LATER, Mom sent Uncle off to the airport. He would be going to a conference in DC for a week and then returning to Beijing, where he lived. Emily was sorry to see him go. She enjoyed hearing his stories of China.

"How come my mom doesn't have stories like yours?" she asked while watching him pack.

"Oh, she has more stories than you can imagine," her uncle said.

"Only Grandma tells me any stories, and I don't even understand them half the time."

"I suppose the kinds of stories your mother has aren't the ones that are easy for her to tell," he said.

"What do you mean?" asked Emily.

"Well," he said, "we were the ones who survived. The ones who lived through so many changes. The ones tossed about by history, like leaves in the wind. Sometimes, the past isn't easy to remember. Sometimes, it's best to move on." He smiled. "That's what most of the ones who left China were trying to do. In all different kinds of ways."

"How come Aunt Hong never came over?" Emily asked.

"That I don't know," her uncle said. "You'll have to ask her."

Emily remembered meeting her aunt when she was nine. Aunt Hong flew from China to shoot on location in New York and had squeezed three days out of her schedule to visit them in Massachusetts. When her aunt arrived, she had held Emily in her arms. But it wasn't long before Emily squirmed away. It was a version of her mother that was not her own. A more glamorous version, with rouged lips and cheeks and hair that was curled in beautiful waves down her back.

The strangeness stayed with her, but there was reassurance, too. Emily realized she would never be able to mistake her aunt for her mother. Even their mannerisms were different. Aunt Hong's smiles lit up the whole room, and her laughter rang out like a bell. In comparison, her mother felt like a paper version of her sister. A kind of backdrop to her sister's illumination.

"When are you planning on settling down?" Grandma had asked Aunt Hong.

Her aunt had blushed then. The pinkening of her cheeks made her look even more youthful, and a smile crept across her lips.

"So you have found someone," Grandma said, knowingly. "Then what's the holdup? You should hurry up and get married soon."

"Don't you know you can't get married in show business?" Aunt Hong had shot back with a wry smile.

The two sisters were different in spirit. And now, after talking with her uncle, Emily realized there was yet another difference between them. One had stayed in China, and the other had left.

EMILY TRIED TO imagine leaving everything behind. First, she'd have to say goodbye to her family. Her mother, grandmother, and father.

Then, she'd have to say goodbye to her home. Her bedroom. Her dresses hanging up in the closet. The dark spots scattered like moles across her dresser mirror. The summer light on the windowsill. Perhaps even herself. Shedding her memories one by one as she walked toward another country.

And then she imagined another version of herself. The version of herself who was the daughter of someone who stayed. A daughter who grew up in China. Who might that girl have been?

GRANDMA AND MOM drove Uncle to the airport. For the first time since her uncle had arrived, Emily was alone in the house. As soon as the sound of the car faded away into the distance, Emily began searching for the trunk. It was so large that she was confident she'd be able to find it. And indeed, she found the trunk shoved into a little crawlspace in the basement, behind some old paintings and picture frames.

She quickly flipped the bronze latch. Even if there was a hungry ghost hidden somewhere inside, her curiosity won out over her fear. Once the lid was open, Emily began rifling through the trunk. The animal smell, as strange as it was, had become familiar now and a little comforting.

Some of the contents seemed like junk—spare buttons, used-up spools of thread, old blouses, letters on the verge of falling apart. There were pages and pages of these letters, all written with neat, tidy characters. Emily shifted a few of the letters aside. At the bottom, she found a little bell and lifted it. She gave the bell a shake, but it didn't ring. The clapper was stuck and rusted over. She set it aside and continued searching.

But the photo album she'd seen last time was missing. Instead, Emily lifted out a silk handkerchief folded into a square. When she examined the handkerchief, she discovered embroidered red clouds all along the border. She could tell it was the same handkerchief as the one Grandma had given her, for it was still stained with mud and dirt. When Emily carefully unfolded it, a lock of hair fell into her lap.

The lock of hair was bound together with black thread on one end, while the other end fanned out. It was about the length of a handspan, and most of the hairs were a dark gray. She placed it in the palm of her hand and stroked her fingers along its length. Was this what she had felt that night? Emily wondered who it had belonged to, and why her grandmother must have wrapped it up so tenderly in the handkerchief. Did it belong to her grandmother's mother?

Emily set the handkerchief and lock of hair aside, along with its mystery, and looked again for the photo album. After half an hour, she had to admit defeat. She had turned the trunk over from top to bottom. The album was nowhere to be found.

Disappointed, she put the lock of hair back in the trunk. She held on to the handkerchief. It had been hers once, and it was of no use to anyone tucked away. She folded it up and placed it in her pocket.

BUT A FEW days later, the photo album turned up. It wasn't Emily who found it. It was her father. His angry voice woke her up, and she got out of bed to see what was wrong. She passed by Grandma's closed door and followed the yelling to her parents' bedroom. It was still early—barely morning—and the sun was cold and pale. Through the open door, Emily could see her mother sitting quietly on the bed. She was looking down at the album in her lap as if she were a child. In her right hand, she held a photograph. She didn't seem to be listening to what Dad was saying.

She would be happy if he hurried up and died, wouldn't she? That's what she wanted, all these years. His eyes were fixed on Mom.

"What's going on?" Emily asked.

"Go back to your room," her father snapped.

At this, Mom roused herself, and she stood up.

Dad lunged forward and snatched at the photograph in her hand, tearing it in half. One half fell to the ground. Mom drew in a sharp breath. She started forward, as if she were going to pick it up.

But his word stopped her.

"Don't you dare," he said.

Mom stared at him for a long time. Then, she turned around and grabbed Emily by the hand.

"Let's go," she said.

"Where are you going?" Dad asked.

"Out."

"When will you be back?" he asked. Although his words were filled with anger, there was a hint of pleading in his voice.

"I don't know," her mother said.

EMILY AND HER mother were silent in the car. Emily was too afraid to ask her mother where they were going. Her mother gripped the steering wheel tighter and tighter, until her knuckles turned white. But soon, Emily recognized the winding road her mother was taking. They were heading toward the flower nursery in the nearby town of Harvard.

The twenty-acre plot where the nursery was located had been a riding stable before her mother's friend, Rebecca, bought it five years back. Since then, Rebecca had torn down the rings and transformed the grounds into a garden center and apple orchard. Every fall, around Thanksgiving, children climbed into horse-drawn wagons for hayrides across the fields.

But Mom liked the nursery best for its roses. When Rebecca had first started the garden center—after her divorce—she had begun breeding roses of her own. Mom had always marveled over the hybrids that Rebecca produced. She wouldn't sell the roses she bred. She kept the nursery well-stocked with the classics instead—Mr. Lincolns, Earth Angels, Boscobels. But every year, without fail, Rebecca would gift one of her hybrids to Mom.

"It's nice to get out, isn't it?" Mom said. Her hands loosed on the wheel.

Emily agreed. Sunlight flickered on the dash. Maple trees lined both sides of the road, which was empty and quiet.

Her mother turned on the radio. "Your father's just been tired lately," she said suddenly, over the music. "Because of work." He worked hard for the family, Mom always said. It was the picture she painted to outsiders.

Emily's mood soured. She jabbed her finger at the button to roll down her window. The wind whistled through the car, sweeping away Mom's voice.

"THESE BLOOMED JUST this morning, May," Rebecca said, gesturing to the pots of roses on the ground. Rebecca was a few years older than Mom, though the carefree way she carried herself seemed more youthful. She and Mom had been seatmates on their first plane ride to the States from China. The both of them had come over, along with their families, in the early nineties, in that wave of students who had been disillusioned and disappointed. Many of them settled in Boston, and Mom had adopted the English name May, for the month she had arrived.

"They're incredible," Mom said, admiringly. Emily could always sense a tone of admiration in her mother's voice whenever she spoke to Rebecca.

"I thought so, too." Rebecca reached out and fingered a deep red bloom. "I bred it for vigorous growth and strong disease resistance. You could even grow it as a climber. If you don't keep an eye on it, it'll take over everything. And the fragrance—" Rebecca leaned down and placed her face close to the bloom. "Here, smell for yourself."

Mom leaned down to press her nose against the petals. She looked up in surprise. "Like lemons."

"Yes, and honey, too, beneath the myrrh. The coloring belongs to the father, but the fragrance is all the mother's."

Mom leaned down again. 'What are you calling this one?"

"I was thinking 'Forever Red.'" Rebecca looked at Mom out of the corner of her eye.

Mom straightened up. Her eyes were wide. She looked as if she wanted to say something but didn't. Instead, she burst into tears.

"I'm sorry," Rebecca said, looking worried.

"I'm just being silly," Mom said. "I'm honored." She tried to compose herself. "Thank you."

Emily decided to give the two of them some privacy, so she wandered off, making a slow loop of the nursery. Emily knew that her mother was born at the height of the Cultural Revolution and that her name, Yonghong, meant "forever red." She shared the red of Hongxing's name—they were twins, after all, Grandma said.

By the time Mom was born, Grandma said, the dragons that flew across the skies were not the ones setting fires. Instead, the fires burned because of the Red Guards, who marched in the streets. They had such hopes for the children, then, Grandma had said. In their righteousness. They were sure the children would be the ones to unify the country. To heal the old, festering wounds.

When Emily completed her loop, her mother and Rebecca were still speaking to one another in low voices.

"I fought with Aiguo again," Mom said to Rebecca. "I just don't know what to do."

Rebecca listened sympathetically.

"Sometimes, I wish I'd never married him."

At her mother's confession, Emily's eyes widened. She hid herself out of sight behind a pair of cypresses.

"Everyone feels regret from time to time," Rebecca said. "No one knows that better than me."

"But I never loved him," Mom said. "And I don't think I ever could. Not in the same way—" She broke off.

There was a pause. Then, Rebecca bent her head closer. "The same way you loved someone else . . . ?" she offered.

Mom began to cry again. Emily felt as though she was witnessing something she wasn't supposed to. She quickly turned and walked away toward the fields on the outskirts of the nursery.

As Emily picked her way to the wagon at the center of the field, a numbness spread over her entire body. She had always believed her mother and father were college sweethearts. Once, after having had a bit of wine, Mom had even told her the story. Dad had gotten into a fight with a fellow college student, and Mom had found him bleeding from the mouth. She pulled a handkerchief from her pocket. He had thanked her then and looked at her. (Here, in the telling of the story, Mom stopped and smiled.)

Emily often wondered about the moment of the meeting of eyes, the pulse rising in the underside of the wrist. She had always thought her mother had loved her father—more, even, than he had ever loved her. At least, it always seemed that way. The tenderness with which Mom treated him. The anger she received in turn. Emily felt a sense of guilt, which slowly built to anger. If her mother never loved him, why had she married him? Why had she built a family with him? Why had she had Emily? Now, Emily's birth felt like proof of some wrongness—some kind of mistake—of the past.

"WHERE DID YOU GO?" Dad demanded when they got back, peering at the both of them with his blue eyes. He was standing in the doorway of the garage, his arms crossed over his chest. He fixed his eyes on the potted rose in Emily's arms. "Don't you have enough?" he asked Mom.

"Rebecca gave it to me," Mom said softly, walking up to the door.

Dad's mouth tightened.

Emily set the pot down on the workbench in the garage. Her father watched her disapprovingly as she unwrapped the shiny vinyl paper from around the pot. Already, one of the buds was falling off, and its colors seemed dull and flattened. Would the rose bloom like Rebecca had promised? Emily hoped it would grow and grow into a wall of thorns, keeping her mother safe behind it.

When Emily went to throw away the packaging, she found pieces of the torn photograph in the trash. Carefully, she collected the pieces in her hands and brought them up to her room.

AT NIGHT, in bed, she turned on a flashlight and pulled the covers over her head. She laid out the pieces of the photograph before her and slowly put them back together. When she was finished, there was a gap in the middle—a piece she hadn't pulled out of the trash. She taped the photograph together as best as she could. It was an old photograph, yellowing, curling at the edges. Within the frame, her mother smiled out at her in black and white. She must have been a teenager, Emily guessed, from her bookish outfit and shoulder-length hair. Beside her stood a young man. He leaned against the railing of a bridge with a grin. He had a friendly, open air about him. Half of his face was missing in the gap, but Emily could tell he was not her father nor her uncle.

Emily flipped the photograph over. On the back were handwritten characters in Chinese she couldn't recognize—other than her mother's name. Her mother's name had been traced over, again and again, so that each stroke was dark and bold. Emily could tell it had not been done out of anger, but love.

The Birthmark That Was Also a Scar

WHENEVER IT RAINED, Grandma would always tell Emily that Leigong must be making a fuss up in the heavens.

As the god of thunder, Leigong punished evildoers down on earth with strikes of his hammer and his drum. But his justice was imperfect, Emily knew. He struck in darkness after all. He didn't care if his strikes were true or false. He only cared for vengeance. His wife was the one who brought the light. She used her mirrors to reflect lightning across the skies.

Emily watched as the rain fell relentlessly. She pressed her cheek against the window.

"What are you sighing for?" Grandma asked, sitting in her recliner in the living room. She was still watching Aunt Hong's new show, Emily noticed. It was the third time she had watched the show since Uncle brought her the DVD last summer. Emily caught a glimpse of familiar dark eyes before the scene changed to a snowy landscape.

"Didn't you just watch this episode?" Emily asked. She remembered seeing the exact scene in the morning. Suddenly, the scene changed, and the character her aunt played darted behind a tree.

"It's my favorite," Grandma said.

"All of the scenes with Aunt in them are your favorite," Emily said wryly.

"This scene about love I like the most."

On the screen, there was a wedding. A woman and man crossed their arms and drank from each other's wine cups. Grandma leaned forward in her recliner, her eyes fixed on the figures moving across the screen. "Come here," she said, pointing to the television. "Watch."

But Emily couldn't focus on the show. There was a storm raging on inside the house as well. The dark cloud of her father's mood filled every corner.

Lately, Dad had started coming home early and cutting back his hours. He would enter without a word and throw his bag down on the counter. Often, he'd call out for Emily to make him some tea or to tell Grandma to turn down the television. When her mother returned from work, his eyes would follow her wherever she went. There was a haunted look in his gaze. In the past year, he had become thin and gaunt. Even his hair turned gray. The blackness of each strand seemed to have washed out, like a drop of ink in water.

ON GRANDMA'S SEVENTY-SEVENTH birthday, Mom took her and Emily to the Peabody Essex Museum in nearby Salem to see an old Chinese house built over two hundred years ago. A girls' trip, Mom had said on the ride over. The sky was a dull, flat gray when Mom pulled into the parking garage.

Inside the museum, there was a quiet hum of voices. After picking up the audio guides at the front desk, Mom led Grandma and Emily through the main atrium toward Yin Yu Tang, the family home from China that had been carefully disassembled, piece by piece, and then reassembled in its entirety.

Emily held the audio guide up to her ear as she walked through the main courtyard. The audio guide took them through the entire house, leading them through all the rooms. Generations of one family had lived in the house, she learned. Each room was preserved in the way the family might have used it. In the kitchen, a cupboard was half open, revealing beautiful blue-and-white bowls inside. In a bedroom, a poster of Chairman Mao was pasted on the wall.

This is where the head of the family slept, the audio guide informed her. Notice the wallpaper from Europe. Notice the signs of each era in history. And here, on the wall, is a poster from the Cultural Revolution— bright and striking. At a time when Chairman Mao was your father and the nation your family, these kinds of posters took the place of family photographs.

"There's your father's name," Grandma said, pointing to the poster. "Aiguo. It was a common name back then."

Ai, Emily knew, was for "love," and *guo* for "country." China was *zhong gou*—the "country at the center of the world"— and America was *mei gou*—the "beautiful country." Her father's name was "the love of one's country." Jack, however, was his second name. Once, Emily had asked him how he had gone about choosing an English name, and he had shrugged. Like so much else, Emily had to fill in the past with her imagination. She liked to imagine that he had chosen it while studying English nursery rhymes.

On the second floor, Emily turned down a narrow hallway and looked out through the carved window. In the shady courtyard below, visitors milled around, stopping from time to time to peer into a room or examine the details of the dark wooden beams and paneling.

Emily walked further down the hallway and slipped into another bedroom. There was an ornate moon bed pushed up against one wall, and a desk and chair against another wall. A silk duvet covered the bed, though the pillow was slightly askew. Who would have slept in the bed so many years ago? And who might have sat at that desk and written a letter to send to someone far away? Emily imagined figures sitting, standing, lying down. She imagined the barest profile of a face, turned ever so slightly away.

"Isn't this place wonderful?" Grandma asked. She walked around the room without waiting for Emily's answer. "I grew up in a house similar to this one. Not as luxurious, of course, but it also had a courtyard in the center," she said. "It was my grandparents' house." She focused on the items on the desk and examined them carefully. There were books scattered across the table, along with a calligraphy brush and inkstone.

"Sometimes," Grandma said, "I wonder if my father also grew up in a house like this."

"He never told you?" Emily asked.

"I never knew him," Grandma said. "He died before I was born."

Emily was taken aback. She had never known that about her grand-mother. Had always just assumed she had grown up with her father and mother.

"How did he die?" Emily asked.

"In the revolution," Grandma said. "My mother always told me he had the most beautiful handwriting." She reached out a hand, almost touch-ing the brush on the table. "My mother raised me by herself—though I only knew her for much of my childhood as my older sister. I was her little sister, her mei mei. Her family passed me off as a cousin's child. They had hoped she might be able to remarry one day, and her chances would have been slim as a single mother." Grandma paused, before continuing. "But, she never remarried. I grew to admire her for that. I, too, wanted to find that kind of everlasting love—with someone who wasn't ashamed to call me theirs."

"When did you find out she was your mother?" Emily asked.

Grandma frowned. "She didn't tell me until I was nine years old, when we were fleeing Japanese soldiers." She shook her head. "I suppose she thought it would comfort me, but it only made me confused and resentful. And eventually, I would have figured it out myself—seeing how she gave me this." Grandma gestured to the birthmark on her chest, which was also a scar.

"The birthmark?"

Grandma thought for a moment. "A stain that can't be denied. She tried to cut it out of me, once. I remember it, even though I was a baby. I think I'll always remember it."

Grandma turned abruptly. She walked out into the hallway and down the stairs. Emily followed her. They stood in the open courtyard, listening to their audio guides in silence. Grandma tilted her head back and closed her eyes.

And here are the fishponds that once might have been teeming with flashing golden carp.

Now, there was only water, still and dark.

THERE WAS A bottle of wine in her classmate's hands.

"Where'd you get that from?" Emily asked. Everyone else seemed to be drinking out of beer bottles or colorful aluminum cans.

"It's a secret," Alice said, mischievously. They had become friends over the past year, as they had been assigned seats next to one another in homeroom. Alice was the one who had invited Emily to a party on the banks of Walden Pond. Being a freshman, Emily had never gone before, though she knew it was a tradition among the students in her high school to host a party at the start of the school year.

The day was already darkening, and someone passed out handfuls of sparklers. Around them, flames traveled slowly down in bursts of little stars. Alice twisted off the cap and sniffed at the dark red liquid. "Want to try?" She passed it over to Emily.

The wine smelled bitter. It reminded Emily of the medicine her grandma had made her once as a child. The medicine had been black then, and thick and syrupy, whereas the wine flowed like blood. Emily tilted back her head as she took a sip, and then another.

Emily could feel her heart pulsing in her throat. Her cheeks warmed, and the flush spread all the way through her body, starting from her chest. The skin around her eyebrows throbbed. It was still tender from earlier, when she had plucked the hairs of her brows for the first time.

"You got a lighter?" another girl asked. "The one Jackson has is broken."

Alice dug into her bag and pulled out a lighter. She got up and followed the girl to where the others had built a pile of kindling. Emily watched as Alice flicked open her lighter. Her small flame burned slowly down a twig.

Emily dug her hands into the sand. Around her, the laughter was growing louder. The voices, more raucous. Someone started playing music. The song seemed to come from the fire itself, though Emily knew it didn't. Someone leapt into the lake. Another followed.

From the distance, there came a whistling sound, soaring higher and higher. A lone firework exploded in the sky—red and white sparkles smudging against the night.

Alone, Emily could hear the waters of the lake colliding with the banks. She got up, sand sticking to the back of her thighs, and walked along the shoreline. The banks grew rockier—rougher beneath her sandals. She stumbled over a boulder—perhaps the wine had gotten to her head, more than she realized—and sat down, extending her legs into the water. Some weeds were clinging wetly to her ankle, which she tried to pick off. Emily watched her legs move around in the water. They were just dark shapes, like snakes swimming up to the surface.

Someone was setting off fireworks again. A whole burst of them. Emily leapt into the water, and instantly, she was chilled all over except where the wine had touched the inside of her throat.

Emily swam deeper. Bubbles escaped from her nose, her mouth. They floated up in a ribbon of air. Underwater, the human body moved slower, subject to the currents.

Swimming at night, there was just the sound of water and her own breath. Across the lake, she could still see figures moving, the edges of their bodies illuminated. The darkness was shimmering now. She felt, suddenly, sorry she had come. She wanted to rewind the evening like one of her aunt's tapes, the actors undoing all their work:

Alice's lighter snaps shut. Emily brings the wine bottle up to her lips. The wine rises through her body. Emily hands it back to Alice. The shimmer runs up the sparklers, instead of down. The sky lightens. Emily stands up from the sand, walks backwards to the parking lot. She gets into Alice's car, which speeds back to Emily's home. Emily keeps her eyes open. Her cheeks dry again. Alice parks her car in the driveway and opens her door. Dad stands on the lawn, Emily's name returning to his lips. He lowers his arm. Emily and Dad return to the house. The front door slams shut. . . .

No, rewind it even further. Rewind through the past, rewind through her father calling her ungrateful. Through him demanding she stay home to keep him company. Through his raised voice, leaping back down his throat. . . . Rewind farther back. Back through all the beginnings. Through a torn photograph, reassembling. Through a wooden trunk returning over land and sea. Through a handkerchief passed from hand to hand. Through a scar on the chest, unwounding. Through another father rising out of the fire. Through a revolution.

What Is Inherited

WHEN EMILY RETURNED from Walden Pond, her mother was waiting for her in the darkness.

"Where were you?" she asked. Her voice was filled with anger.

"I told you," Emily said. "I went swimming with friends."

"We were supposed to spend the day together. All of us."

Emily stared in her direction. She could only make out the vague outline of her mother's shape, sitting on the couch. She didn't understand why her mother still wanted to pretend. They weren't happy. None of them were.

"Why would I want to be stuck at home?" Emily demanded.

"He's your father," Mom said.

"Why?"

"What do you mean?"

"Who was the man in the photo?" When her mother didn't answer, Emily lowered her voice. "The one you loved?"

At that, her mother turned her face away. The both of them stayed silent for a long time, a silence that crystallized between them. Her mother was the first to speak again.

"Your father loves you," she said.

"It doesn't feel like it."

There was another pause. "When he was young," Mom said quietly, "the Red Guards came to his house and burned down everything. His parents died in the fire. Afterward, he was sent to the care of a distant relative who treated him more like a servant than a son." Mom shook her head. "So you see," she said, "he doesn't really know what it's like to be part of a family."

But the story only infuriated Emily. "You're just making excuses."

"Maybe I am," she admitted. "But, you don't have much time left together. He's sick, Emily."

Emily peered at her mother's face in alarm. "Sick, how?"

"Lung cancer." Mom closed her eyes.

Emily tried to process what she had heard, but the words rang emptily in her head.

"When I decided to marry him," Mom said, "I was certain he would never die. Never leave me. I was certain his anger would keep him alive." She sighed. "How wrong I was," she said.

IN THE SUMMER, the waterline dropped to the lowest that Emily ever remembered. A brown sandy strip ran around the edge of the lake. Emily wandered down the trails of the conservation land, going further than she had ever gone. Past the tall pines and the large gray boulder. Past the unmarked paths through the slant of evening light.

But no matter how far she walked, she could not escape her father's body. She witnessed him in the desiccated berries clinging to the branch, in the black mud at the edges of a brackish puddle. She felt the weakness of his muscles in the papery bark she peeled from the birches. She heard his breath in a rustling pile of last autumn's leaves.

Once, Emily came across a clump of white mushrooms growing out of a rotting log. Over the span of just a few days, as she retraced her steps along the path, the caps flared out, exposing dark brown gills. A white veil broke away from the underside of the caps. Then, the mushrooms softened and shriveled. Their stems darkened, their caps as well. Soon, the clump collapsed into the ground, and by the next time Emily returned to the log, all traces of the mushrooms had disappeared. She pressed her fingers into the log, which was soft and damp. She brought her face close. It smelled of dirt and decay. The smell lingered in her mind, and her dreams.

WHEN EMILY RETURNED home from her walks, Dad would often be asleep in the bed the hospice nurse had ordered. It was a special kind of bed, with a mattress that would inflate and deflate by itself. The alternating air pressure would help prevent bedsores, the nurse said, though they were inevitable to some degree.

During the rare times Dad was awake and lucid, Emily might sit beside him. She'd listen to the mattress breathe in and out. She didn't know what to say. She had never known what to say when he was healthy. Now that he was dying, words felt even more useless. But Dad didn't require her to say much. In this, he was as consistent as he had ever been.

MOM SPENT HER days on the phone. She called his doctors, the pharmacy, the insurance company. Whenever she was placed on hold, the sound of the music over speakerphone would echo through the house. Often, it was pop or country rock. Other times, it was classical. Once, it was opera, and the sound of a woman's voice seemed to weep from the other end.

"A good doctor is hard to find," Mom would say. "You'll be the best doctor, Emily. I know it." She would smile at Emily with obvious pride. It was one of the few moments that could bring a smile to Mom's face.

BUT EMILY WASN'T planning to become a doctor, despite what her mother and grandmother believed. In her sophomore year of high school, she dropped out of her biology class and took earth science instead. She didn't want to examine the human body anymore. She preferred losing herself in the landscape.

For her final project, Emily conducted a study of animals that lived within the Eastern white pines in the conservation land. She learned what species of squirrels preferred its seeds over others, and what birds liked to nest among its branches. She spent hours in the woods, documenting what she found with a camera and a notebook. Only the present was observable, she reminded herself, again and again.

At times, when she had walked deep enough into the forest, Emily laid herself on the bare earth. She closed her eyes and tried to focus on the sounds of the forest. She counted down from ten and imagined the muscles all over her body relaxing, one by one. First her toes, then her ankles and calves. She imagined all her muscles loosening until she felt as if she couldn't move at all. Until she was a puppet, lying on the ground with her strings cut.

But her mind always drifted back to the past. To the lives of those that had passed before she was born. To the ways that history had already shaped who she was—and who she might become. Once, Grandma had called her birthmark a stain. Only now did Emily understand what she meant. It meant that the past was forever etched into their bodies. That the past could never be escaped.

IT WAS DECEMBER when it happened. The darkest part of the year. In the funeral home, an inescapable compulsion brought Emily to the edge of her father's closed coffin. It reminded her, suddenly, of the trunk that her uncle had brought over from China. The one that had held so many ghosts.

"He loved your mother in his own way," Grandma said, walking up to her. "He was a faithful husband and father."

Emily bit back a retort. She wanted to ask her grandmother if she had ever even liked her father. She wanted to ask what she really thought of her parents' marriage. But Emily stayed silent. She knew she wouldn't get a straight answer.

The Choice She Made

IN HER FIRST year of college, Emily's birthmark began to darken from red to black. She worried at it with her fingers, and soon a rash bloomed across her chest. Hives appeared, then blisters.

"Do you have any family history of skin cancer?" the dermatologist asked.

Emily shook her head. "But many of the women on my mother's side of the family have the same birthmark as me."

"Ah, a hereditary birthmark," the dermatologist noted. "And what about your father?"

"He passed away almost four years ago," Emily said. "Lung cancer." She paused. "But it was likely due to chemical exposure when he was a teenager. He worked in a factory when he was young in the countryside in China." As one of the sent-down youth, she had learned. But no one had told her this. Not her mother or grandmother. Emily had pieced together the story herself from his medical files that she had found the last time she was home.

The dermatologist recommended a biopsy of the birthmark on her chest. He'd give her a shot of local anesthetic to numb the pain before taking a slice of her skin. If she didn't want to undergo the procedure, they could also continue to monitor the mark. The choice was entirely up to her.

"Cut it out," she said.

PART FOUR

BEIJING

2018

What Is Left Behind

"COME VISIT ME at my new place," Xiaoyan cajoled over the phone. "We haven't seen each other since the wedding."

Sprawled across her bed, Hongxing stared up at the light fixture on her ceiling. It was an ugly, dated chandelier, with cups of frosted glass. Ever since she first moved in, a decade ago, Hongxing had been meaning to change it. She had grand plans for her entire apartment and had made improvements, bit by bit. A new chandelier was supposed to be the last, finishing touch. One dripping with crystals that reflected flecks of light all around the room. But after everything that had happened, Hongxing never got around to it. And now it seemed almost fitting that the first thing she should see when she woke up each morning was another sign of her failures.

"It'll be good for you to get some air," Xiaoyan said, somewhat sternly.

And so, Hongxing dutifully made the trek over to Beijing's third ring where Xiaoyan lived, near the embassies. The taxi dropped her off at the entrance of a gated apartment complex—one of the those complexes that was filled more with American expats than locals.

After her wedding last year, Xiaoyan had uprooted all of her belongings in the fourth ring and moved in with her Chinese American husband—the Diplomat—in Chaoyang District. She had given up her career as an actress, too, along with her old apartment. "Well, it's not like I'm giving anything up," Xiaoyan had said with a laugh at the wedding reception. "The roles aren't exactly coming in like they used to." She had given Hongxing a conspiring glance then—the one she always gave whenever they discussed younger actresses or the latest scandal. Hongxing had forced herself to keep smiling and raised her champagne glass.

Xiaoyan's wedding was the last public event she had attended with old colleagues from the industry. The wedding had taken place two months after Hongxing realized she had been erased from public memory by the government. Her name had been stripped from the internet, from the movies and television shows she had acted in. Old friends distanced themselves, and directors stopped calling. Her life's work gone—just like that. All because of how she had loved her. Her, Hongmei.

Hongxing liked to call what had happened her Disappearing Act. The shame had still been fresh and painful. But still, she had made herself go to Xiaoyan's wedding. They had been such good friends, had climbed up together from the early days when they were both naïve and hopeful students at the Beijing Film Academy.

It had been almost four decades since Hongxing had moved to Beijing after her stint in the army. They had been a trio back then—Xiaoyan, Hongmei, and Hongxing—and would stay up all night watching films. During the day, the three of them would take classes and practice reciting lines. In between all of that, Hongxing and Hongmei would steal kisses in the abandoned dance studios of the Film Academy.

They had been young then—with the whole world at their feet. There was no need for money or men—only dreams.

HER NAME, XIAOYAN—MEANING "Little Swallow"—truly suited her. Her parents must have foreseen she would go into show business, for her birth name made a perfect stage name as well. She had gotten a later start than Hongxing after the Academy. She never held it against Hongxing, though, and was always a true friend, through and through. She had gone with Hongxing to see Ma off at the airport when she'd left to help Yonghong take care of Emily. She had helped make arrangements for Ba's funeral so long ago. And Xiaoyan had been there, too, in the days after the Disappearing when everyone else seemed to disappear.

Xiaoyan had always been good to her.

Xiaoyan had married a cinematographer when she turned thirty-eight, but, less than a year later, she divorced him upon discovering he had purchased a house for his mistress. And now, she had remarried and voluntarily retired.

"I am ready to spend the rest of my life enjoying it," she told Hongxing when she arrived at her apartment on the thirty-first floor. Xiaoyan had been in the middle of putting together sandwiches—"American sandwiches, Xing Xing!"—with a panini press she had bought at the Shimao Department Store. Hongxing had never seen her cook before. The thought crossed her mind that Xiaoyan's new life was just another role for her to play. An uncharitable thought, Hongxing admitted to herself. But if it *was* a part, she was playing it perfectly. Even her gestures seemed full of joy.

The Diplomat had been called away on urgent business to the embassy, so the two of them had the apartment all to themselves. Xiaoyan gave her a tour—the first floor, with its balcony overlooking the courtyard; the second floor, with two bedrooms and a sitting area; and the third floor, with its master bedroom. There were only a few pieces of furniture that

Hongxing recognized from Xiaoyan's old life. A lamp here. A nightstand there. A handful of books. The rest were in the latest fashion.

"He thinks he'll be transferred back, maybe even in the next few months," Xiaoyan said as they sipped their cocktails.

"So soon?" Hongxing asked. "But you just moved in."

"Maybe I should call up your sister," Xiaoyan said. "Is she still living in Boston?"

"Just outside the city." Hongxing stared down at the red maraschino cherry at the bottom of her glass. "Are you really thinking of moving to America?" she asked.

Xiaoyan smiled. "Who knows?" she said evasively. "And even if I do, it's not like I won't ever come back."

Hongxing picked the cherry out of her drink and placed it in her mouth. Chewing slowly, she let the sickly sweetness of it curl around her tongue. Most who left, she felt, never came back.

"Don't worry," Xiaoyan said, sensing her disquiet. "We'll always be friends—just like we promised."

Her words provided no comfort. Hongxing had no faith in promises anymore.

THE SUN WAS setting by the time Hongxing left. When she heard the gate creak behind her, she looked back, hoping it was Xiaoyan. But there was no one there to call her back—to ask her to stay a little while longer. Not like in the old days, when there was always some reason or another to linger in each other's company. Now, when Hongxing turned her head, there was only a white cat, slipping out between the bars of the gate.

As Hongxing stood on the corner of the street, a bus came to a shuddering stop in front of her. The doors to the bus opened, and Hongxing moved aside as people got off. There was an advertisement for a movie pasted on the side of the bus. AFTER HEARTBREAK, the movie was called. Hongmei's eyes stared out at her, lined in kohl.

It would be Qingming—Tomb-Sweeping Day—the next day, Hongxing remembered. The day of remembrance for the dead. It was natural for ghosts to come visit you. Ghosts of the dead, and the living.

IT WAS DARK when Hongxing reached her apartment at the edge of the fifth ring. Inside, the kitchen window had been blown wide open by the wind, filling every corner with the chill of the night. As Hongxing closed the window, she saw that someone had painted a new image on the building opposite. An astronaut, descending a long white ladder made of bones.

During Qingming, Wai Po had once explained to Hongxing, the boundaries between the worlds of humans and spirits were at their thinnest. Sometimes, troubled spirits slipped over into our world as well. They could be warded off with prayers and branches of willow. Still, the strongest spirits among them—the most restless—were able to walk among everyone, invisible to most but seen by some.

That night, Hongxing ate dinner alone in her living room. On the television, the newscasters were reporting on the state of things in America. Look at the social unrest, they were saying. Look at the disharmony. The president over there was standing behind a podium, pointing out at the crowd that was a sea of red caps. His words were angry—and full of accusation. The people in the audience cheered wildly. He would change their lives, he promised them. He would raise the nation to great heights. Hongxing turned down the volume. The newscasters were always going on and on about the collapse of American democracy. But it wasn't so different, Hongxing thought, from her childhood. They had worn red then, too, had held red books in their hands. They had placed their fists over their hearts, beating red.

WHEN HONGXING WOKE, her hands were clenched into fists. Her phone was buzzing beneath the pillow. With great effort, she uncurled her stiff and swollen fingers. There was an ache in her hands, running to her shoulder blades. A dancer's fingers, Hongmei had always said, before kissing them tenderly. Outside, it was still dark.

"Hongxing?"

Her back straightened at the sound of her sister's voice. "Yes?" Her voice came out scratchy and hoarse. Hongxing tried again. "It's me."

"I didn't wake you, did I?" Yonghong asked.

"No," Hongxing said.

"It's so late where you are."

"It's fine." Hongxing reached for the glass of water on the nightstand and drank deeply.

Outside, the city had settled into the quiet of the night. A car drove past, its wheels dipping and rising as it rolled over a manhole. A pair of heels clicked down the sidewalk.

The last time they had spoken, six months ago, neither had known what to say. Hongxing hadn't ever told her sister about the Disappearing, but she knew Yonghong must have known about it. In her last few calls prior to this, Yonghong's words had been stilted. She hadn't asked Hongxing about work or her personal life. Instead, they spoke of more general things—the state of the economy in America or the latest corruption scandal in China. It had been more painful to Hongxing than if her sister had simply asked her about what had happened.

Hongxing set the glass firmly down on the table. "Is there something you want?" she asked.

Once, they had known each other better than they knew themselves. Now, Hongxing could only imagine what her sister was up to. Perhaps she was looking out her window, too, at the expanse of sky. One sister under the sun, the other in darkness.

"Ma—" Yonghong said. She hesitated, her soft breathing resonating over the line. "Ma wants to see you."

"Ma?" Hongxing asked, frowning at the strange tone in her sister's voice. A sense of dread was creeping in. "Did something happen?"

Somewhere outside, in the darkness, the heels were clicking again, as if they had never stopped. Soon, they would be at Hongxing's door. Maybe they already were.

"She hasn't been doing well," Yonghong finally said. "She's asking for you."

A House Made of Paper

MA HAD NEVER fully recovered from the bout of pneumonia last winter. The doctor's report that Yonghong sent over WeChat described in clinical detail the deterioration of her lungs as a result of her illness. Her blood pressure had also flared up. Ma was beginning to talk to people who were long dead and buried and see places and buildings that no longer existed. It was time to start thinking about making her comfortable, was how the doctor had put it to Yonghong.

Twenty years earlier, Hongxing had done the same for their father, whose condition after open-heart surgery had taken an unexpected turn. Doctors had been optimistic about his recovery, and so Hongxing had not called Yonghong or their mother to inform them about the surgery. It was what Ba had wished for anyway, telling her not to worry them.

Later, Hongxing thought that if she had been a better daughter—a kinder, more forgiving one—she would have gone against his wishes, and they might have all been able to see one another one last time. But, instead, Ba had passed with only her beside him, watching the last fall of his chest.

BUT BA MUST have known he was going to die that day, the day he called her in to sit by his side. Nothing could have prepared Hongxing for it. Indeed, Hongxing had made all the arrangements she could to ensure a smooth and swift recovery. The private hospital room she had paid for, out of the salary from her last movie, was a spacious one. It had all the creature comforts a patient could ask for. And, most importantly, the surgeon who had operated on Ba was a friend of Xiaoyan and paid special attention to them, frequently checking in.

Hongxing tried to distract Ba from pulling at his bandages by reading from a popular novel, one that was currently being adapted into a television script. Her agent had recommended it to her, hinting that she would have a chance to audition for one of the leading roles. From time to time, Hongxing would pause in her reading to remind her father not to scratch at the staples running down the center of his chest.

A breeze carried the sound of children playing through the open window. From where she was sitting, Hongxing could make out the large plum blossom tree in the courtyard, its pink blooms trembling when the wind swept through its branches. The hospital was insulated from the noise of the city by its surrounding gardens and extensive rows of trees. That had been another point in the hospital's favor when Hongxing had made the arrangements.

When Hongxing glanced at her father, Ba seemed to be asleep. But the second she stopped reading, Dad opened his eyes again.

"Why did you stop?" he asked.

"You should get your rest," she said. Hongxing got up and went to close the window.

"Don't close it," he said.

When Hongxing turned around, her father's eyes were filled with tears. Hongxing had only seen him cry once, many years ago when she was a little girl—when the plum blossom tree of her childhood had put on its last and final bloom—and the sight of tears now running down her father's face disturbed her. She didn't know what to do, so she pretended she hadn't seen them.

"You're tired," she said, though she didn't know if it was Ba or herself to whom she was saying those words.

"Sit down," Ba said.

Hongxing obliged and watched as her father took several deep, rattling breaths and began to cough.

"Shall I call the nurse?" she asked him.

He waved away her concern. "When I'm gone," he told her, "take my ashes and bury me beneath the tree." Ba didn't have to specify which one, for Hongxing already knew in her heart.

"Just focus on getting better," Hongxing said, brusquely.

"Promise me."

She tried to ignore his hands, which were reaching toward her. "Don't think about these things," Hongxing added.

Ba caught her hand in his and squeezed it once. "We both know the pain of not being able to be with the ones we love," Ba said. His gaze was knowing.

Hongxing flushed and she averted her eyes. She wondered if he knew about Hongmei and, if so, how? Hongxing felt unsettled that her father might know more about her than she had realized. That he might have, in fact, seen right through her. She stood up.

"I've got to run some errands," Hongxing said. "I'll be back with your dinner."

When she returned with his favorite takeout, Ba was fast asleep. The nurses had pumped him full of painkillers, and any chance of finishing the conversation was now long gone.

That night, Hongxing stayed up watching the rise and fall of his chest. She kept the window open. It was not a cold night, and she thought that the scent of the plum blossoms would help him sleep better. Was his health failing faster or slower than the doctors had predicted? How did one measure a life as it left the body? Hongxing leaned forward. She wanted to capture every breath that escaped him, though she knew it was impossible.

He slept deeply, so deeply he never woke again.

AFTER BA'S DEATH, Hongxing had gone to see the old plum blossom tree of her childhood again. The parking lot of a supermarket filled the space where the tree once stood. She took her father's ashes back with her.

THE CAB FELT weightless driving along the banks of the Charles River that wound through Boston. Cars in the other lanes sped even faster, passing them on their way from the airport out of the city. Narrow streets widened into larger ones. The highway was black and glossy in the drizzling darkness, looking almost like a sheet of ice.

By the time the cab arrived in Concord, the sky was lightening again. But the light was gray and cold, a reflection of the fog drifting off the ground. They pulled off the turnpike and onto a smaller street. White houses with black trim lined the streets. Flag bunting hung beneath rows of stately windows.

Hongxing looked out the window, half-awake. She had visited her sister's house once before, several years ago, for her brother-in-law Aiguo's funeral. It had been a brief trip, then, and she hadn't stayed overnight. Hongxing had been surprised at how much older Yonghong had seemed. Her twin hadn't said much—even less than they usually said over the phone. She had spent most of the time silent, with red eyes.

The fog grew denser the deeper into the neighborhood they drove. The driver turned on his windshield wipers and rolled down his window. Crunch of gravel. Smell of pine and the cold, morning dew.

Eventually, a red colonial house appeared. As they pulled to a stop at the edge of the lawn, Hongxing looked up at its dark-screened windows, one after another. Beyond the house, the trees of the conservation land rose up in a foreboding wall.

After being deposited in the driveway with her bags, Hongxing checked her appearance in a little handheld mirror. There was a touch of lipstick on her lips, and her shoulder-length hair was permed into curls. When she was younger, permed curls had seemed the most glamorous of hairstyles. Now, the look was somewhat dated. She frowned at the flecks of gray at her roots.

Slowly, Hongxing began walking toward the front door, through the garden that took up most of the front lawn. She passed the tulips and budding peonies, wet with the morning dew. Thorns from the roses pulled at her clothing, her skin. One caught on the hem of her dress. Another scratched her ankle, drawing a line of blood. The door was painted a green so dark it was almost black. It was death that had brought her here the last time. And now, it was the promise of death that brought her back again. Hongxing raised her hand to knock.

THE FRONT DOOR swung open. A woman in a bathrobe stood in the doorway. Hongxing took in the curling ends of her sister's loose braid, the lines at the corners of her eyes, the softening of her jawline. Proof of all the passing years.

Hongxing searched her sister's face. There was surprise there, then happiness and relief.

Yonghong embraced her. "I didn't know you would arrive so soon," she said. "You should have told me."

"I got the earliest flight here," Hongxing said.

"I would have come to pick you up."

"How is Ma doing?" Hongxing asked, stepping into the entryway. She set down her bag and bent down to take off her shoes.

"She's holding on," Yonghong said. "She's strong." She led Hongxing deeper inside the house. "She's sleeping now. But she'll be so glad you're home."

Hongxing followed her sister, winding past the living room toward the kitchen. The house was dark, filled with a subterranean silence. There was a stillness in the air, disturbed only by the dust motes drifting down.

"You didn't need to rush down." Yonghong said again in the kitchen. "She'll hold on for a few more weeks." A pause. "Maybe even longer." But her voice was not filled with hope—only wistfulness.

"I'm not busy these days anyway," Hongxing said.

Yonghong poured her a cup of tea and the two of them sat down at the table.

"Where's Emily?" Hongxing asked.

"She's driving over from New York tomorrow."

"It'll be nice to see her again," Hongxing said. "She was still in high school the last time I visited."

"She's busy," Yonghong said. "She hasn't been back home in years."

As the two of them sat in silence, Hongxing observed the face across from her. Forehead to forehead. Nose to nose. Chin to chin. Every line and angle of their faces was the same, only framed differently by their hair, the years.

QUIETLY, HONGXING OPENED her mother's door and made her way over to her bedside. Ma was already stirring, her eyes opening slowly.

"Yonghong?" Ma reached out to touch her face.

Hongxing caught her hand. "It's me, Ma. Hongxing."

Ma's eyes cleared. Her face was much thinner than Hongxing had remembered. Her smile, however, still lit up the room. "I knew I would see you again."

Hongxing bent down to kiss her on the cheek. Then, she felt her forehead. It was damp with sweat but cool to the touch. Ma asked for some water. Hongxing lifted the cup on the nightstand and brought its straw to her mother's lips. Ma took long, deep sips. She drank half the cup before she turned her head slightly to the side.

"How are you feeling?" Hongxing arranged the pillows against the headboard and helped her sit up.

"I'm glad you're here," Ma said. "I wanted to tell you something." There was an excited flush in her mother's cheeks and a glow in her eyes.

Hongxing waited. In the silence, her mother's eyes drifted closed.

"Why don't you rest now," Hongxing said gently, rising from the bed.

But Ma grabbed onto her hand. "I dreamed that you were coming, you know," she whispered, as if she were confessing a secret.

"Did you?"

Ma looked toward the curtained window, framed with light. "I dreamed of her, too."

"Who?"

"My mother—your wai po—losing her husband to the revolution, to the flames on her wedding night," Ma said. "Last night, all of us were in my dream together." She frowned. "You remember, don't you?" She stared hopefully up at Hongxing.

THROUGH THE WINDOW of the guest bedroom that evening, Hongxing could make out a house with a red door across the field. Hongxing stood beside the window, watching the house light up from within. She and Hongmei had once imagined living in a house like that—a house across the sea where they didn't have to hide their love. Hongmei dreamed of a wide yard, tall trees, birdsong. "And a nice chandelier," Hongmei had said, "But you'll have to let me pick it out since I don't trust your taste." Hongxing had smiled and promised she would.

In those early days after graduating from the Film Academy, they had still been sharing an apartment together. The jobs weren't coming in yet, and so they had cobbled together a life out of second-hand furniture.

There was a wobbly table they had bought from the previous tenant of the apartment. Two mismatched chairs gifted from a friend. A bed frame whose wood-grain pattern looked like ripples in water. They had done their best to make the apartment a home. Neither of them had much to their name then. Only each other.

One morning, lying in bed beside her, Hongxing had the thought that if she had shared her sister's birthmark, she might have been more afraid to fall in love. When she was little, she felt as if she didn't belong to their family. After all, Ma and Wai Po and Yonghong all had the mark on their chests. But later, after Leap Forward's death, after witnessing her father's infidelity, after learning of the murder of Wai Po's husband, the birthmark seemed more like a curse than anything. In her eyes, the red thumbprint was the print of heartbreak, and she felt grateful she didn't have one. And so, when the fear came, it came too late. But perhaps, it would always have come too late. There was no other possible past in which she would not have fallen in love in Hongmei.

"What are you looking at?"

Hongxing turned from the window at her sister's voice. "Nothing," she said.

Yonghong came over to stand by Hongxing, and showed her the photo album in her hands. "Look what I found," Yonghong said. She began flipping through its brittle, yellow pages. Then, her hand stilled, and she passed the album over to Hongxing.

Hongxing peered down at the page. On it, two girls in identical floral dresses sat facing the camera. Both wore the same sullen expression. She smiled.

"When is this from?" Hongxing asked. She examined the photograph more closely for any marks or notations, but there were none. It had to have been well before Wai Po's death. Before the Cultural Revolution, too, when family photographs and personal portraits were banned.

"I found it in the trunk our cousin brought over one year. Wai Po's trunk."

Hongxing couldn't think of the trunk without thinking of Wai Po draped over it, her eyes closed and her hair falling down her shoulders. The trunk had seemed to Hongxing like a coffin then.

"I must be the one on the right," Yonghong said.

"I thought that was me," Hongxing said. She looked again. This time, she saw more. One girl had thicker eyebrows. The other, longer hair. But still, she couldn't tell for certain. Hongxing shook her head helplessly.

"We used to get so angry when called by the wrong name," Yonghong said, smiling. "Now, look at us—not knowing ourselves."

"Back then," Yonghong added, closing the album again, "it was such a luxury to have your picture taken. I still remember all the excitement of that day Wai Po took us to the studio for our birthdays."

Hongxing turned to look at her sister. "Who could forget?" she said. The memory came flooding back. They had worn little red dresses and lacy hats.

"And how she'd always—"

"Of course—"

The sisters smiled at one another.

"The other month," Hongxing said, "I went to visit Wai Po's grave in the new plot. I brought her favorites—fennel cakes and lotus seeds." Hongxing had placed the offerings before Wai Po's stone marker in the cemetery. She had burned a bundle of incense and bowed three times before her.

Buying the family plot was one of the few things Hongxing had been able to do after the Disappearing. One of the few things that still held any urgency for her. In those first few months after being shunned by the public and friends, Hongxing had started thinking again about the past, about family. She had pulled some strings to secure a plot in a private cemetery on the outskirts of Beijing. There was enough space there for all of them to be buried there, even after relocating Wai Po and Ba. It had been an expensive purchase—second only to her apartment. A peaceful afterlife didn't come cheap.

Out of a sense of duty, Hongxing had even planted a plum blossom tree at the new plot. She had hoped it would appease her father's spirit.

Xiaoyan hadn't been able to understand why Hongxing had been so adamant about the whole thing. "Most kids these days do what they can to get away from their parents," she joked. "And here you are wanting to be with them for all eternity."

Hongxing admitted it did seem strange to want to bring them all together in death in ways they hadn't ever really been in life. But she had never understood how truly alone she was until after Hongmei had left. It was then that Hongxing realized she had no one—save for those who shared her blood.

"It's practically impossible to get a burial site there," Hongxing said. She paused. "But don't worry, I've already reserved a plot for Ma. For all of us."

"What do you mean?" Yonghong asked, furrowing her brows.

Hongxing frowned. "She'll be coming back to China, won't she?" Her hand curled at her side.

"She's staying here," Yonghong said firmly. "With me."

The East Is Red

THE LAST TIME Hongxing searched for herself on the Internet had been about a year ago. She typed in the characters of her name, *hong* and *xing*, then tried the words *actress*, *film*, and *movies*. The character *hong* was from Wai Po's name, "red" for good fortune and luck, and then later, for the Red Guards, the Red Army, the red flag of the country. The character *xing* was drawn from her mother's name, Yuexin. But instead of the *xin* of the dawn, her *xing* pointed to the stars. Although she didn't bear the red birthmark of her sister, mother, and grandmother, her name was a kind of equivalency. Hongxing was the red star of the sky—the sun that shone forever and ever. Until it didn't.

A year ago, Hongxing had clicked through twenty pages of searches before admitting defeat. So it was true after all—she had disappeared. Had been wiped away off the Internet as if she never existed.

It wasn't as if she hadn't expected it. First, it was the online rumors, then it was the investigation into her taxes. They were common strategies used against one's political or social enemies. She just never thought Hongmei would have ever used them against her.

But Hongxing didn't fight back, for there was a part of her that thought she deserved it. Hongxing was the one who had phoned her, day after day, when Hongmei stopped returning her calls. Hongxing was the one who had gone, uninvited, to her wedding to that well-known politician. Hongxing was the one who had showed up to her door, begging to be let in—just to talk, one last time. Hongxing was the one who had refused to let go, even as Hongmei had already broken away, like an iceberg from its glacier, implacably drifting into the blue.

Her disturbances were beginning to raise too many questions about the nature of their relationship and their past. Unsuitable for Hongmei and her powerful husband and their new, perfect life.

How could Hongmei throw everything they'd had—everything they'd been through—away? Hongxing had given her everything. She had been prepared to grow old together and could imagine no other future. Hongxing loved her, even now. But it had seemed so easy for Hongmei to let her go. "This is the only thing my parents have ever asked me to do," Hongmei said after telling her of her engagement, and nothing more.

HONGXING WOKE AT dawn. She checked the time on her phone then closed her eyes again. She tried to will herself back to sleep but knew it was no use. Her heart was still racing from whatever had woken her up.

After their disagreement the night before, Yonghong and Hongxing hadn't spoken for the rest of the evening. Hongxing had been stunned that Yonghong wanted to bury their mother at the local cemetery here, and not in the plots she had reserved for them all in China. And she now realized that Yonghong herself would also remain here in death, next to her husband. It felt as though she were being abandoned all over again.

Many of Hongxing's friends had moved away in the last few years—some to the US, but others to Canada or Australia. And if it wasn't them, it was their children. Hongxing envisioned them all leaving, one by one. A slow, quiet exodus out of the city until she was the only one left.

Hongxing couldn't deny that she had thought of leaving in the past—even before the Disappearing. She had imagined leaving by herself. She didn't know where, exactly, she would go. Maybe she would walk and walk until the air grew heavy with fog and mist and the sound of running water came to her. The paths would be made of dirt, not pavement, and there, in the distance, she would see a bridge. And where the bridge might lead her, she couldn't begin to guess.

HONGXING BORROWED A pair of jogging sneakers and a light jacket she found in the downstairs closet and made her way into the conservation land behind her sister's house. She plodded down a trail and crossed over a wooden bridge. To the side of the trail, someone had carefully balanced the stones on top of one another in little towers.

Hongxing raised her face toward the sky. Clouds were passing by. The smell of forest debris, the pines. The air was so sweet here. Would Hongmei have loved it here? Once, she would have answered yes. But now, she didn't know what Hongmei loved.

The last time Hongxing had seen her was at Xiaoyan's wedding. She had known Hongmei would be there. She had tried to steel herself. But nothing could have prepared her for the vision of seeing them together again before her—Hongmei in a sparkling pink gown and her husband in a sleek, black tuxedo. A perfect couple.

Hongxing knew she was staring but couldn't help herself. She felt as if she were frozen, the whole of her distilled into this one moment. Someone laughed. Someone called her name. Then, Xiaoyan was there, leading her away.

As an actress, Hongxing had played the part of being in love; she had imagined it. But she could have never imagined what it felt like to be denied love. Like a ghost, hungry and full of desire.

In the taxi ride back after the wedding, Hongxing had pressed her cheek against the window and looked out at the people on the street. Teresa Teng was playing on the radio, singing of everlasting love. Hongxing was suddenly struck by the memory of watching Yonghong and Leap Forward listening to cassette tapes of Teresa beneath the plum blossom tree. The tree had been barren of blossoms, though it didn't seem to matter to Yonghong and Leap Forward, who curled up blissfully beneath its bare branches.

After Miss Wu's death, Hongxing had seen Ba watering the roots of the tree, day after day for a week. Once, she spied him mixing salt into the watering can, before taking it with him to the tree—surely the reason it would never flower again. She hadn't understood then why he would do such a thing. But now, she thought she did.

WHEN HONGXING WALKED back to her sister's house, a black sedan was parked in the driveway. She went in through the side door and, as she slipped off the sneakers in the mudroom, she heard voices coming from the other room.

In the kitchen, there was a young woman sitting at the table. She was talking to Yonghong with brief, quiet words, but the two of them fell silent once Hongxing entered the room.

"Emily?" Hongxing said in surprise, before embracing her. "How you've grown."

At first glance, Emily seemed to take after her father's family who were from the north, in Tianjin. She shared their strong eyebrows and sharp, bony shoulders. But there was something of her mother—and, by extension, Hongxing, too—in her eyes.

"How long will you be able to stay?" Hongxing asked.

"A few days. Maybe more."

From what Yonghong had told her, Emily had been working for several years now as an environmental biologist in New York.

"When was the last time you were home?" Hongxing asked.

"Two years," Yonghong cut in. "And the last time you were back, you only stayed for a few hours."

Emily looked down into her cup and watched the leaves settle at the bottom. She took a sip. "I was busy with work," she said shortly.

"She's too busy to come back home," Yonghong added. She looked at Hongxing, though Hongxing knew she was really speaking to her daughter.

"Young people lead different lives than us," Hongxing said, trying to lighten the mood.

Emily stood up abruptly. "I'm going to go unpack," she said. "Let me know when Grandma wakes."

"I'll help you carry your things up," Hongxing offered. She followed her niece up the stairs. Emily hadn't brought much, only an overnight bag. Hongxing wondered how long she was really planning on staying.

Emily stood in her childhood bedroom, looking around the room. It didn't look as if Yonghong had changed the room at all since her daughter had moved out. The stuffed animals and books lining the shelves belonged to a younger version of her niece than the one who stood before her. Emily sat down on her bed, then stood up again. She looked as if she didn't know what to do.

"I'll bring some fresh sheets in," Hongxing said.

When Hongxing returned, she found Emily brushing out the tangles in her hair.

"Do you need help?" Hongxing offered. "I used to brush your mother's hair for her when we were little," Hongxing said. She couldn't help but smile at the memory.

"That's alright," Emily said, putting down the brush. "I need to get it cut."

Hongxing tilted her head as she considered Emily. "You know, you really do look like her."

"Like who?" Emily asked.

Hongxing was about to say Yonghong, but she paused at the last moment. Was it really Yonghong that Emily resembled? The way that Emily was looking at her now, eyes wide and filled with the light from the window, brought to mind the image of Wai Po.

"A little like my wai po," Hongxing finally answered. "Your great-grandmother."

"My great-grandmother?" Emily asked. "Grandma's mother?"

Hongxing considered her again. She wasn't so certain anymore. "Maybe," she said, with a self-deprecating laugh. "I'm at that age where I only think about the past."

"DRAW THE CURTAINS," Ma commanded from where she was lying in bed. Emily got up to oblige, but Yonghong stopped her.

"Why?" Hongxing asked. "It's such a beautiful day out. Don't you want to see the sun?"

Clouds drifted across the frame of the window like a scene out of an oil painting. A cardinal flew by—a shot of red in blue.

"Draw the curtains," Ma said again. "They're watching us."

"Who?" Yonghong asked. "There's nobody out there."

"They've always been looking at me," Ma said. "Pointing fingers. I'm not like the other children, and they know that."

"There's nothing to worry about," Hongxing said.

Ma shook her head and closed her eyes. She turned her face away as if she could hide from those she imagined were looking at her in judgment.

"They say I don't have a father. They say I'm just an orphan," Ma said, "but it isn't true." Her eyes flew open and focused on Hongxing. "My parents loved each other, you know."

"I know," Hongxing reassured her. "I know."

"You were always so perfect," Ma said, smiling. "My sweet little girl. No one would dare criticize you."

"I know," Hongxing repeated, though she felt a deep, abiding sense of shame. Ma didn't know anything about the Disappearing, but better she remained as she was in Ma's memory.

"A perfect little girl," Ma said. "If only your sister could be more like you," she added, turning to Yonghong. "How you make me worry. There's something inside you that won't be stamped out. That can't be. Don't you see?" She looked at Emily and held her gaze.

Emily perched on the edge of the bed, her body tense. She looked as if she were on the verge of setting off in flight. Yonghong's eyes, too, were full of sorrow.

"Don't you hear her crying?" Ma asked.

"Who?" Hongxing asked.

But Ma only looked more confused.

"Rest, Grandma," Emily said soothingly.

Ma suddenly tried to sit up. "When I think of my mother," Ma said, "her face comes to me in bits and pieces. Fragments of her smile. The mark like a thumbprint on her chest. The way she'd brush my hair. Every year, she'd hold remembrances for my father, her parents, her brothers. She never forgot them." Ma paused and grasped Emily's hand. "You will remember me, won't you?"

"Of course," Emily said.

The expression on Ma's face remained doubtful. "But the photographs," she said. "They're already fading."

The Torn Photograph

ONCE, DURING HER academy days in Beijing, Hongxing had been invited to a gongfu tea ceremony in honor of a classmate's great-great aunt's eighty-eighth birthday party. Sitting at an immense circular table, Hongxing watched as the tea master held a pot with a long, golden spout. With a series of arcing gestures and flourishes, the tea master wove an intricate dance with the pot in his hand. At the end of his performance, everyone's delicate cups were filled with the perfect amount of steaming, amber tea. For a long time, Hongxing remembered that tea as the most fragrant she ever drank.

But a year ago, Hongxing learned that to be "invited to drink tea" was something else entirely. In this case, men in suits showed up at your workplace to invite you to drink tea in a discreet governmental office building. Once seated, there was no tea master or long, golden spout. Instead, there were a series of questions—a "casual" interview. They pulled out old social media posts of yours from decades ago, or even an essay you once wrote as a student. They looked into your family background and history. Who were your great-grandparents? Who were your grandparents? Who was your father? Your mother? Your sister? Oh, a sister in America? And what about your tax returns?

Hongxing had long suspected that an invitation might be coming. Weeks earlier, she had been informed by her publicist of a wave of negative comments posted about her on message boards and social-network microblogging sites like Weibo. Someone made the connection that she had a cousin who had been jailed for embezzling money from the construction of high-speed trains. It wasn't true. Hongxing had never believed it could be true, though he had been fined and imprisoned. She had always suspected he had been the scapegoat. But once the connection had been made, the anti-fans became unstoppable.

"Don't worry," her publicist reassured her over the phone. "They're clearly being written by some water army." The publicist had suspected it was a rival actress who had hired the army of online users who flooded the forums with negative comments.

It wasn't the first time something like that had happened, so Hongxing didn't pay it much mind at first. Her publicist would counter the negative comments by hiring ghostwriters of their own. After the negative publicity had been quelled on social media, a few well-placed articles would be released detailing Hongxing's charitable contributions and time spent volunteering at home and abroad.

But when Hongxing called Hongmei to tell her what had been happening, a man's voice had answered instead.

"Don't call here ever again," he said. "Or things will get worse."

HONGXING'S LAST POST on Weibo: *The tea was cold and very bitter.*

THAT NIGHT IN Massachusetts, Hongxing had the most vivid dream she'd had in a long time. In her dream, Ma was shutting the curtains again. Hongxing and Yonghong followed close behind, trying to open every one that she shut. It was no use. Each open curtain revealed only more shut curtains behind it. "Let her do what she wants," Wai Po said. Wai Po didn't have a body—she was just a voice. A voice that echoed all around the room. It was Wai Po's voice that reminded Hongxing she was dreaming. It was Wai Po, after all, who had taught her how to dream. In her dream, Hongxing closed her eyes and imagined that when she opened them again, all the windows would be open—and they were. It was so easy. The easiest thing to ever come to her. She just had to think it, and it would be. And in fact, there were no walls, no windows at all. Just the blue sky surrounding her and Wai Po's voice.

Hongxing opened her eyes. She had always had a talent for lucid dreaming, a talent that Wai Po had helped her cultivate. When they were children, Yonghong had been jealous of how easily it came to her. But was it a gift, as Yonghong had always thought? It brought the burden of choice even in dreams.

Hongxing knew she could be free, just as easily as she had chosen to be in her dream. She knew that nothing was holding her back from moving on from the past, from Hongmei. She knew she didn't have to live hidden away, like Ma had tried to live. She didn't want to be haunted by the past, like her mother still was—even on her deathbed.

Hongxing looked out the window to the house across the field. It stood with its red door, silent and dark. She got out of bed to get a glass of water. As she walked through the hallway, she paused at the sight of Emily's open door.

"Aunt Hong?" Emily called out softly.

Hongxing startled. "Yes?"

"I want to ask you something."

"What is it?" Hongxing asked, entering her niece's room.

Inside, Emily was sitting at her desk, peering at her laptop. On the screen, there was a photograph in black and white.

"You're up early," Hongxing said. She studied the photograph on the screen. Yonghong and Leap Forward were standing in front of a bridge, the two of them smiling. She remembered, suddenly, that she was the one who had taken the photo of them together, on the day she had learned of her acceptance into the military's art troupe. Someone had lent her a camera, and Hongxing, in celebration, had taken many photos—and had been photographed in turn.

"I wanted to restore this," Emily said. Seeing the photo album earlier that day, Emily explained, had reminded her of this photograph that she had kept hidden in her room. So she had scanned the photograph and was fixing it up on her computer. "It was torn, you see."

Hongxing could see that the photo had once been torn, for there was a gap in Leap Forward's face.

Emily moved her mouse around. Eyes darkened again in the photograph. Faces lost their yellow cast. The details on Yonghong's school uniform sharpened into focus. Leap Forward's hair shone again.

"Who was he?" Emily asked.

"A childhood friend of ours," Hongxing said after a pause.

Emily studied his face. "Where is he now?" she asked.

"He was sent to the countryside during the Cultural Revolution," Hongxing said. "He died there."

Leap Forward's death had not been quick. A tree he had been ordered to fell to make way for new rice fields had crushed him to death. The other students had tried to lift the tree, then—when it became apparent that it was no use—had stayed with him until he died. They never knew how long it had taken—but according to the students, it had been long enough for Yonghong's name to be one of the last words he ever spoke. After the fields had been flooded with water and the rice sprouted and harvested, one of the students had brought back a sack of rice for Leap Forward's family. They had all eaten from that sack of rice, Hongxing remembered—spooning soft white grains into their mouths.

But Hongxing didn't tell any of this to Emily. "He was special to your mother," Hongxing said.

Outside the window, morning light was spilling over the edges of the forest.

"She loved him, didn't she?" Emily asked.

Hongxing didn't know how to answer her niece. "For days after his death, your mother wouldn't speak to anyone." Hongxing could still remember trying to persuade her to talk.

Emily scrutinized the photo on the screen. "I wish she had told me about him," she said eventually.

"She used to be the talkative one, but his death changed her."

"Was that why she came over to the States?" Emily asked. "To escape the past?"

"For you, of course," Hongxing said, though there was some truth in Emily's words. "For you to have a better life, a better future than one we could have imagined—than anyone could have imagined."

"Was it really for me?" Emily said.

"Of course," Hongxing said. "Even my mother came over for you."

Emily looked at her sharply then. Perhaps Hongxing hadn't disguised the bitterness in her voice as much as she had wanted to. It seemed ridiculous after all these years to be jealous of her niece. But her regret had only intensified after Hongmei had left her.

"Mom was always telling me how much she missed you," Emily said. "I grew up hearing your stories. She and Grandma would always watch every single DVD you sent over."

"I'm not making any movies anymore," Hongxing said.

"Do I really resemble her?" Emily asked.

"Who?"

"Your wai po," Emily answered. "Grandma keeps saying that I do."

"You have the same birthmark."

"Not anymore," Emily said. "I cut most of it out. The doctors were worried about it."

Hongxing was silent. Then, she said, "But you can't cut out blood, you know." It was why she had bought the family plot. Why she wanted them to all be together.

The morning light was spilling through the windows now, and the sunrise was almost blinding.

"If that's the case," Emily asked, "then why do I know nothing about the blood that runs through me?"

"Maybe there are some parts of your mother's life," Hongxing said, "she just wants to keep to herself." She knew how true that could be.

AS SHE WALKED downstairs, Hongxing heard the buzzing undertone of the television. In the still-dark living room, Yonghong was asleep on the couch, her face flickering with blue light, a blanket fallen beside her. She looked at her sister's face. Was it still the same face? Was it still the face they shared? Some days, Hongxing wondered if they shared a childhood, and nothing else.

On the screen, the American president stood behind a podium. He was telling the enraptured crowd how much he loved the country, how much he loved them. But China, he said. China, China. The Chinese, you know. A frown crept to her face. In such a country, Yonghong still wanted their mother to be buried here?

The crowd cheered wildly, overcome with passion. Hongxing remembered how the people had cheered in the same way during her youth. They cheered and marched in the streets, declaring their love for the motherland. They had cheered, too, while listening to Hongxing sing.

When they were children, Yonghong had once asked if she would sing a love song just for her. Hongxing had nodded, though it had been a lie. She wasn't singing it for her sister. Not exactly. She had sung it for the memory of Miss Wu. For Ba, whom she had spied weeping after her teacher's death, clutching a white silk scarf.

Hongxing stared down at Yonghong's face. If only she could sing again—all that she felt—as she had that year. Would Yonghong understand her loneliness then? Her fear of being alone in life and the underworld, too? Hongxing bent down and touched the blanket with her hand. But just as she began to pull it up, her sister stirred. She dropped the blanket and left.

"THERE—THERE YOU ARE again!" Yonghong pointed at the hand of a woman on the screen. "Rewind," she directed Hongxing. The hand retreated again from the frame. "Yes, there."

On the screen, her other self was walking across a bridge, hair blowing in the wind.

The sound of the erhu rose from the television in Ma's room. Its notes arrived sweetly, then stridently. There was something in the vibrations that always reminded Hongxing of someone singing. Wai Po had once told her and Yonghong of how beautifully her ge ge had played the erhu. "His arm swung back and forth like the wing of a bird," she said. "Even the light seemed to dance at his music."

"What are you all doing?"

Hongxing looked toward the door of Ma's bedroom, where Emily was now standing.

"We're watching one of your aunt's old films," Yonghong said. "Join us."

Emily came in. She perched at the edge of the bed, where Ma was propped up against some pillows. Hongxing restarted the scene. The scene froze—skipped—jumped back—played again.

"This looks like a sad movie," Emily said.

"It has a happy ending," Ma said.

"You remember it?" Hongxing asked, surprised. She peered closely at her mother's face.

"Emily's seen it before," Ma said.

"Have I?" Emily asked.

"You used to get so upset, watching Hongxing's films," Yonghong said with a laugh. "You would always think it was me on the screen."

"I remember that," Emily said solemnly. "I felt betrayed."

Ma smiled. "Filled with fire, just like your mother."

"Am I?" Emily asked.

Ma didn't answer. Instead, her eyes drifted over to the window and widened. "Do you see her?" she asked Hongxing.

Hongxing turned her head. "Who?" she asked.

"The one who's crying outside. The one standing there. The beautiful one," Ma answered. "She's crying. Can't you see?" Her voice was rising in agitation.

"Miss Wu?" Hongxing asked.

Ma's eyes filled with tears.

"Do you want me to draw the curtains?" Yonghong asked.

"It's not her eyes I'm afraid of," Ma said. "She doesn't love your father. Not really. She thinks she does, but she's so young. I feel sorry for her. I feel sorry for all of us—loving the wrong people."

Now it was Hongxing's eyes that welled up with tears.

"Loving those who can't love us back," Ma said. "How wrong we were." Suddenly, Ma smiled. "But it wasn't all wrong," she added. "I loved you. All of you." Ma's eyes were already closing. She was drifting back to sleep.

Hongxing turned to her sister. "Can't you give me this at least?" she asked. "Can't you let me take her home? To be buried next to Ba?"

"Ba?" Yonghong said with a frown. Then, she added, "There's a space for her here."

"At the cemetery?" Emily asked.

"Yes," Yonghong answered.

"And you have a space there, too?" Emily's words were sharp and pleading at once.

"I do." Yonghong's voice was carefully blank again.

"Next to him?" Emily asked, though she looked like she already knew the answer. "Why, when you never loved him?"

A Birthday for the Future

"Wait, Emily!" Yonghong called out as Emily ran out of the house. Hongxing went after her.

Outside, there was a soft drizzle of rain, the thinnest of veils falling from the sky. Hongxing barely felt it on her face as she chased after her niece.

In the driveway, Emily was standing by her car, keys in hand.

"Where are you going?" Hongxing asked.

"It's not that I'm trying to stay away," Emily said to her mother. "It's just that I don't know how to get back to how we were."

"What do you mean?" Yonghong asked.

Emily looked as if she wanted to say more, but shook her head instead. "Maybe I shouldn't have come back," Emily said, getting into her car. "I'm going for a drive."

THE ROADS WERE dark and inky with the increasing rain as Yonghong and Hongxing pulled out of the driveway.

"Where do you think she went?" Hongxing said.

Yonghong didn't seem to have heard her as she fiddled with the windshield wipers. There was music coming out of the speakers. An old song from their childhood.

"There's one place I have in mind," Yonghong said at last.

"She asked me about Leap Forward, you know."

"She did?" Yonghong furrowed her brows.

"You never told her about him?"

"How could I?"

"It seemed important for her to know," Hongxing said.

"What use is it to speak of him?" Yonghong asked.

"Perhaps it's worse to keep him a secret."

"And what about your own secrets?" Yonghong asked.

"What do you mean?"

"What happened to you a year ago?" she asked. "I read what I could online, but nothing made any sense."

Hongxing hesitated for a few moments. Then, she spoke. "I loved someone I shouldn't have," she said. It was the most she had ever said out loud about what had happened between her and Hongmei.

"I'm sorry I never asked," Yonghong said. "I didn't want to pry. And a part of me wanted to pretend that you were doing well—that I had nothing to worry about."

Hongxing stared out the window. Yonghong turned out of the neighborhood and onto the main road. They passed by several old colonial houses with signs staked in their yards. MAKE AMERICA GREAT AGAIN, they proclaimed in white lettering on a background of red. They called for a return to an imagined past—a past that never was nor could be again. Hongxing frowned. She looked at the signs through the rearview mirror until they disappeared from sight.

"You don't have to worry about me," Hongxing said. She was surprised to find she truly meant it. "I'm like a newborn now, without a past to tie me down." After being effectively erased from public consciousness in her home country, no one had any more expectations of her. Not even herself. She could do anything. She could be anyone.

The sky was beginning to turn a deep orange with the sunset.

"It wasn't you I wanted to leave," Yonghong said as they pulled into the cemetery. "I just wanted to escape my memories of Leap Forward. I knew I wouldn't be able to live for myself, when everything reminded me of him. So, when I married Aiguo and came to America, I thought it would be a fresh start. Not just for me, but Emily, too."

"Was it a fresh start?"

Yonghong parked in the gravel lot. There was only one other car in the parking lot, and it was Emily's.

"No," Yonghong finally answered. "Even if I tried to forget, I couldn't."

THEY STEPPED OUT of the car. Hongxing peered into the fog that filled the grounds of the cemetery. She couldn't see anything around them—not the way forward, nor the way back.

"Don't worry," Yonghong said. "I know the way."

Yonghong forged ahead with a red umbrella. Hongxing followed with one in black. A heavier fog rose from the ground, reaching their knees. They passed several markers: a crabapple tree, laden with white buds; a weathered mausoleum with a shadowed doorway; an angel in stone, its face stained green, gazing downward.

"After Emily left for college," Yonghong said, "I used to turn on the television in the mornings and play one of your tapes. I would let it run in the background. It was comforting, hearing your voice fill the house." She glanced at Hongxing. "You seemed so happy on the screen." She paused. "I never wanted to take Ma from you," Yonghong said. "I never knew that's how you felt."

At first, Ma was going to stay for a few months. But then, at some point, she had decided to stay for good. A choice had been made, one sister over the other.

"I know," Hongxing said at last. It hadn't been about her—or at least, not only her. It had been about them both—and all the ones who lived before.

The fog thinned, revealing row after row of graves. Eventually, they spotted Emily, standing in front of a tombstone. When Emily noticed their approach, her eyes widened.

"What are you doing here?" Yonghong asked.

"I wanted to see for myself," Emily said.

"See your father again?" Yonghong asked.

Emily looked away. "I couldn't find the right one," she said, her cheeks flushed with embarrassment.

Yonghong turned to Hongxing. "If you want to bury our mother back in China, I won't stop you," Yonghong said. "But I want to show you something first." She turned to Emily. "The both of you." She began to walk off.

The rain had stopped, and now Yonghong carried the collapsed red umbrella beneath her right arm. The way she marched forward reminded Hongxing of the way her sister had looked leading the students in their class to and from the school. Her posture was so reminiscent of their childhood days that Hongxing thought she saw, for the briefest moment, another walking beside her—following her, as he always had.

At some distance away, Yonghong stopped at a plot. There was a singular tombstone there, with the name *Aiguo Sun* written on it. It was surrounded by several empty plots. "I've reserved spots for everyone, too," Yonghong said, looking over at Hongxing, then Emily.

"But wherever you decide to rest," Yonghong added, "I'll be waiting for you in the underworld. Because there'll always be a space for you beside me." She turned to Emily. "Have I ever told you, Emily, how I picked your name?"

Emily tore her eyes away from the empty plots and shook her head.

Yonghong looked saddened for a moment. "We named you 'Ai Mei Li.' 'Ai' for the love that drove me across the ocean. Love was what I hoped would fill your life. What I felt that filled me to the brim when you were born. 'Mei Li' for how beautiful I hoped your future would be in a new, beautiful country."

There was a hopeful lilt to Yonghong's voice as she spoke. Emily looked as if she were hanging on to every word.

"After Leap Forward died, I thought I could never love again," Yonghong said. "But I love you," she said to Emily, "more than you could ever know."

The sky was already darkening to night, and stars shimmered overhead.

"Let's go home," Yonghong said.

AT HOME, MA was awake and sitting up in bed when they entered her room.

"I have something for you," Emily said to Yonghong. Emily handed over a printed photograph along with the torn original, now taped together. "I restored it," she said.

Yonghong peered closely at the new picture and the old one. Her eyes darted between the face with a missing half and the one that had been filled in and reimagined. The crack through a cheek, now healed. Both pairs of eyes, dark and bright again.

"Is this how you remember it?" Emily asked nervously.

Yonghong didn't answer, but she was smiling. "Thank you," she said. She gave Emily a kiss on the cheek, then turned away. Only Hongxing saw how her eyes welled with tears.

Yonghong left the room, and when she returned, she was holding an ice-cream cake on a large tray. "I know it isn't your birthday just yet," she said to Ma. "But I wanted to celebrate while we're all together. A cake for your future birthday, for whatever is to come."

"A birthday for the future," Hongxing said.

Ma laughed then.

"Will you light the candles?" Yonghong asked, handing Emily the matchbook.

Hongxing placed a wax candle in the center of the cake. They gathered around the bed, watching as Emily struck the match. She touched the flame carefully to the wick. When the candle began to flicker with light, Emily extinguished the match. The scent of smoke slowly filled the air—heavy and sweet.

Hongxing looked around at all their faces, illuminated by the flame. Shadows danced across their cheeks. There was something so beautiful about the flickering light, so inviting, that she couldn't help but inch closer. She wanted to hold the flame in that moment—the moment before it was blown out—the moment when it felt like it would burn forever.

Acknowledgments

THIS BOOK WOULD not have been possible without Sarah Bowlin, my brilliant agent and advocate, and Kathy Pories, my wonderful editor. Thank you to the team at Algonquin, whose tireless efforts turned my dreams of publishing a novel into reality. I would like to express my gratitude to the members of my long-running workshop, whose feedback has transformed my writing: Anna Mebel, Megan Clark, Ally Young, Lindsey Skillen, Bruna Dantas Lobato, Jacquelyn Stolos, Annie Trizna, Rucy Cui, Melia Jacquot, and Kate Doyle. In addition, thank you to early readers of my work: Vivian Lee, Emma Borges-Scott, Elizabeth Bruce, Margaret Diehl, and Amy Bishop.

Thank you to MacDowell, the Rice Place, and the Kimmel Harding Nelson Center for the Arts for the time and space to write and think.

I would not be the writer and artist I am today without the guidance of my professors at the University of Denver, Syracuse University, and Wellesley College: Graham Foust, Patrick Cottrell, Selah Saterstrom, Kristy Ulibarri, Joanna Howard, Scott Howard, Donna Beth Ellard, Tayana Hardin, Lindsay Turner, Brian Kiteley, Brooks Haxton, Mary Karr, Bruce Smith, Chris Kennedy, Michael Burkard, George Saunders, Dana Spiotta, Jenny Offill, Dan Chiasson, Carlos Dorrien, and Phyllis

McGibbon. Thank you also to the members of my doctoral creative writing cohort, Elisabeth Booze and George Kovalenko, for the conversations and laughter.

Thank you to my dearest friends, many of whom were also early readers, who have supported me on this long journey: Alexandra Chang, Michael Prior, David Whelan, Anna Babcock, Echo Yue, and Zoee Kanellias. Dylan Davids, thank you for your love and kindness.

Lastly, I would like to thank my family, whose enduring love has allowed me to pursue my dreams. Thank you to my grandparents, my parents, my aunt, my brother-in-law, and my darling niece. A special thank you to my mother and sister, for always supporting me with all their heart. Your love has given me the wings with which to fly.